CLOCKWORK,

CURSES, AND COAL

STEAMPUNK & GASLAMP FAIRY TALES

A Punked Up Fairy Tales Anthology

Edited by Rhonda Parrish

World Weaver Press

Published by World Weaver Press, LLC
Albuquerque, NM
www.WorldWeaverPress.com

Cover layout and design by Sarena Ulibarri.
Cover images used under license from Shutterstock.com.

*

First edition: March 2021
ISBN-13: 978-1-7340545-1-4

Also available as an ebook

CLOCKWORK, CURSES, AND COAL

CONTENTS

INTRODUCTION

Rhonda Parrish

I first heard of steampunk twelve years ago at the World Fantasy Convention in Calgary. A friend and I were walking through the vendor room and there was a book called 'Best of Steampunk' or 'Ultimate Steampunk Collection' or something like that. When we asked the bookseller about what steampunk was she basically said, "Buy the book and find out." Which was spectacularly unhelpful and gave me the impression she didn't actually know the answer.

I'm not sharing this story just to throw shade at some unnamed bookseller, but because I think that since then steampunk has become pretty well-known. Even if people haven't read much of it, they know the aesthetic—gears and goggles, steam and airships. Wild west and Victorian settings. We all get it. Gaslamp fantasy might be a little less common, but it is pretty much exactly what it sounds like. It's set in the same Victorian/Edwardian era as steampunk, but with a focus less on tech and more on the supernatural and magic. Often with an obvious gothic influence.

That gothic influence shows itself in a lot of the stories in this collection. In fact, this is probably the darkest anthology I've ever put together for World Weaver Press. I think it's partly a reflection of my personal tastes, partly because of the influence of the genre, but probably mostly a sign of the times. Submissions for this anthology closed about two weeks after my city started to lockdown as a response to COVID-19. That means while North American authors probably didn't have the new coronavirus front of mind when they were writing their stories, I definitely had it front of mind when I was reading and selecting them. There's no way that couldn't have played a part in which stories I chose to include, even though it wasn't a conscious part of my decision making.

The good news, though, is that dark doesn't mean depressing. While these stories do tackle some serious issues in fairy tale form (imperialism, equal rights, racism, exploitation), and they absolutely go to some dark places, many (most?) also find a spark of optimism or hope in the darkness. There aren't a lot of traditional happily ever afters in these fairy tales, but there are a lot of satisfying endings and these days that is a thing to be treasured.

Rhonda Parrish
7/31/2020
Edmonton, Alberta

The Iron Revolution,

OR

A Multiplicity of Fairy Curses.

BEING AN ACCOUNT OF THE INFAMOUS EXHIBITION CONTEST OF 1851

Christina Ruth Johnson

Our story begins in many places.

In the heat of Bombay, an artificier, keen to show his skill, embeds tiny strands of copper into the hands of his youngest daughter in an intricate *mehendi* pattern. Tears prick at the pain, but she bites her lip and keeps still, studying his method.

In the cold of Moscow, a young woman, left to die as a babe in the harsh winter snow, is fitted by her adoptive parents with her first prosthetic toes and fingers, all metal and glass and gears. She abandons her crutches with a happy sigh.

In the heart of the Cape Colony, a barefoot girl in a backyard shed delicately tightens a screw on her newest innovation: a mechanical arm to press and powder medicinal herbs. She cranks the handle and breathes deeply the scent of malva and wormwood.

In the most fashionable dress shop in Paris, the owner personally fits a young woman with the latest steel-boned corset, while her assistant proffers hat after hat trimmed with ribbons made of thin sheets of brass and flowers made of industrial-grade glass. The girl's mother chooses for her, while her daughter stands still and breathless, a perfect ornament for society.

In the office of the most prosperous steam-powered mill in the greater London area, a young man sits engrossed with a blueprint of Watt's atmospheric engine, making small notes and calculations in the margins. He jumps when his father drops a pamphlet in front of him, reads what it says, and scowls.

To the Nations of the World:
Their Royal Highnesses Queen Victoria
and Prince Albert of Great Britain

And other Sponsors of the Great Exhibition of the Works
of Artifice of All Nations

Invite one maiden from each nation to enter

A Contest Most Unique!

Only the most modern maidens may enter!
Each must exemplify the progress of our Age of Artifice
in their pedigree, on their person, or in their accomplishments.

Their elegance and talents will be judged by

Master Thomas Clarrett,
Young Artificier Extraordinaire!

The winning young lady will have the honor of riding in the
opening procession of the Great Exhibition with the Royal Family.
She may also earn the love and hand in marriage of
England's most eligible bachelor—who knows?!

Master Clarrett will announce the winner at the

Exhibition's Grand Ball

the evening before the Exhibition's opening

at Mr. Paxton's "Crystal Palace"
on the first of May, 1851.

"Must I?" the young man asks his father.

"All publicity is good publicity," is the rote reply. "Also, your mother insists."

***

Reactions to the invitation differ across the nations. Some recipients look for honor and choose their best to attend. Others dismiss it as mere advertising, halfheartedly searching for an inoffensive girl to send. Not many ask the girls if they want to go, but they all do anyway. A few complain to their fathers along the way about being publicly paraded before a foreign boy in so crass a fashion.

"All publicity is good publicity," is the rote reply. "Also, your mother insists."

***

The girls arrive in London at the dirigible docks or train station or (a lucky few) by direct carriage within the same week, a rather dreary one in April. Each makes her way to the designated hotel, where she is greeted at the door by a butler and staff hired to see to her every need and by the hotel matron hired to watch her every move.

Inside the grand lobby is a concentration of the modern splendors of the glorious Age of Artifice. Textiles, art, mechanized furniture of the highest quality, and cabinets full of exotic curiosities suffuse the space with their unusual patterns, bright colors, and symphony of clicks and whirs. Each girl passes by the objects with either awed or assessing glances, following the butler toward her room.

The house's tasteful luxury is tipped over the edge into ostentation once the full chattering mass of young women—all wealthy, most socialites, some noble, a handful royal, and not a few the daughters of newly-great men of artifice—gathers in the ballroom on the day the contest is set to begin.

There is an unconscious separation of the contestants into two groups after a brief period of informal introductions. One group is marked by porcelain skin and the latest European silhouettes. The other boasts darker complexions and more vivid fabrics draped in native styles from the Colonies.

They eye each other, some friendly, some not.

Maids enter the room with mechanical tea trolleys and begin to crank the handles to set the kettles boiling. Girls seek out couches and chairs, spreading across the luxurious room like so many scattered gemstones.

The girl from India holds her teacup delicately by the handle and rim to avoid the scalding sides, which might quickly conduct heat into the strands of metal sunk into her gloveless skin. With the advent of such convenient heating, many places are switching from traditional British teacups to Russian-style tea glasses with handled, metal holders. She does not see any here and is admittedly not surprised. This hotel with its Georgian façade and old-fashioned furnishings will be British until it dies.

In the center of the European crowd, the petite, fair-haired girl from Russia unselfconsciously converses and sips at her tea, also without gloves, displaying fingers sculpted entirely of glass, braced by steel, with gears at the knuckles allowing them to bend naturally. She does not seem perturbed by the overly hot teacups. The Indian girl gives a half smile at the irony and spends a solid minute staring, for the glass fingers are stunningly beautiful. (Others acknowledge her lack of living fingers with looks of disgust.)

The theme of metal and glass pervades the room. Most of the girls' jewelry is metal, delicately forged of brass or bronze. Gears are a repeating motif. The Irish girl sits on the edge of the European group wearing an over-large pendant of an actual functioning clock.

On the other side of the room, the taciturn princess from China wears an elaborate gilded headdress from which dangle modern glass pieces tinted pink and molded to resemble cherry blossoms.

Next to her sits a young woman from Africa, whose entire neck from jawbone to clavicle is wrapped in a metal collar decorated with incised lines mimicking a band of thick rings. The subtle overlapping of small plates on each ring, like snakeskin, allows her to move her neck and head just as freely as if she wears nothing there at all. Currently, her neck is bent over a lapful of small tools and cogwheels, perhaps a dismantled pocket watch.

Never have the other girls seen a woman do an artificier's work. Shocked whispers start to circulate.

The maids return to crank the trolleys for a second round (just when the first is finally cool enough to drink), followed by the hotel matron, who in turn is followed by three strangers.

The woman is tall, dressed in an elegant if slightly old-fashioned gown. Her husband is shorter but robust with a laborer's physique trending toward fat, and he wears the very latest in men's suits from the Continent. Their son, however, claims most of the ladies' attention.

"Mr. and Mrs. Clarrett and Master Thomas Clarrett," announces the hotel matron.

The maids courteously usher the young ladies into a receiving line.

The matron presents each girl in turn to the Clarretts. She announces their name (with dignity if not accuracy), their country of origin, their parentage (if notable), and their personal claim to modernity.

"Mademoiselle Juliette Latour of Paris, France."

She wears the most extravagant ensemble of the European group by far with small beads in the shape of gears decorating her bodice, a manufactured glass flower in her hair, and a waist so tiny, a silhouette so stiff, her corset has to be made with steel boning. Protruding from the back of the corset, just above her bustle, is the handle of a large steel key.

The Indian girl, last in line, finds herself wondering what exactly might happen if she tried to turn the key.

Second is the Russian girl with the glass fingers, who walks with an odd little mince to each step—glass toes as well?—but seems sweetly eager to meet the Clarretts.

"Duchess Anechka Stepanova of Moscow, Russia."

Her curtsy is quick but not perfunctory, and her demeanor seems to immediately endear her to young Mr. Clarrett, who smiles and asks her questions. The duchess seems happy to answer them, holding out her hands between them and turning them this way and that.

Time and titles shuffle by. All are tired. The younger Mr. Clarrett, though, is pulled from his apathy when he sees the wearer of the stunning metal collar presented before him.

"Miss Zibusiso Mandla of the Ndbele of the Cape Colony, apprentice to Master Artificier John Smythe."

The whispers immediately start again, and Mr. Clarrett begins to pelt Miss Mandla with nuanced questions about her training. She answers a bit stiffly but courteously, her back proudly straight. The conversation ends, she steps away, and then,

"Miss Reena Kapoor of Bombay, India."

She assesses the people before her. The Clarretts are proud, that much she can tell, but it is not the innate pride of entitlement. It is the kind of pride achieved only with work and determination. The young Mr. Clarrett's eyes are intelligent, and, yes, she admits to herself, he is handsome in a continental sort of way with his dark hair and intelligent black eyes. She has heard a rumor that his father has Italian blood.

"Was it painful?" he asks before anything else, surprising her. For a moment, she does not understand but then lifts up her hands for his inspection, as Duchess Stepanova did before her.

"Yes."

He frowns.

"I do not understand the pain women go through for beauty."

She draws her hands back, clenching them slightly.

"Do you not? Is it not painful to stare at blueprints in the candlelight or write calculations until your hand cramps from the effort? And all of that to achieve something beautiful."

"You know how an artificier works, then?"

"Of course. I have watched my father work for longer than I have memory."

"Do you know whose theory he employed to graft the copper without disturbing the tendons?"

"A combination of Gerhardt's, Strabel's, and his own."

"You know Gerhardt?"

"Yes." She lifted her chin. "My father cannot read, so I do so for him."

"From the German?" His tone is surprised, and Reena's defensiveness grows.

"Yes. I learn whatever language he requires me to learn, though do not ask me to speak it." She says the last with a tiny smile that is more a baring of teeth. He smiles back, genuinely, irritatingly, and the interview is over.

Before she can step away (quite intent on having her cup of tea), there is a sudden moment when her breath stalls in her chest, and the very air of the room turns solid and bright for a heartbeat.

And there is one more girl.

The other contestants blink away the light and stare, for this girl wears a full cloak and hood; not to mention, she has appeared from nothing.

The newcomer pushes back her hood to reveal a stunningly beautiful face, old of eye but young of skin. Long auburn curls cascade past her waist. Her voice is loud, carrying to all corners of the large room.

"I am Vivianne of the Fair Folk. I come on behalf of my people. Our land received neither an invitation to your contest nor to your Great Exhibition. I declare these are slights that will not go unaddressed."

The elder Mr. Clarrett's mouth falls open, and Mrs. Clarrett turns quite pale. They know who stands before them, for they witnessed firsthand the fallout from the christening of the queen, when a curse was laid, spindles were made profane, and the Age of Artifice had begun. Unaware of his parents' reactions, Thomas Clarrett crosses his arms.

The elder Mr. Clarrett finds his voice first.

"My dear lady, I offer sincerest apologies for any perceived oversight," he says with a low, diplomatic bow. "Forgive me, but my wife and I have no say in who is invited to the Great Exhibition. I doubt that those who do ever imagined that the Fair Folk would have any interest in a show of artifice and industry."

"Then your imagination is small. And you may not have a say in the Exhibition, but you certainly did for this contest. Have you so little knowledge of the Fair Folk? Do you not know our love of beauty and display? It is made worse by the fact that you have slighted our people twice now in your living memory, first at the christening of your queen. One such slight might tell only of guileless ignorance, for which you were given a warning."

Realization falls across the room as each girl remembers the stories from their youth about a curse, a prohibition, a deathly sleep, and a kiss. Reena feels her ire rising. A *warning*? The queen had almost died!

Vivianne continues. "Two slights, however, is no error made in ignorance, but willful disregard for the relationship between our nations."

Mr. Clarrett loses whatever confidence had spurred his first response. "Bu—but you disappeared! You were defeated, and you disappeared!"

"Defeated!" she hisses, her cloak flinging itself behind her on an invisible wind.

"You think us cruel, inflicting revenge for a slight? Yes, your precious Victoria slept, but let me ask you this: had the young prince not kissed her, had he not been the one to wake her, would she have been allowed to wed him? A second son of divorced parents from a minor state? And now he is the mind behind your lauded Exhibition!"

Her voice lowers.

"Within our warning was blessing, a guarantee for future prosperity if relations between our nations improved. And yet, they have not."

A girl gasps softly behind her, and Reena turns her head to see Thomas Clarrett do something quite astonishing. Unnoticed, he has stepped away from his parents and picked up one of Miss Mandla's stray tools. Swiftly, he presses the tip of the pliers against the bare neck of the fairy, the only part of her skin showing other than her face and hands.

"Iron," Reena breathes.

But the iron does not burn, and Vivianne laughs. She plucks the tool from Mr. Clarrett's hand without fear.

"And you must be Thomas, the boy with his heart for sale."

He flushes.

"I thought you were a great artificier, *an artificier extraordinaire.*" She scoffs. "Not a fool who believes in old cottage tales. What do the Fair Folk have to fear from anything that comes from the earth—from which all power comes, even yours?"

Still holding the iron pliers, she flings wide her arms and turns to address the entirety of her captive audience.

"Hear this. One among you is not as she seems. She is a daughter of the Fair Folk in human guise. If your dear Thomas does not choose this Fair Child as the winner of the contest, your Crystal Palace will go up in flame and all innovations of your so-called Age of Artifice will turn to rust and dust." Her mouth smirks. "You will have to return to spindles."

She turns back to the young Mr. Clarrett.

"For your insolence, not only must the Fair Child win the contest, but you must take her as your bride, symbolic of an alliance between our nations. You have until the ball." Graceful as a dancer, she tosses him the pliers. All eyes follow its trajectory straight into his hands. When they look up, Vivianne is gone.

***

Many girls leave that very afternoon, bags packed hurriedly with no care for creases. Others quietly disappear over the course of the week, eager to return home and escape fairy curses. The Clarretts encourage it, arranging travel and expenses as needed, for surely the girls who wish to leave cannot be the fairy in disguise.

"Unless she does not know her own heritage." But Reena's rumination goes unheard by those with any influence in the matter.

A small handful of girls sneer at those who leave, claiming Vivianne's performance to be just that: a hoax to weed out the cowardly. But fear is a funny thing and spreads even to those who at first repudiate it. By the end of the week, only five girls remain.

They sit in the ballroom once more, though it is much too big, the empty seats a constant reminder of the threat hanging over them. Excess chairs are quickly removed, the remaining ones clustered around a single fireplace. A thick rug laid under their feet keeps their voices from echoing around the cavernous space.

The girls are silent and awkward, unsure of one another.

Reena has not left, as she (with her hands) is to be part of India's display during the Exhibition the following week and does not have the money to purchase earlier passage home. Duchess Stepanova from Russia and Miss Mandla from the Cape Colony also remain, likely for similar reasons. Mlle. Latour from France sits with lips pressed together next to the girl from Ireland, a Miss Elizabeth Brannon, who is a less ostentatious version of Mlle. Latour, though quite a bit prettier. Having lately become fast friends, they are the only two yet claiming that the curse is a trick.

Thomas sits in an adjacent room with his mother, also unsure of himself, not quite knowing what to say. His father has spent every waking moment in contact with those in charge of the Exhibition, trying to convince them that a fairy had appeared out of legend and laid a new curse. So far he has met with incredulity, though today he is to meet with the designer of the Crystal Palace himself, Mr. Paxton.

"Thomas, we will find a remedy for this. Let us take it one step at a time. We *must* find a way to discover which of the remaining girls is not who she seems."

He nods.

One by one, over the course of the day, they bring each girl into the private room for an interview.

Reena's invitation comes first. Mrs. Clarrett and her son await her, the former sitting stiff and proper in a wingback chair and the latter in a more relaxed pose on the sofa. He stands quickly when Reena enters. They politely wait to begin the interview until a trolley has been cranked and tea has been poured. Again, the cups are ceramic, and Reena avoids hers for some minutes.

"Where were you born?" Mrs. Clarrett asks.

"Bombay."

"Your family?"

"My father is an artificier, and my mother is dead. I have two older sisters."

There is an unexpected pause. Mother and son look at each other. She nods. Her son speaks.

"Miss Kapoor, I wish to be honest. I do not believe that you are Fae."

"As relieved as I am not to be mistaken for a fairy, I do not understand why."

"Iron."

"Iron?"

"You whispered it when I pressed the pliers against Lady Vivianne's neck, and you were as surprised as I when it did not burn. I saw your face. There was no reason for you to dissemble so subtly if you were only pretending at humanity."

"For what it is worth, I will emphatically state that you are correct."

Thomas gives a small, tight smile.

"I would ask a favor of you."

"I am happy to oblige."

"I would like for you to spy for me."

Mrs. Clarrett clears her throat. "Thomas, really."

"That's what it is, Mother."

"Spy?" Reena presses hesitantly.

Mrs. Clarrett explains with a resigned sigh. "On the other contestants. We have ruled out Mlle. Latour and Miss Mandla due to their notoriety. They are too well known and their faces too well documented to be someone else in disguise. That leaves Duchess Stepanova and Miss Brannon as the only possibilities. Personally, I am leaning toward Miss Brannon, as she is Irish, and the Fae have always preferred that country, but I have been recently informed that Duchess Stepanova is a foundling. We would like your help in discovering who is true and who is not."

"How should I spy?"

"No protest?" asks Mr. Clarrett.

"Not really. I would like to know as well and am quite pleased to help in any way."

"Thank you. We will have you watch the other interviews from the room next to this one, if you are amenable to the idea, by way of a rather ingenious contraption if I do say so myself."

Reena leans forward.

"A mechanized camera obscura? Hunt's variation on the Franklin optical device?"

Mr. Clarett leans forward just as eagerly and whispers, "A hole in the wall."

She sits back with obvious disappointment, and Mr. Clarrett laughs.

It is, of course, slightly more than a hole in the wall. Mr. Clarrett has installed a small device like the back end of a telescope against the hole, allowing the viewer to use it comfortably without flattening their face in an unseemly fashion against the wall's surface. He has left enough of a gap, however, for sound to travel clearly through it.

Mrs. Clarrett arranges for the maids to leave Reena with tea and a few small iced biscuits. There is no tea trolley, as the crank would be too loud. Instead, there is an old-fashioned tea cozy snugged around the kettle to keep it warm in lieu of mechanized power. Reena even thinks it is handmade, perhaps from before the Spindle Ban. It suits her perfectly.

Over the course of the afternoon and into the early evening, Mr. Clarrett and his mother ask the other four girls deep questions about their past, not neglecting Miss Mandla or Duchess Stepanova, in case they discuss their interviews with one another afterward.

Miss Mandla's story fascinates Reena the most. Her accented English is at first somewhat difficult to follow, but Reena focuses intently to pick up on the quirks of the South African cadence as quickly as she can. She herself has a small accent and cannot fault another's.

"My parents were slaves, freed in 1834. They stayed with their old master, as he offered them good wages. I was born a year later. I began to help my father with mending broken clockwork starting when I was five years old. When I was older and better at it, as good as my father, his old master commended my skills to his brother, who is a Master Artificier. His wife had been a missionary and he an abolitionist. They did not mind taking a Ndbele girl as apprentice into their home, even if others were quite against it."

The end of the telescope device is hard against Reena's eye, certainly leaving an indentation. She forms a makeshift cushion out of a napkin while Duchess Stepanova is settling in.

"I do not know my true parents. I was found abandoned in the snow as a child." She fiddles with her glass fingers. "Do you think they could be Fae? I have been anxious since that horrible announcement, wondering if the fairy in disguise even knows whether or not she is a fairy. Could it be me? Please believe that I do not wish to be one!"

The Clarretts are quick to reassure her.

"Certainly the fairy in disguise knows who she is," says Mr. Clarrett.

Reena wonders if he is right, but the duchess leaves with a lighter step. Mlle. Latour is next.

The napkin keeps slipping and covering her view, so Reena entwines her thumbs and forefingers around the circular end of the device instead. She switches to her left eye.

The Parisian girl's English is perfect but heavily accented. With a sigh, Reena concentrates again to catch every word.

"I do not need to tell you of my past. My father is Frederic Latour. Of course I am not Fae. It is but silly bedtime stories meant to frighten children. I think it is a hoax. She was not even that good an actress. If this is your idea of a contest, I think it is in rather poor taste. All the same, I have my honor. I am not frightened. I will not leave."

"Thank you for your time, Mlle. Latour."

She is dismissed, and Mr. Clarrett paces the room.

Reena has discovered that the copper grafts on her fingers have left their own pattern around her left eye. At least now she is symmetrically indented. She sighs and presses her right eye directly back onto the device when Miss Brannon arrives.

"My father is Irish, and my mother is Scottish. I was raised in Dublin with my six siblings. Four brothers, two sisters. My father opened a textile factory after the Spindle Ban. He redesigned the mechanical loom, making it more efficient, and sold the design to other factories. We might not be a noble family, but we are honest. My father sometimes told stories of the Fair Folk when I was a child. I never much liked them. My mother dismissed fairies as fanciful, and I do not think my father truly believed in them. They did not even allow us to read the Grimms' stories. I cannot believe in them now, whatever that Vivianne claims to be. I am certainly not one of them."

"Thank you, Miss Brannon."

She leaves, and Reena quickly asks a maid for the location of the necessary. She needs a mirror, cold water, and a soft towel before the Clarretts see her in her dented condition.

Dignity intact, Reena reenters the parlor, where she finds mother and son in heated debate over which girl is Fae. They quickly ask her opinion.

"Duchess Stepanova seems the most likely, though I believe that she truly does not know the identity of her original parents. It would be just like the Fae to arrange a Fair Child to be among us without even knowing it herself."

"Despite my assurances to the contrary to Duchess Stepanova, I agree with you," replies Mr. Clarrett. "But we cannot rule out Miss Brannon."

"Nor can we rule out Alice, Tamsin, or Elizabeth."

Both Clarretts turned to her quizzically.

"Who?"

"The maids."

"The maids?" Mrs Clarrett repeats, not comprehending.

"The Fae are known for their silver tongues, are they not? What Vivianne said was 'one among you.' Not: 'one among the contestants.' She could have been including any young woman in the room."

Thomas lays his face into his hands and mumbles.

"Why must this be so complicated? Why is this happening at all?"

He looks up.

"But truly, why now? Why disappear for fourteen years and then return to punish us? Despite recent notoriety of a small degree—and I am not being overly humble—we Clarretts are not of any grand importance. If the Fae are offended by not being invited to the Exhibition, why not go straight to Prince Albert?"

Mrs. Clarrett puts a comforting hand on his shoulder.

"There must be something about this contest that is important to them. Vivianne did mention their love of beauty and display."

"Does anyone else think that sounded like a flat excuse? That sort of generalization comes from the same cottage tales that promote iron as a weapon against them."

There is an awkward moment, which Reena does not feel adequate to fill. Finally, Mrs. Clarrett breaks the silence by sitting up and brushing off her impeccable skirts.

"Well. Let us face one problem at a time. How shall we test the girls?"

Mr. Clarrett pinches the bridge of his nose.

"Whatever method we choose, I wish to keep it to ourselves as much as possible. No sense in showing our hand too soon. If we even *have* a hand to show."

"So, we need a method that is subtle but empirical," Reena states, standing and beginning to pace.

"Do you have something in mind?"

"No, I do not."

Mrs. Clarrett begins to think out loud. "Lady Vivianne gave an explanation for why the iron did not work—do you remember it?"

"That she fears nothing that comes from the earth," her son quotes, taking his turn at standing and pacing.

"Hardly helpful," quips Reena.

Mr. Clarrett throws himself back down onto the sofa.

"What I do not understand is how so many men of learning, who believed in the Fae and studied them, wrote about the efficacy of iron as a weapon against them."

"One source wrote it and the rest copied it?"

"Many were written around the same time from disparate corners of the Isles. No common source. I double checked this morning."

"Could it be a certain type of iron? A particular alloy?" Mrs. Clarrett offers.

"Every alloy is still 'from the earth,'" her son argues.

Reena shoots to her feet.

"Oh!"

The Clarretts stare at her.

"Egypt!"

"Egypt?"

"Yes! Napoleon!"

"My dear Miss Kapoor, are you quite well?"

She begins to pace again.

"My father wished to study the Egyptian's use of metals, so I read accounts from Napoleon's expeditions. They used metals quite ingeniously to create pigments. There were a few hieroglyphic texts that I studied, from translations done later by Champollion. Of course, I searched for any mention of metal, and one in particular struck me."

"Yes?"

She turns to her captive audience.

"They called it 'star metal.'"

Mr. Clarrett goes still.

"A meteorite," he breathes.

"A meteorite," she repeats. "Not from this earth."

"But where *on* earth are we to find one?" Mrs. Clarrett interjects as the voice of reason. Her son smiles.

"I know a shop that might sell them. They deal in exotic imports."

"Whatever do people buy them for?"

Mr. Clarrett shrugs.

"Everyone wants a piece of the sky. Iron from the heavens."

Reena lets out a breath.

"Iron that will burn."

***

The plan is Mrs. Clarrett's idea. If her son returns successful, she will knock in a particular way on Reena's door and then pay a visit to the hotel matron, Mrs. Hill, to discuss the maids. Miss Kapoor meanwhile will collect the other contestants for a special meeting with Thomas Clarrett in the ballroom. The maids by then will have been sent to clean the rooms most recently vacated by former contestants, while those that remain meet downstairs. Reena understands that this will leave all of the girls' bedrooms (maids' included) open for some sort of test to be put in place, but Mrs. Clarrett would not explain fully.

The knock comes. Reena jumps to her feet, heart racing with the thrill of Thomas' success. She quickly fulfills her part.

During the entirety of the hour spent in the ballroom, Reena can barely stop her toe from tapping in anticipation. Thomas casts a quick smile toward her when she enters, but conversation with the other contestants' takes his attention.

On their way back upstairs to dress for dinner, Reena catches a glimpse of Mrs. Clarrett descending from the back service stair. Mrs. Clarrett nods across the distance and is met by her son, who escorts her out the front door.

Apparently, Reena is not to know the finer details. Frustrating family!

She does not see either of them again for an entire week, raising her frustration to full blown anxiety. Nightmares begin to plague her sleep, in which the fairy in disguise reveals herself, and the knife of star metal Thomas has forged does no good against her. Reena always thrusts herself into consciousness before the evil Fae can turn the knife back on him.

At breakfast each day, the other girls seem to be feeling the pressure as well. None except for Mlle. Latour and Miss Mandla look well rested, and Miss Kapoor is not so sure that in both cases it is not just sheer force of will creating that illusion. Duchess Stepanova carries dark bags under her eyes, which do nothing for her fair coloring. Miss Brannon appears thinner and tenser, jumping at the slightest noise.

That first evening after the day of interviews, Miss Kapoor finds a note slipped under her door.

> *I know you must be frustrated not knowing. Mother has protested keeping you in the dark, but every experiment must have its control. I told her you would understand. Keep heart!*
>
> *TC*

She tucks it inside her pocket each morning afterward, the feel of it crinkling beneath her fingers enough to give her mind a moment's quiet.

The next shock comes the morning of April 29th, two days before the Crystal Palace opening and just a day and a half before the ball.

Miss Brannon has left in the night.

Mlle. Latour breaks into open tears.

Duchess Stepanova exclaims in a moment of nervous silliness, "But what if she has been kidnapped by the fairies?!"

Miss Mandla gives her a light slap on the cheek. "Of course she was not kidnapped. I saw her carriage through my window."

The duchess presses her cheek in shock but then apologizes.

"I am not myself these days."

"None of us are." Miss Mandla offers as an olive branch.

Reena just stares into space, thinking, *I dearly hope she was not the fairy*, but she is too tired to feel much emotion over it.

Now it is down to seven.

That evening, another note is pushed underneath her door. Reena quickly unfolds it and is disappointed. It is not from Thomas.

> *My son and I have investigated the matter you brought to our attention. The three additional possibilities are no longer such. Each is known too well in their particular circles.*
>
> RC

It takes Reena a minute longer than it should to ascertain the meaning behind Mrs. Clarrett's vague wording. When she does, she mutters.

"And then there were four."

That night, the last before the ball, Reena's nightmare is the worst yet. Duchess Stepanova reveals herself as the fairy, her prettiness transforming into unearthly beauty. This time there is no knife. This time, Thomas smiles and reaches for her hand. Reena wakes in tears.

The next day is a haze. That afternoon, Reena brings her formal sari out from her traveling trunk, to ready herself for the ball. She is almost too exhausted to wrap it properly, but it gets done. She adds an anklet with little bells that rest just above her silk slipper and bangles that clink against the metal *mehendi* in her hands.

She dozes for most of the carriage ride to Hyde Park, where the Crystal Palace has just been finished. For a moment, it wakes her spirit to see such fantastic construction—a miracle of iron and glass and nothing else. A full-grown tree fits inside the center atrium and fountains tinkle down the aisles of the two wings. Shuttered booths of innovations from every conceivable nation, just waiting for the dawn to be uncovered and shown off to the world, line the aisles. As the sun sets, the glass turns black, the interior gaslights throwing their reflections against it like artificial stars.

Duchess Stepanova sidles up and whispers in a shocked voice. "I hear they have public restrooms! For both men *and* women!"

Reena manages a smile.

The crowd around them is growing. She looks for Thomas in vain.

Hours later, she is dozing again, having found a small chair tucked halfway behind a potted plant, letting the swirl of colored fabrics lull her to sleep as the dancers—the best of British and international society—sweep around the dance floor to an energetic band. Hushed conversations travel to her ears in random bursts. Once or twice she hears the word "fairy." Apparently, rumors are circulating.

And then it is time.

Thomas is on the stage with his parents.

Surreptitiously, Reena flicks cool water from a nearby fountain on her face and pinches her cheeks. As she makes her way toward the makeshift backstage area, her nerves begin to wear away her exhaustion.

There has been nothing out of the ordinary at the hotel, other than Miss Brannon leaving—no sign of a test causing any disruption. Reena concludes that her star metal idea has not worked.

Thomas must be distraught. If he chooses wrongly, every bit of artifice in the world, everything he loves, will turn to dust. She has no doubt that Vivianne will keep her threat. *So he must choose Duchess Stepanova. With Miss Brannon gone, she is the obvious choice.* She swallows past a lump in her throat.

Once all of the contestants are lined up on stage, squinting into the bright lights trained on them, barely able to make out the crowd, the elder Mr. Clarrett introduces himself and with great flourish describes the particulars of the contest. There is no mention of fairies or curses.

When she is introduced, Reena manages a graceful curtsy, bells around her ankle and tiny brass gears decorating her sari jingling harmoniously.

As Thomas steps forward, Reena catches her breath. She spies a hooded figure lurking in the wings, stage-left. Could it be?

Thomas is speaking. Reena's nerves spike, and she cannot quite hear. Until…

"…and my choice is… Miss Reena Kapoor!"

The lights go out.

There are screams in the crowd and the sound of shoving until a soft glow begins to bring order back to the chaotic dark. It emanates from Vivianne, who steps from the wing onto center-stage.

"Well chosen, Thomas."

"But—but I am not Fae!" protests Reena.

Vivianne turns to her.

"Yes, you are. A changeling. You do know that your father traveled to England often for business in his youth. He found one of our… doorways and took advantage of trading that we offered." She frowned. "We allowed him too much. During one dealing, we discovered that he had behaved in a less than honest way, in order to return quickly to his wife, who believed she was pregnant with a son. His heir at last. You."

"But—"

"No, you are obviously not. We exchanged the child in the womb for a girl of ours as punishment for your father. It is the only time I have ever traveled to India. I did not care for the heat."

Vivianne turns back to Thomas, leaving Reena gaping.

"You must tell me how you discovered her true identity."

Thomas smiles, but it is not kind.

"Meteoritic iron."

The fairy's eyes widen.

"Yes, we know your secret now."

His voice rises to include the captive audience straining to follow what is happening on stage.

"It is my mother who deserves credit for the test. As we had discovered a substance that is inimical to fairies, we wished to keep it secret. Our test needed to be discreet but with concrete proof. My mother said to me, 'Let us place one piece of the substance under each girl's mattress as they sleep. The one who spends restless nights will provide us evidence of her heritage.' As you might imagine, I was skeptical."

Thomas was warming up to his audience.

"I queried whether or not the girls would feel such a small thing under a thick mattress. My mother, ever the pragmatist, explained. 'My dear,' she said. 'The hotel might have delusions of grandeur, but they are just delusions, as the thinness of the mattresses will attest.'"

This drew laughter from the crowd.

"'Short of sewing the substance into their clothing, this will afford it the longest time possible in as close contact as possible to our contestants. Or do you have a better idea?' Obviously, I did not, so I bowed to her wisdom.

"At first, the hotel matron reported that all girls were showing signs of sleep-deprivation, understandable with a fairy curse hanging over our heads. We began to lose confidence. But then—"

Thomas steps toward Reena and takes her hands gently, pulling her to the front of the stage.

"Then I heard that Miss Kapoor was crying out in her sleep, that nightmares plagued her, and that there were faint bruises on the back of her shoulders and arms, which she may not have noticed, but others did. And I knew."

Reena grips his hands more tightly.

"But what if you were wrong?" she whispers. "There must have been a seed of doubt. What if you were wrong, and the fairies destroyed artifice and everything you love?"

"Well, they would not have destroyed *everything* I love." His smile is the smile she saw in her dream, yet this time it is directed at her.

Vivianne interrupts, "Yes, this is all very touching, but there is more to discuss."

"What else is there?" Thomas demands harshly.

Reena answers for him. "We must discuss *why*."

Vivianne smiles slowly, like a cat finding cream. "Your chosen bride is intelligent, Thomas."

"Obviously," he retorts. "Now, explain. Why did you do this?"

She throws out her arms in a familiar way.

"Business, my dear artificer. Business. Do you think the Fae have retreated to our lands, ignoring the power that humanity is gaining? We want to be part of it. We will *not* be lost to time." Her eyes are fierce.

"That is why you did business with my father."

"Yes. His dishonesty set our plans back some years, for the more conservative among us saw it as a sign that we *should* retreat."

She squares her shoulders.

"But *I* am Lady of our Woods, and I say no."

Reena's thoughts spin. She releases one of Thomas' hands and steps them both toward Vivianne.

"So what is it that you want from *me*?"

"If you are this intelligent when tired, then Thomas should let you run the business when he inherits."

"Willingly," he murmurs. "I'll work; you'll manage?"

Reena flashes a grin back at him then faces Vivianne once more.

"We wondered why you chose to curse the contest. It is hardly the most exciting thing happening during this Exhibition. It made no sense to us, at least at first. I now see a little more clearly. It is me, is it not? I am the common factor bringing you here, now, today."

"Of course. Had you not joined in the contest and merely been on display in the Exhibition, we may have needed to lay a curse on the entire Crystal Palace. It would have been difficult, so I thank you for not making that necessary."

"What do you want from me?"

"A child must help pay for the sins of the father, do you not agree?"

"Apparently, I am not his daughter."

Vivianne waves a hand, as if brushing the words away.

"Nonsense. You are as much his daughter as you are a child of the Fae. That is how the magic works. The debt remains."

"You want me to work for you?"

"In a way. You will be our ambassador to the human world. You will help us negotiate our business affairs, help us integrate into your magnificent world of artifice. It is beautiful, and we can add to it beyond your wildest imagination. Imagine this building, but no iron—simply glass. Or no glass and simply iron, open to the elements that empower it all."

In this moment, Reena sees the heart of Vivianne, a heart full of wonder and grand ideas. The heart of an artificer, if she only has the chance to become one.

"I agree."

"Miss Kapoor!" protests Thomas.

"First of all, please call me Reena. Secondly, it is truly fine. I will be the fairies' ambassador. But—"

She locks eyes with Vivianne, staring into their green depths, pushing her will against the fairy's in a way that she does not quite understand but, she is beginning to discover, is her birthright. Being a changeling might bring its own rewards. She drops her voice, so the still-rapt audience cannot hear.

"But the fairies will always know that we know their secret. If there is ever again a fairy curse as long as I or Thomas lives, as long as our children or children's children live, we will give that secret to the world."

Vivianne stands still for a moment, her cloak fluttering in an unseen breeze, never breaking eye contact. Finally, she nods, and in the next moment, is gone. There is a moment of sweet silence heralding the ending of the curse.

Then, in full view of everyone, Thomas spins Reena around and kisses her soundly, and Reena realizes that she is not so tired after all.

Christina Ruth Johnson is an avid fan of fairy tales and fantasy fiction. She spends her days teaching art, art history, and ancient history to middle and high schoolers and her evenings daydreaming, reading, and birdwatching. In the summers you can find her on an archaeological dig in Israel. She is absolutely thrilled to be a part of this anthology. Her story "The Iron Revolution" puts a steampunk spin on The Princess and the Pea with dashes of Cinderella and Sleeping Beauty thrown in for fun.

CLOCKWORK TEA

Joseph Halden

From the diary of Robert Fortune, 1848

My loneliness has progressed such that I now long after the automata. Do not judge me, dear reader, for had you travelled as an unwelcome foreigner for as long as I have, you would also lower the standards to which you hold company.

Then again, I should hope neither you nor anyone are reading this, for it is more likely than not these private musings would cost my livelihood.

To stop writing my thoughts altogether, however, means forfeiting my sanity. I choose, therefore, to continue. As they say here in China, "Go forward, go backward—both difficult."

A dull emptiness had already begun to set in the day the steamship landed in Hong Kong. Open markets all around, bustling with conversation that, despite my previous visits, I struggled to follow. Why could they not adopt one mother tongue?

Bowls of tea were pushed at me, none I trusted. People beckoned from the fish markets whose stench always made me gag. Lining the muddy streets were a handful of vile opium dens.

And everywhere, automata trinkets.

Countless demonstrations of wooden and metal figures: some as large as oxen, some as small as thimbles, all engaged in some mimicry of humanity. The larger ones moved to the whirring and puffing of steam, sustaining the market's fog.

An automaton boy drew Chinese characters on a sheet of paper, the craftsman having taken such pains as to make the fake head look up and blink every so often. Another automaton handed out bags of purchased tea while staring into oblivion. Built only from the torso up, these automata sat propped on vendor's tables as novelties to attract passersby.

Other automata in the market included merry-go-rounds, flat cases that opened magically into birds, flopping fish beneath a fisherman's rod… all manner of snapshots into the lives from which the automata would remain forever distant.

Seeing them gladdened my heart, though, for it signaled that Britain's efforts to penetrate the Chinese market, with our superior automata craftsmanship, were succeeding. This suggested my own mission had better chances now, too.

Up until quite recently, China had been squeezing the Queen's silver out of Britain, for they alone possessed the secrets of growing and processing tea. The country was said to be the graveyard of silver, for all flowed in and none out, in order to feed the Empire's tea addiction.

That was the reason for my quest: tea. I was tasked to find out tea's secrets, and bring back enough samples to enable full-production plantations in India.

I wondered how many of the teas in the stalls around me were stained with cyanide to make them a vibrant green.

Cyanide. Such treachery had resulted in the untimely death of my dearest cousin Patrick. How I wish he were still alive, and that we could enjoy a Sunday afternoon biscuit with some of the tea—*safe*, better tea kept for China's internal consumption—I'd vowed to bring back.

I had to see it all, learn it all, and bring it all back by myself, for I could trust no one here.

For who could poison—murder—all for the sake of making a few more sales? Such acts removed one's claim to humanity, in my view.

After escaping the hordes of hawkers, I seconded to a private hotel room where I began the transformation to mark myself as loyal to Emperor Daoguang. Shaved forehead and sides, and long hair tied back into a braided ponytail. From my suitcase I unfolded the long-sleeved, long-waisted traditional garb that completed the façade.

If anyone now inquired of my provenance, I would say truthfully, "From beyond the Great Wall."

You might think this is not enough for me to pass as a Chinaman, but the country is so vast that there is a surprisingly large amount of diversity. Mongolians are almost as pale as me, and in the Southwest of China, among the Hmong, the Chinese even have blonde hair. Therefore, to the majority of countryfolk who have had limited experiences with the breadth of what it can mean to be Chinese, saying "I'm from beyond the Great Wall" in a strange accent does not preclude the idea of me being a Chinaman, for they have glimpsed enough variance within their borders but are not yet experts.

This is not the case with the more worldly traders in the mercantile cities, where they've had far more interactions with foreigners and have learned to be more discerning about who is Chinese and who is not. I shall have to be more careful among them, and be sure that no such merchants recognize me once I go past the treaty ports where foreigners are allowed to walk.

It is both a blessing and a curse this country is so big, for once in the countryside I can move about as a sheep in wolf's clothing. However, the country's vastness also means my journey into the

North, to get the best green and black teas, will be arduous and time-consuming.

Once I donned the garb, the veil came over me, a curtain of deception that also rent me from myself. Would you believe, dear reader, that lying rearranges you, bit by bit, with forces so small you can't tell what's happening until your nose is askew and your mouth crooked? A small fire that spreads and alters everything in its path? If there is magic in this world, it is found through truth and lies.

This lie began the slow erosion of loneliness.

Here the urge to speak the truth, to tell someone of my true purpose, began in earnest, for it is only so long that one can maintain a lie without it burning a hole right through the centre.

***

I reached the village of Shanghai before the first difficulties. Hiring local porters and boatmen to ferry me was tiresome, because there are so many dialects, and I had to be sure I had a guide for each dialectical leg of the journey. My own mastery of the language is not strong enough to hold great conversation with them, so I was in many ways at their mercy.

I told the men the moment we departed Shanghai, that we had to avoid the city of Hangzhou. Many times I emphasized this, although I did not outright state that I didn't want to set foot in a bustling trade city where I would be recognized by the more worldly traders as a foreigner, and hanged for going beyond the treaty ports.

I had learned to read Chinese well enough that I recognized the signs for Hangzhou the moment we drew close. Cursing my recalcitrant guides, I demanded a palanquin before we went any farther, because to turn back now would waste considerable time and invite follow-ups from the watchful guards.

My guides carried me in the palanquin, passing bribes to the guards along the way. Soon I found myself in the middle of the city—too late to turn back. Robert Fortune, helpless. If the guards at the entrance hadn't taken bribes, I would be dead. I prayed the guards at the exit would be just as remiss in their duties. The sound of the busy markets, that I couldn't see, stabbed daggers in my ears. Every outburst from an enthusiastic vendor rang accusatory, as though each one was a member of a jury to unearth my guilt.

All my autonomy had vanished. I felt shackled and bound for the entire journey.

We reached the other side, where by some grace the guards were able to be bribed just as the ones at the entrance had. As I emerged from the lowered palanquin and inhaled as though surfacing from a lake, I realized it was in fact two sophisticated automata that had carried me through the city.

They looked so much like real Chinese people, that were it not for the tufts of steam spouting from the napes of their jackets, and the whirring of gears, even I could have been deceived. Their eyes blinked, and their bodies bobbed in a small rhythm reminiscent of life. Although they did not speak, their heads turned in the direction of sound.

They could also walk across terrain, following simple instructions, even navigating rough surfaces.

Such a remarkable creation far surpassed anything I'd ever seen back home. Maybe this was yet another secret the Chinese had hidden from us. Perhaps this is where the so-called graveyard of British silver lay, in the automata they had bought and then improved upon.

Our whole troupe seemed jovial, having been revivified by their passage through the city, joking with one another and bargaining for food.

And me, removed from it all, forced to merely march when needed, not unlike the automata.

By the time night had fallen and we'd set up camp in a forest, the urge to connect, to speak truthfully to someone, overtook me.

You might think me a liar, but I swear the automaton they call Baozhai tilted its head more and more in my direction, as though it could sense my great consternation.

All my other companions were soon asleep, and I remained with Baozhai who sat rigidly upright, head still tilting to sounds.

You will probably think me foolish, dear reader, but a most delirious urge struck me, an urge to unwind the secrets knotted about me. And the automaton presented as the perfect medium to unfetter this land's coils.

I told myself the machine is not human, so it had no opinion that could be taken into consideration. Its comprehension was likely not greater than what was required for simple directions. Yet I should have seen the contradiction in that moment, because the automaton was the only one who seemed to have noticed the effect of the day's stresses on my psyche.

I told her absolutely everything in a broken mix of English and Cantonese, with several words from Mandarin and other dialects that had blurred into my vocabulary. She listened with black eyes lit by the fire, tilting toward the sound of my voice, blinking just often enough the illusion of life could be maintained.

I found, with each word spoken, she grew more human, which drew the words from me as a medic wresting poison from a wound.

It felt good to unwind some of the twisting my spirits had endured under the weight of the long-maintained lies. Through the truth I felt realigned by subtle forces, a quelling of the fire that had burned and rearranged unseen parts of me.

I finished with a dry mouth despite the jungle around.

Baozhai grew still and elicited a louder whirring of gears. Then, to my great astonishment, my own voice emerged from her throat.

What devilry was this? She'd somehow captured—recorded— every single word I'd uttered.

What a fool I'd been.

There was no choice what to do next. Baozhai had recorded far too much. I doubted she herself could understand it, but that didn't matter—the Chinamen would.

I will not say I killed her, because to kill implies something is alive. I disassembled her, violently.

So many gears. So many incredible gears and interconnecting tubes and pipes, I thought a surgeon's license may be needed to make sense of it all. I will admit there was a lingering sense of unease in my heart, especially as she twitched during the disassembly but I reminded myself that Baozhai was nothing more than a glorified spanner. After digging and coating my hands in black oil, I discovered a key linkage, a gear or cog—I'm not certain of the correct term—whose absence caused her motion to stop altogether.

That convinced me, more than anything else. In other places in her body, the gears and linkages seemed to have some redundancy, some capacity for failure that wouldn't be catastrophic. A mimicry of homeostasis. Yet this cog, this single bit of molded metal, was enough to halt her life completely.

Nothing living could be that fragile. Life was fragile in some respects, but always there was some capacity for withstanding hardship. Even part of the heart could die without causing an entire system failure.

Such a weak, fragile thing as this automaton, dependent on a single cog, could not be deemed living.

After washing off the oil and disposing of all the evidence in the swift-flowing Qiantang river, I tried to gather sleep, and further convince myself of my righteousness.

To dispel all lingering doubt required subtle rearrangements, refinements to my thoughts, as though I had grasped the minute spiritual forces and tuned them for my own designs. I was right, though, and that certainty won through.

***

My goodness, what wondrous relief! A great weight has been lifted. I feel as though the air is cleaner, and our quiet journeys on the river are now bearable.

My companions were satisfied by my hypothesis that a

malfunction had caused Baozhai to wander off during the night. It seems even they are wary of the newness of the automata.

Even more invigorating than the mere confession last night was the sense of authority, autonomy, that I regained in those final urgent moments with Baozhai. I was a master again, albeit of a small domain, but a master nonetheless, and that was enough. It would sustain me, and reverse the transformative effects of the daily lies.

I have kept Baozhai's cog, as a memento of that power, and when I feel lonely now, I thumb the teeth of the gear like a rosary.

***

The loneliness has sunk in once more, like sediment to the bottom of a jar of swamp water. Thankfully we will soon be stopping by another village, where I pray there will be more automata to replace the one I disposed of last night.

I kept its cog, too, and it forms a matching set with Baozhai's. Curiously, they are not the same—I wonder how many different models there are?

***

The journey has been horrendously long. Yes, the vistas are at times breathtaking, with rolling hills and mountains covered in such a deep green, and with forests banded as though a creator painted them with a thick brush.

Most days, however, the beauty is not enough. The diversity is not enough.

I record and catalogue the plants, and want to share the wondrous progress I'm making, the discoveries I know will change the lives of every British man and woman. Yet there is no one with whom I can share it.

The nearest I've come to camaraderie was during passage through a canyon, when my companions said the region held dead spirits that were calling to them. They explained that they must call back then proceeded to make bestial calls that echoed for miles, and I joined them.

I've dispatched several more of the pack-carrying automata. Do not judge me, for they are serving in their demise a higher purpose as councillors than they ever were as pack animals.

Most remarkably, their cogs are all unique. Cataloguing the intricacies of their interiors is as fascinating an enterprise as is cataloguing the local flora, and I only wish I could share it all.

***

Finally, I've reached the plantation. The knowledge and secrets that have been withheld for so long now pour over me. A long, dangerous journey has paid off, and it seems I will have ample enough supplies and samples to send to the plantations in India.

The fields are lush and so thick with humidity in the mornings you can put out your tongue and taste settling droplets. Yet in the afternoons, it all dries in a baking heat, made worse by the steady flames with which the workers roast and churn the tea leaves.

Beyond the secrets of the tea making, it seems the Chinese have been hiding far more advanced automata in these remote mountains. The entire plantation is run by walking clocks who shuttle up and down the rows of plants, bowing to each one before they pluck it. The cooking, the stirring, and the spreading are all done by wooden machines that would make Britain's greatest artisans redden with shame, and Joseph Merlin's Swan look like a toy.

Their liveliness is uncanny. The tender grace with which they carry themselves about, and seem to gaze into the sunlight, evokes competing emotions within me. For I recognize in them a subtle humanity. I feel a kinship through their seemingly strong love of nature, a kinship stronger than any I have felt so far with my fellow Chinese travelers.

Yet I know, at their heart, these intricate creatures possess a single cog upon which their entire worlds pivot, and such a fragile homeostasis cannot be said to be alive.

***

It seems I've spent all of the fortune which is my namesake, for I am cursed. Cursed!

This morning, with foolishly naïve high spirits, I was whistling the tune of *God Save the Queen* as I walked about with the automata gathering samples. And would you believe it? Their blasted infernal cogs must've once more contained some means of not only recognizing but storing a catalogue of sounds, for out of the gaped mouth of a porcelain-white automaton came a recording of *God Save the Queen*, by a full symphony, no less.

Our own desperate exports have become my undoing. Were we not so overzealous to penetrate the Chinese market and recuperate some of Britain's lost silver, our advanced automata might not have migrated so deeply into the Chinese culture. Although these automata seem to have far outpaced our own capabilities, there appear to be some lingering relics of British influence.

As soon as the song came out of the pile of gears, one of the nearby boatmen widened his eyes and lifted an accusatory finger toward me. By his expression of abject horror, I could see he finally realized that I was not, in fact, a Chinaman. Chasing him down was easy enough, being a full head and shoulders taller than him. Gagging and binding him in the forest was obligatory.

I wanted to smash the automaton who had given me away, but the opportunity was robbed from me, for upon returning to the plantation, more of the boatmen were milling about. Perhaps I should be grateful only one of them had heard my witless patriotism.

The rest of the day was spent in utter terror that I would be discovered, or that the missing boatman would wriggle free of his bonds. I copied down notes as normal but my mind was in another world, a world replete with cliffs and precipices, where a single sigh in the wrong direction could send me plummeting to a rocky demise.

I could not kill the boat man, yet I could not let him go, either, without ruining everything I'd fought so long and hard for.

What other options were there? If I took the path of moral righteousness, then my dear cousin Patrick, and so many others who'd perished at the hands of cyanide-laced green tea would surely haunt me in the afterlife. Yet if I killed this boatman, I would be descending to the same level, committing an atrocious murder for the sake of my own industry.

I ruminated the day long over what to do, and had not a single solution when the sun finally set. The smoke from roasting tea leaves, normally a cleansing tonic for my spirits, tasted more like ash.

***

I did it. By some miracle, I did it.

It took me all night, and the bones of my fingers are exhausted from intricate surgery, but it is done.

They say that higher powers often give us problems at the same time they give us solutions, and this was one of those fortuitous occasions.

By the time everyone had gone to bed the path was as clear and obvious as the endlessly glowing lights of the automaton's lamplit eyes.

You would not believe the intricate cams and gears inside these automata. Their spines consist of a thousand vertebra, shining golden, irregular shapes each crafted for a different movement, a different sound, and—dare I say it—a different thought. It is as though their brains have grown beyond the confines of their skulls and extended all the way down into this long series of interconnecting disks so thin that if you squint it appears as a single pulsating wave of life.

In this wave lies the mutability of the automaton's existence.

My encounters with automata up to this point seem to have prepared me for this moment.

I traced the interconnecting gears by candlelight through long hours until it became clear just how I could modify them to my own designs.

If you teach a man to fish, are you then responsible if he kills all the fish in the lake? At some point there must be separation between creator and created. Just as I had taken responsibility to deal with the aftermath of the lies' power, the automaton had to take ownership of the subtle adjustments I had made.

Am I responsible if an automaton picks up an iron fire stoker rather than a clump of tea leaves? Am I responsible if they take many more paces out of the plantation and up the hill, rather than into the sheds to stir the sacs of dried leaves?

I say I am not. Thus I walk, and maintain, my tread on the path of righteousness. My own spine tingled as though something had tried to shape me, but I had emerged unscathed.

***

I have another of my keepsake cogs, and I didn't even have to dismantle the automaton myself. Once the other boatman discovered what the clockwork creature had done to their compatriot, they tore it apart in much the same way it had their friend.

Now all that remains is to pack the tea specimens into the Wardian glass cases that will allow moisture to recirculate and keep the plants alive on their long journey to India. I will tuck my keepsake cogs into these cases, for I believe the Chinese may be even more reluctant to have these leave the country than their precious green tea.

To top it all, I will be able to return and delight my colleagues with newfound knowledge of advanced automata.

***

The journey back was uneventful, or so I thought until I saw all the shipments.

Someone had opened the Wardian cases. What fools! Almost all the plants were absolutely, utterly ruined, and I have nearly nothing to show for my long toils.

The handful of samples that have survived are all ones in which I have buried my cogs.

Now, I am not known to be superstitious, and consider myself a true man of science, but even if this effect were correlative rather than causal, my fragile psyche needed a means of channeling all the disappointment, frustration and creativity that had been destroyed.

So began my foray into the construction of an automaton.

Perhaps I am trying to prove that a Scot can do just as well as a Chinaman in crafting these into near-humanity.

Nevertheless, I have been working long hours in an effort to get my automaton ready for my trip back to China. This time, I will not only get more samples of the green tea, but black tea, too.

***

I have returned to China, accompanied by my automaton good-luck charm, whose innards of gears, cams and cogs include all those I collected during my last trip.

I have named it *Ping Nuo Cha,* meaning "Peaceful, warm tea."

It can traverse rough terrain, carry any odd object placed in its purview, and record notes so I can replay some of the more challenging dialects to translate. The hardest oak makes up its body. The bone structure of its limbs is the inverse of a human's. Where we have skin and flesh, it has hardwood, and where we have bones, it has cavities filled with malleable cams and rods. It needs very little oil; such is the precision with which I have arranged its motions.

Best of all, I have carefully designed its gears so there is not a single one without which it cannot function. It is far closer to achieving a true homeostasis like that of a real boy.

I am proud to say that its outward likeness is remarkable. The artist I hired to texture its Chinaman skin, paint its lips and mount a long black ponytail to its head did a magnificent job. *Ping Nuo Cha's* narrow, glass-beaded eyes track my motions well, with just enough white in them to dispel the impression of marbles. Its articulate cheeks and eyebrows are capable of the subtlest motions, elegantly combined with natural, almost imperceptible tilts in the head, that I shall be not struck by loneliness again, nor will I be shaped by the long-term effects of my necessary lies.

This trip, everything will go smoothly.

***

The journey has gone well so far, but not without issues.

I'd hoped having *Ping Nuo Cha* around would keep me from feeling the pressing grip of loneliness, and he has. The boatmen have taken to him quite well, included him among their own automata and even complemented *Ping Nuo Cha's* competence at carrying without staggering. *Ping Nuo Cha* has successfully replayed conversations to me, so that I can clarify those I could not follow the first time. His eyes seem so eager for acceptance, for approval, that I cannot help but speak to him, teach him, in the late hours when everyone else is asleep. He is a rapt listener, and has helped me keep the truth alive and flowing in my body.

Yet even *Ping Nuo Cha* is not enough to combat the rising pressure I feel as the weeks grind by. I cannot help but feel at the mercy of my environment.

Perhaps it is my overall impatience throughout the long travels, or my hunger for retribution this time around, that is driving me harder, making my mind whir when it should find peace in the surroundings. I feel like everything is winding out of control with each moment that passes without more tea samples in my hands.

How else can you regain a sense of control when you cannot tune the clockwork of your own life? Were the lies bearing down on me with greater force?

Thus, in desperation after weeks of travel, to avoid falling into an abyss from which I might not emerge, I have stripped several more automata of their essence. I've taken their key cogs.

To my delight, they are as unique as the rest of my collection, and I have put them into *Ping Nuo Cha* to build up his expressions and enhance his capacities. With each addition he grows more and more like—dare I say it—a son.

As a result, his face seems to have bulged a bit near the nose—I'll have to look into that in the coming days. Perhaps I am merely redirecting the subtle forces that seek to shape me, but even if so, it's better on him than me.

***

What can I do, dear reader, what can I do?

I thought to keep these words hidden from everyone, absolutely everyone, but like my yearning to speak and be heard, I am at last desperate for someone, anyone in the far reaches of this god-forsaken land, to read these words and offer aid. Perhaps if more people read these words of truth, it can wrest me from the entrapment of so many lies.

I have traveled beyond the green tea plantations and acquired all the samples I'd gotten before and more. I've gone even further and reached the temples where monks brew black tea.

I've even added more cogs to *Ping Nuo Cha* (whose nose continues to extrude more and more despite my best efforts).

Fortuitous, you would probably say. Good fortune for Fortune, no?

Yes, in all other circumstances, it would be. But *Ping Nuo Cha* has betrayed me, has rebelled against his father in the most hideous manner possible.

As I've said, there is powerful magic in truth and lies.

Between bouts of prayer and calligraphy with the monks, *Ping Nuo Cha* began playing recordings of my voice.

"I am squeezing every last drop of knowledge out of this country, and brewing it into a delicious tea for the British Empire."

The monks frowned at these words, yes, but thankfully none of them spoke English.

When he played recordings of similar words in different Chinese dialects, bearing my voice, I had to act.

It pained me in that moment, deep in my sternum, with the sudden realization I would have to get rid of *Ping Nuo Cha*. Up to now, he had served me quite well, but I couldn't rightly let my many years of hard work and subterfuge be ruined.

How could he have done such a thing? I'd never constructed any such behaviour in him. It was as though the humid, low-pressure air had recalibrated him.

Or had I merely made him a vessel to be shaped by the force of my lies? Surely that was an absurdity, wasn't it?

I excused myself and found *Ping Nuo Cha* gazing in through a nearby window, clearly wanting to partake in the ceremonial activities.

I felt tremendous anger that such disaster could be sown from *Ping Nuo Cha's* unfathomable childishness. I wished we were closer to the cliff's edge, so that I could shove him off and be rid of him forever, but we were on the side of the temple surrounded by rock, and there was nothing I could do but to try and dismantle him then and there.

The monks, the cursed monks, came upon me before I could make any real progress. Thankfully at that point *Ping Nuo Cha* had deigned to stop playing the recordings.

I could see in the monks' eyes the horror at the thought of me being so violent with what was, in their view, a hapless automaton. There was no way I could destroy *Ping Nuo Cha* right in front of them and still retain enough of their respect to learn their ways.

It is late into the night now. I wish the monks didn't drink so much tea! Will they ever go to sleep? They laugh around the fire with *Ping Nuo Cha* among them and the other automata.

***

I write this with the last of the control left to me, in the hope someone will find and understand. I am not a monster. I am a human, and if you are reading this, then I beg of you to save me.

Last night, by the light of the crescent moon, I cornered *Ping Nuo Cha.* He was as compliant as he usually is.

I had built him with a mind to making him achieve a truer homeostasis, and not depend on a single cog anywhere in his design. It required careful tuning and calibration of multiple redundant gears, but I'd done it. Then I'd added more cogs, pouring my stifled energy into him so that I might feel the healing power of truth again.

In my frantic state, however, I couldn't recognize any of my designs among *Ping Nuo Cha's* innards. There were shadows of memories, perhaps, but nothing clear, and I started to remove things frantically to try and find a way to stop his whirring motion.

Only several gears in, my hands covered in oil and rags all about me, *Ping Nuo Cha* grabbed my hand.

"What are you doing?" he said, playing a recording of my voice chastising a boatman whom I'd caught lazing about in the previous weeks.

"Let go," I snapped, wrenching my arm free and shoving my hands back into his torso.

Ping Nuo Cha's nose seemed to grow. I told myself maybe his head just cocked in a way that the shadow grew longer and twisted. However, with every inch my hands pushed into his body, his nose extended likewise.

Our fates, our essences, seemed bound, but I refused to believe it. My actions could not reshape an automaton in such a manner. My lies could not have invoked such power.

"When left with no option, any living thing will protect itself."

My words again. I had been lecturing *Ping Nuo Cha*.

He had clearly been listening.

His hands were on me again, but this time I grabbed a turnscrew I intended to jam into him, even if I knew it would only slow him down.

I shoved the turnscrew toward him, and *Ping Nuo Cha* shoved right back. Stabbing pain in my stomach. We wrestled and with each dart forward I made, *Ping Nuo Cha* retaliated and turned my own devices against me.

I fell to the floor, bleeding and defeated, my consciousness draining from me.

When I awoke, I lay on a bed, my notebook on the side table, with *Ping Nuo Cha* bent over me.

"All beings have something that turns them," he said, in my voice, from one of my speeches to the many automata I'd slain. "It's just a matter of finding out what."

I cried out in agony as lightning arched up my spine. My limbs grew tingly and I lifted my head just long enough to see that Ping Nuo Cha had cut me wide open.

Blood pooled at my back, draining from me, while Ping Nuo Cha's nose receded, closer to its original size and shape. Inside my abdomen, where my bowels ought to have been, were scores of interconnected gears. And as they began to spin, my sense of control drifted away.

I grabbed for my notebook, and wrote these words, so that someone, anyone, will know the truth, and will please for the love of Great Britain help me.

I am human; you must remember! I am hu—

***

Exhibits Bearing Humanity the Most Captivating
From The Illustrated London News, 1851, by Herbert Ingram

While Prince Albert's *Great Exhibition of the Works of Industry of All Nations* sought to highlight advances in iron, steel, machinery and textiles, the exhibit that most captivated me was an automaton that, upon first description, might seem like nothing out of the ordinary, but upon closer inspection, bears incredible details strikingly close to humanity.

Whether from the taut life-like skin covering the model, the gel-filled eyes, or the natural movements that transcend all the stiffness of much mechanical clockwork, I dare anyone not to be transfixed by this marvel from the Orient. The automaton does not carry out many complex motions, but what it does perform it performs magnificently. From the pouring of tea, to the carrying and delivery of a cup, you will be delighted as though you've been served by a true English butler. This delightful lie will bewitch you for countless hours!

Joseph Halden is a wizard in search of magic, an astronaut in need of space, and a hopeless enthusiast of frivoli-tea. Pinocchio seemed to him the perfect candidate for a clockwork fairy tale, which then just needed an appropriate setting steeped in lies. The British Empire's resume was a perfect fit for the job, in particular the first case of industrial espionage. To be honest, though, Joseph's massive tea addiction probably played a larger part in this assam story's realization. You can mix and matcha from Joseph's e-sencha reading at www.josephhalden.com.

A Future of Towers Made

Beth Cato

I sat across from my husband as our carriage bobbed to and fro, the night breeze through the curtains teasing tendrils of hair loose from my pins. I wore one of my best brocaded gowns, but I'd have given anything to trade my finery for my grubby day dress and precious time on the solid ground of our home laboratory. Instead, social obligation required that I attend a party at Jordan's side.

"Wear your gloves, dear." Jordan tried to straighten his cravat as the carriage heaved.

"My gloves are right here. I'll put them on once we arrive." I did the majority of our laboratory work and had the stained cuticles and calluses to prove it, but heaven forbid I be anything less than his ideal of pretty in public.

"Well! Don't forget, Rapunzel. And the lace along your décolletage has folded inward. Fix it."

I forced my face into neutrality as I inwardly seethed. He hadn't ceased fussing over me ever since I'd returned from shopping with the household staff.

"Is anything on your mind, Jordan?" I asked in my lightest tone as I fixed the lace. It had been years since one of his mistresses had arrived at our doorstep, pregnant and insistent on monetary support. Was I to expect another surprise of that nature?

"I always have things on my mind," he replied loftily as he glanced out the curtains. "Good. We've arrived." He nodded approval as I pulled on my gloves.

We exited the carriage. He required only a moment to program our automated driver to park itself in a nearby lot, and together we entered the estate.

I manufactured a smile as readily as I could an automaton and soon found myself ensconced by women who chattered about children, shopping, and holiday plans for the continent. I had nothing to offer on the subject of offspring—what a mercy!—and contented myself with nodding as my mind wandered to the project that currently stimulated me more than a barrel of tea.

For some months, I had deliberated upon the central problem of the burgeoning airship industry—persistent crashes during ground landings which were all too often followed by dreadful conflagrations.

The solution recently came to me as I stood at the top of the octagonal tower central to my own home. The deep blue sky put me in mind of the sea and ships, and I thought, if a dirigible could dock up high, the vulnerable belly of the ship need never touch the ground.

My design soon shifted away from a house-like structure to a mast akin to an oil derrick of bare steel beams. Access to the top would be achieved by stairs and an automated lift system.

I continued to develop the idea as time permitted—when Jordan fell soundly asleep with the help of sherry, or ambled off to the public house midday—and it had now been two days since I'd had the opportunity to put pen to paper. This tormented me as if I were starving and forced to stare at a magnificent display of patisseries on the far side of strong glass.

"Zela. Zela!" A hand waved before my eyes.

I blinked. "Oh, Naomi!" We hugged. "I haven't seen you in ages. Oh, your hair looks wonderful."

My roommate from my boarding school days wore her hair in the modern fashion, trimmed to highlight her high cheekbones. In stark contrast, mine dangled past my waist when loose but was most often pinned up as Jordan preferred—the trend of our grandmothers' time.

Naomi held me at arm's length, lips pursed as she inspected me as if she sought bruises. A vain effort—Jordan hadn't been that careless since we were newlyweds. "Thank you. Now, if you came to one of my book salons…"

"I wish I could."

She gave me a look that said she knew exactly why I didn't come. It wasn't simply because Jordan disapproved of my socializing without him, though he did. The practical reason why I didn't attend was that I usually worked fourteen-hour days managing his business affairs, laboratory, and household.

"I'm glad you continue to ask, however," I added softly.

Her head tilted in thought as I broke our usual script. "Then I'll persist in my invitations." Her gaze followed mine across the room, to where our husbands were cloistered, amber drinks in hand. By the loudness of his guffaws, Jordan had busily slaked his thirst. "My husband stumbled across something curious in a case of late."

"Oh?" I asked. Naomi worked as law firm secretary and would make an incredible barrister herself, were women allowed such an occupation.

"Yes, we know of a woman bound in a marriage rife with… unpleasantness." She said this in a wide-eyed performance of gossip, but she wasn't wont to prattle, especially about clients. "She suffered beneath the unequal yoke for years, never knowing that when her parents had passed years prior, they had left their property to her, to the specific exclusion of her spouse."

My heart ticked faster, thoughts of my invention pushed aside as new fears and possibilities swirled in my brain. My home—dubbed the Tower—was mine? I love the place as I loved little else in life. As a child, I believed the cozy old estate to be outright magical in nature. To my dreamy eyes, the science my father worked in his laboratory tower was surely the purview of wizards and fairies! Even as an adult, mired in a miserable marriage, my home had never ceased to provide comfort.

But a place of refuge can also become a prison.

"How was this information discovered after so long?" I asked.

"By happenstance. Such paperwork must be filed in duplicate with the district records office. While searching for other papers, Daveed noticed the familiar name."

"How could a woman expect to act on such information?" My voice rasped, anxiety like a hand around my throat. "A person needs more than a domicile to survive on their own."

"I think, perhaps, many women underestimate their capabilities." Naomi chose her words with the care of one treading upon an icy walkway.

I shook my head, frustrated. My ability to invent meant little when I couldn't own my own concepts, much less market them at industrial symposiums.

As if responding to my thought, my husband's laughter boomed out from across the room. I resisted the urge to cringe.

"Perhaps you overestimate their capabilities," I murmured, not adding that Naomi's own experience distorted her perspective. She had a prior marriage herself, begun and ended at age sixteen, but had the fortune of meeting Daveed soon after. I had zero desire for further experiments in matrimony.

"I truly wish you could make it to the next book salon." She smoothly changed the subject as other women sidled close. "Our novel will be about—"

"You think that concept's something? Poppycock!" Jordan's voice was a trombone among flutes. "My next symposium presentation will be the grandest yet! The innovation of our age! The cure for the ill that plagues the nascent airship industry!"

Heads turned his way. Many of those present worked within the airship business, invested in it, or desired to fly. Dread stewing in my gut, I walked toward Jordan, Naomi as my shadow.

"Really? Do tell!" challenged a walrus-like old man.

"I have contrived brilliant new means of landing the crafts!" The room had gone quiet, his announcement clear to all.

"Surely you can tell us more?" cried a man.

"Not until proper patents are filed!" He wagged a finger and grinned, cheeks flushed from pride and drink. "Attend my symposium in two weeks to learn more about my incredible creation!"

His incredible creation. Rage consumed me in an instant.

"Zela? Are you all right?" Naomi's face loomed near mine. "Oh. It's yours, isn't it? The innovation?" That said in a breathy whisper.

We were in the middle of the room. I sensed the scrutiny of others upon me. I afforded her a tiny nod. "I should get my husband home."

"Keep in mind what I said. We can help you."

My usual polite dismissal rose to my lips, then I heard Jordan's continued braggadocio.

I had tolerated his claims upon my previous inventions, but this, this—my mooring tower was special, my best idea yet, and he had stolen it. And he *knew* he was stealing it. His earlier clinginess now made sense. He must have moved my papers and hadn't wanted me to discover the theft.

"Do you suppose you could send me an invitation for your next book salon, so that I might check the date against my appointment book?" Thus giving me an excuse to respond.

Naomi understood my need for subterfuge, bless her. "Of course. Look for it this week."

"Thank you," I said, and advanced to where Jordan held court.

"Ah, here's my beautiful wife!" He regarded me with delight. "Such a lucky man I am, to be wed to her! Just look at her!"

They looked. I concealed my grimace. I felt like a broodmare for sale. "Come, dear. We had best get home." I entwined my arm with his.

"But I need to tease them with more reasons to attend my symposium hour!" he cried, staggering as I pulled him away. Thank goodness the man was little more than a stick. It's a wonder his thick mustache didn't throw him off balance.

"They know to come, dear." I practically carried him out, attracting glances of pity and amusement the way a gas lamp does bugs. Jordan fancied himself a great intellectual. He had no concept of the modest regard that his peers truly held for him.

I withheld further commentary until we sat across from each other in our carriage, directed toward home. "The innovation is mine."

"Hmm?"

"The mooring system. It's mine, as you're well aware."

"Yours means ours." He yawned, nuzzling against the wall as if it were a cushy bosom. "You really are lovely, Zela. Your hair. Face. All of you." His smile turned dreamy, eyes closing.

Had I a pair of shears at that moment, I would have hacked off my hair then plunged the blades into his chest. Instead, I formed my hands into fists and let my tears fall as he blubbered and snored. I thought on what Naomi had said.

If I could contrive an innovation that would bolster the nascent airship industry, could I also invent the means of my own independence?

***

I knew every nook and cranny of the Tower as I knew my own skin. Without need for a lamp, I walked the cavernous wooden corridors on a midnight expedition.

I ventured to the trunk where my project had been hidden. As I expected, it lay empty. I continued to the laboratory. There I found my papers scattered upon a table. Jordan had scribbled notes atop mine. Some of his observations were astute, but most could be refuted with ease. The man was not stupid, but he had become increasingly lazy and prideful over the years.

Instead of trying in desperation to make up for his inadequacies, perhaps it was time that I let him suffer the consequences.

I straightened the papers and stepped away, perturbed by my dark thoughts, and then annoyed because I *was* perturbed. Why did my brain insist on making his shames into my shames?

I needed to reshape my thoughts, my very perspective.

With grim determination, I went next to his study, to where he hid his mistresses' letters. The most recent correspondence was dated the previous month. I stared at the stack for a foolish amount of time, trying to steady my resolve and abscond with the letters.

Finally, finally, I tucked the pages within my gown pocket and inserted blank sheets within the envelopes. Now I possessed evidence of Jordan's alienation of affection.

I trembled as I exited the room. Where to hide the papers? He had found my usual hiding spot. Where would he never look?

The answer almost made me giggle out loud. Of course—with my monthly girdle and rags! Jordan tried to pretend that women's bodies performed no 'grotesque' functions. Why, he was even discomfited when I drank Mrs. Pinkney's for my headaches.

Mrs. Pinkney's. Most everyone called it by that name alone, but the full name was Mrs. Pinkney's Patented Potion. Could a woman truly hold a patent?

I walked to the larder where medicinal items were kept.

There I found the pink glass bottle half full. The label listed not one but numerous patents under which the medicine had been categorized, all under the name Mrs. Eudora Pinkney. Women *could* own patents.

I put away the bottle, a tingle of excitement expanding within me as a terrifying plan took shape in my mind.

***

Over the next week, I pushed myself to work as never before. I drafted several more iterations of the mooring mast. Jordan wandered in one day, picked up an old version, and approved it without hesitation. That schematic was obsolete with reason; it would get people killed, if anyone were fool enough to actually build it.

After he left, I laughed and laughed and then collapsed in sobs.

I was done with this man. Done.

The next morning, I dutifully kissed Jordan on the cheek as I ventured forth to visit our craftsman regarding the details of our demonstration models. Jordan did not attend such appointments, as he could never explain what we required in a coherent manner.

In the past, that inadequacy had left me feeling most put-upon and exhausted. Now, it formed the wellspring of my hope.

That conference done, I went next to the district records office three blocks away.

Naomi awaited me inside.

"I already retrieved the paperwork and reserved us a private office," she whispered, guiding me through hallways lined with laden shelves.

My recent reply to her salon invitation had provided a tentative 'yes' for the first time, along with a request for this meeting and more assistance.

"I want to pay you for the time you've taken to help me." Emotion thickened my low voice. "Of all of my old friends, you were the only one who never gave up on me."

A blush tinged her cheeks. "You supported me during my teenage indiscretion. I had to return the favor."

"You were wed three months. My marriage has lasted these seventeen years."

Naomi shrugged off the praise. "And will hopefully reach conclusion soon. Here." We entered a small room. Stacked folders awaited me on the table. I set down my own papers and began to review the public records.

The inheritance was as she had described at the party. I felt a fool for not examining it years ago, but I'd fully trusted Jordan and his lawyers amid my grief. Next, Naomi showed me guidelines for divorce filings.

"Different standards for men and women, of course," I muttered darkly. "Fortunately, I brought these as evidence of his improprieties." From among my model schematics, I pulled forth the letters liberated from Jordan's study.

Naomi skimmed them, lips pursed. "How convenient and wonderful, that they so freely elaborate on his indiscretions."

"Even with the will, can he contest my claim for the Tower?" I asked. My future seemed to fully rely on towers, those that moored airships and the one that moored my own life.

"He can contest, of course. He has occupied the house since you were wed and has invested in its maintenance. These letters, though, with their bald statements regarding gifts of jewelry and furs, and aid for children outside of marriage—they demonstrate a proven inequity in your relationship."

How strange, to hear Naomi—to hear anyone—plainly state facts that had been my private shame for years.

I caught glimpse of the wall clock and gasped in alarm.

"I can't tarry. I hate to ask more of you, but do you and Daveed have time to push forward with my…. my divorce filing soon?"

"We can work it in." Her brow furrowed. "But if Jordan knows your intentions for the house—"

"I won't—I can't—reveal my knowledge of the will until much further in the process." I ducked my head, embarrassed anew. Fashion had made it easy for me to hide the few bruises he had given me over the years, but I now feared more for the Tower than my own body. Jordan brimmed with petty spite when he felt wronged. "I would appreciate it if you could submit these papers for me, within the day." I slid a stack of sheets to her.

"What is—oh. Patent filings?" Her eyes went wide.

"Everything will be in order. I've prepared patents many times before."

"Not under your own name, though. These inventions—this is the innovation that Jordan spoke of at the party, isn't it?"

"Yes, which is why it's vital they be filed *now*."

"Oh. *Oh.* The symposium talk next week. What are your intentions?"

"To claim what's mine."

***

I armored myself in satin and brocade, corsetry forcing my posture strong and breaths shallow. I clutched my notebook against my heart as we waited in the wing just off-stage at the symposium. We had been granted the hour slot immediately after lunch. My nerves had prevented me from eating anything more than toast thinly spread with jam. Jordan had praised my light meal, saying it was good of me to watch my figure at my age.

Had I any doubts at that point, his commentary would have eradicated them.

The symposium president introduced Jordan to polite applause. I accompanied him onto the stage, a demur shadow. I raised my head enough to study the seats. Naomi was a bold figure as one of the few women present. She sat third row from the front, Daveed beside her.

"Greetings to my peers and guests!" Jordan said, basking in the welcome. His lectures normally were not so occupied. I set the notes atop the lectern, fingers shaking. I was going forward with this, I truly was. From this moment, there would be no return to my former, complacent life.

With rigid strides, I rolled out the cart with the models atop. Gasps and murmurs filled the chamber.

Jordan glowed. "My innovation will forever change the airship industry with a safe, effective means of mooring vessels!"

My husband parted the cover of the notepad. He flipped past the first blank sheet, then past several. He glanced my way, barely-concealed panic in his eyes.

I did not move, I did not smile. Had I attempted any action, I may very well have fainted.

"Well then." Jordan cleared his throat. "As you, uh, can see here…"

He fumbled onward, describing, quite incorrectly, the construction of the mooring tower and how an airship docked. No numbers or specifics were mentioned, though he inserted plentiful platitudes to reinforce his own brilliance. I might have pitied him more were he a person who required notes to make a presentation—there was no shame in that. But the simple fact was, he only understood my invention enough to know its marketability and value to his prestige, no more.

I waited, hands clasped at my waist, as the murmurs of the audience took on a more ominous tone. Jordan was losing them. Even more, he knew he was losing them. His speech acquired an almost drunken slur as he hastened to explain what he could not explain.

When Jordan paused to guzzle water, I knew my turn had come.

I stepped from the background as I tugged off my gloves. "Greetings to all. My name is Rapunzel Prince. The dirigible moorage system is my creation, patented under my name. I well understand that many present may not believe me." I turned my head to take in the crowd with sober regard, though in truth, my anxiety had rendered everyone into a blur. "Therefore, I will now accept questions from the audience to affirm my complete knowledge of my innovation and its intricacies."

I set my gloves on the display table and flared my fingers to show my stained, callused hands to the front rows. The entirety of the meeting hall fell into a dread silence.

"You can't do this," Jordan sputtered, his fists balling.

He wouldn't strike me in public, but my stomach boiled with nausea nevertheless. Good thing I had already taken precautions for later. Naomi had sent a man to pick up my bags that morning.

"I can," I said with leaden confidence, and turned to the audience. "You heard my husband try to explain the fundamentals. Your reactions were clear. You recognized flaws in his mathematics, in the very functionality of his proposal." I made a point of looking people in the eye. Heads began to grudgingly nod. "I understand my airship moorage system. I will prove it."

Then, without waiting another second, I proceeded with the height, weight, and construction of the mast itself, explaining the required depth of its anchorage so that it could accommodate buoyant craft.

Jordan tried to speak up. I talked over him. Movement across the stage caught my eye. The symposium president, red-faced, engaged in a quiet yet dramatic conference with two men I recognized as representatives of a commercial airship company and the army. The president made to step forward. The others held him back.

I stammered. The president would remove me by a shepherd's crook if he could, like a tone-deaf singer at a talent show. Gazing at the audience again, I saw sneers. Others made a play of mocking me. To them, I was undoubtedly a vindictive woman, a wife betraying and humiliating her husband.

But others took notes. Several engaged in animated whispers as they watched me. More leaned forward, listening, expressions of piqued curiosity.

These men were the ones I needed to heed, the ones to whom I must sell my idea. The others—well, they would continue to hate and scoff. So be it. I never expected to be invited to speak here again. This one time must be enough.

"This is why I would advise that any area considered for airship moorage undergo intense soil stability studies," I said, spacing out my words to handle the alliteration.

"So you say," snapped Jordan, "but—"

"I'm an engineer with Alhambran Steel!" A man yelled from the back. "I missed the specific figures you gave at the start. Could you repeat them?"

"Of course," I said, and did so.

Jordan's face wore the hue of a ripe strawberry. "Well, actually—"

"I want to understand how an airship is moored for passengers and for freight," interrupted a man at the front, an engineer for a fish canning firm.

"I'll be happy to explain," I said, rolling the models to a more central position.

"I can elaborate—" broke in Jordan.

"No, you can't, Prince," called a voice from the back. Some men jeered the heckler, but even more laughed. "Her numbers check out. Let her speak!"

The tension in the room snapped as yells broke out here, there, everywhere, men standing and shaking fists, pointing at Jordan, me, the models, each other.

"Order! Order!" The symposium president stalked onto the stage, the redness in his face almost a match to Jordan's.

The cacophony stopped. From the new silence, a voice boomed out, "We need this invention! I don't care if an alley cat made it. Let the woman speak!"

The president waved his hands to quell new grumbles. He glanced to where the men who had held him back still watched from off-stage, their arms folded.

"In the interest of science," he said, the words strangled, "Mrs. Prince may continue with the fundamentals."

I could have melted into the floor. More shouts broke out, Jordan's enraged voice among them, but the protesters were soon silenced.

"Go on," the president said to me, quite sulkily.

My heart threatened to beat from my chest. I stared into the crowd, frantic, meeting eyes both hostile and curious. And then there was Naomi, radiating faith.

Her support had meant so much to me over the years, but never as much as in that moment.

Giving her a nod, I breathed as deeply as my corset allowed. "Well then. To explain the mooring procedure…"

I elaborated on how passengers would be handled, and how a scaffolding system I had also patented would assist with both maintenance procedures and freight.

A few men stalked from the room. The majority stayed. When I asked for questions, five hands rose. The next time I queried, there must have been a dozen.

A bell rang. The presentation hour was at end.

Jordan had stayed on stage all the while. He hadn't interrupted again, but he had paced behind me like a caged predator in a zoo, ready to pounce if audience sentiment shifted.

He had hoped to intimidate me, and he succeeded. I had kept speaking nevertheless.

"Should anyone wish to confer with me regarding my moorage patents," I said, "find me at the symposium social this evening or through the law firm of Tate and Company. Thank you for your interest."

I curtsied. The applause that followed was restrained, but it *existed*.

As we walked off stage, Jordan gripped my upper arm.

"How could you do that to me, Zela?" he hissed.

"Release my arm," I said levelly. I tilted my head toward other people around us, Naomi and Daveed included.

Jordan released me as if I were coated in pox. "You murdered my reputation in public, before my esteemed peers."

"No. You chose to enter this symposium in ignorance of your own topic. Any loss of respect is yours to own."

"If you had prepared my notes—"

"Jordan. You've relied on me not simply for your notes, but for *everything* these past few years. I've handled almost every aspect of the creative process—and the business side as well!"

He shook his head, as stubborn a fool as ever. "We'll discuss this at home."

"No, we won't. I'm staying elsewhere. Good-bye."

A grinding noise announced the arrival of my forgotten display cart, rolled out by the next speaker's assistant. I gave the young man a tense smile and gripped the handle in his stead.

Jordan opened his mouth. He was not going to let the matter go. "Good-bye," I repeated, and pulled the cart away. Naomi and Daveed followed me. Jordan did not.

"How are you?" Naomi murmured.

"Near ready to shatter," I confessed. We walked down the corridor to where I'd store the display until the symposium's completion.

"If that happens, you'll glue yourself together again. With some help." Her touch on my arm was such a contrast to Jordan's.

"Pardon. Pardon, Mrs. Prince!" A man in a natty suit approached. I recognized the steel industry representative who had spoken in my support. He doffed his hat as he held out a card. "There are murmurings that you may not be welcome at the social this evening. Nevertheless, I would like to discuss business soon."

I accepted his card with bare hands. My gloves remained on the cart. "As would I, mister...?"

"Mr. Durley. I know others who would be interested in hearing you speak as well. Perhaps we can establish our own social gathering." His mustache curved as he toothily smiled.

"I will be in touch soon, sir."

He tipped his hat again and moved onward. I stayed still, robbed of all momentum.

"Of course they won't let me join the usual business social," I murmured. "I was lucky I was not hooked from the stage."

"They let you speak because the majority wanted to hear you," said Naomi. "You achieved what you needed: the opportunity to establish your substratum."

I released a tense, high-pitched giggle. "Yes, a solid foundation is necessary for me, and for my mooring towers as well." *My* mooring towers. I could say those words in public now. "I'm likely to be booted from the premises soon if I dare stay. Should we head to your home now?"

"Yes, let's," said Naomi. Daveed motioned that he could take the cart, but I shook my head. I would exit with my models in my direct dominion. She continued, "We could all do with a spot of tea, and I would love to discuss potential books for my salons. Which you now have no excuse to avoid."

We changed course for the doors outside. "I disagree. If I have business to conduct, that will of course take precedence."

"True enough!" she said, her grin bright.

I felt the weight of other gazes upon us as we exited. Some attention focused on me, but my model airship and mast garnered the most scrutiny of all. Every glance and murmur reaffirmed my faith in my creation and that more good things would come. Soon, I would live within my Tower again, and reclaim its magic and coziness as fully my own. Soon, I would establish my own income. Soon—today, even—I could cut my hair however I wished, without concern of displeasing Jordan.

We stepped outside. I lifted my face to greet the warm afternoon sunlight, the ground firm beneath my feet, my spirit as buoyant as airships on high.

Nebula Award-nominated **Beth Cato** is the author of two steampunk series from Harper Voyager, the Clockwork Dagger duology and the

Blood of Earth trilogy. Her story "A Future of Towers Made" is inspired by the tale of Rapunzel, but with a feminist, steampunk twist. She's a Hanford, California native transplanted to the Arizona desert, where she lives with her husband, son, and requisite cats. Follow her at BethCato.com and on Twitter at @BethCato.

A Bird Girl in the Dark of Night

Sarah Van Goethem

The train chugs into Aldermoor during the night. Jane Windlass stands at her window, watching, a spectre in her white nightgown, her warm fingertips making ovals on the cold glass. She heard the steam trumpet moments before, like always. Every night, trains trundle in and out of Aldermoor, but tonight is different. Jane's eyes snapped open, her limbs tensed, rigid. She's been waiting all this time. Waiting and waiting and waiting. For days and weeks and months and years.

How long has it been since she last saw them? The thought weaves a thread of guilt just under her ribs, plucking at her heart. She gave up counting. At some point she stopped totalling the days and resumed her life.

Without them.

Without her sisters.

But now, finally, the time has come. The circus has arrived and Jane can just make out their forms through the smog-lined streets.

There, in the distance, shadows deboarding. Mulling on the platform, clutching at bags, struggling under the weight of trunks.

The peculiars.

And at the heart of it all, the ringmaster: Perry Featherstone. Jane can't hear him, not from here, not even with her window propped open with a shard of wood. But as his arms gesture, as he commands them all, Jane imagines him as plucking the strings of marionettes. All of the peculiars as toys in his play. *It'll be a good life,* he says. *What else is there for you, really? What else?*

He turns his head in her direction, quite suddenly, and Jane ducks behind the threadbare curtains. Until she remembers he can't possibly see her, not from this distance. He never saw her before, either. He doesn't know she exists. She inches forward again, resumes her place as a voyeur.

The train expels more of them, more curiosities, and Jane swipes impatiently at the patch of fog her breath leaves on the glass, marring her view.

She strains to see, her breath held this time, her lungs swelling. All down the street, lanterns flicker in windows. Jane isn't the only one watching them.

There is an incredibly tall person, a giant, and another so wide, so fat, Jane wonders if he or she needed a special seat on the train. These are the easiest to spot in the dark, though Jane thinks a few others are too hairy or too bony, a werewolf and a skeleton. And there, ambling down the treads, a pair of dwarves, as tiny as children, though Jane knows they are adults. She saw it in the flyer only days ago.

The flyer that listed the sideshow acts.

That's how she knows her sisters have returned. That they're still part of Perry Featherstone's freak show. That they're still being paraded about, exploited for his benefit. Unfortunately, the crowd disappears, blending as one, slipping further down the streets and toward the empty field by the cemetery to set up camp. She didn't see her sisters, but she knows they have to be there.

Did they look for her, too? Jane wonders. *Did they remember to look up, to look for the little attic room above the bakery on Mulberry street? Do they remember?*

Of course, they do. Jane begins dressing in the glow of the gas lamps from the street. Then, she sits on her bed in the silent room and waits for dawn, staring at the empty bed on the other wall, still strewn with pressed flowers and cardstock and balls of wool and knitting needles. And the mannequin head, the one her sisters played with, with her waxy face and pink rosebud lips, Jane's only company now.

Underneath all that, Jane keeps her most prized possession, tucked away against the floorboards. The thing that will gain her admittance.

When the scent of the bread and cakes waft upward and her stomach grumbles, Jane goes downstairs.

***

Jane was born first. That's what Mrs. Lydia Sophronia Dawkins says, and she should know. The baker starts her day at night, when the clock chimes eleven. That's when she makes the bread dough, while the rest of the world snuggles under their covers. Maybe she sleeps while the bread rises, but maybe she doesn't. Jane can't be sure; she's never been witness to it. She only knows Mrs. Lydia Sophronia Dawkins prepares loaves and rolls and kneads dough (sometimes with her feet) in the wee hours of the morning. That's when things happen. That's when whispers spread, babies are born and circuses arrive. And that's why Mrs. Lydia Sophronia Dawkins is always the one to hear everything, to know everything, and to relay all the things she hears and knows.

Jane's Papa grumbles about Mrs. Dawkins being a church bell, but that doesn't stop him from accepting a free loaf, or some biscuits or shortbread. *At least there isn't chalk in her flour,* he says, and that justifies that.

The kitchen is blazing hot this morning, like every morning, and sweat drips off of Mrs. Dawkins' forehead. She leans over the coal range, her face a shade of cherry. "Morning, sweets," she says, somehow always knowing when Jane has arrived, though Jane barely makes a sound. Jane was always the quiet one, the one no one ever noticed. The plain one.

"Morning," Jane says. And then, because Jane doesn't want Mrs. Dawkins to tell her first, she blurts out, "The circus is here."

Mrs. Dawkins raises a brow, retrieving a sponge cake from the depths of the oven while somehow simultaneously cracking an egg and sifting some sugar into a bowl. "Sure is. Little Fanny Cogsmith's been screaming the latter half the night about some armless woman. And Mr. Cuttle says—"

"Mrs. Dawkins," Jane says, quite breathless. And then she pauses, because she doesn't usually interrupt Mrs. Dawkins and everyone knows Mrs. Dawkins prefers to be called by all three of her names. But Jane can't wait, not today. She doesn't have time for gossip and long-winded names. "They'll be here, right?"

For once Mrs. Lydia Sophronia Dawkins is still, a wooden spoon balanced in the air. Then she nods, slowly. "Oh sweets, I surely hope so. For your sake."

"Can I take some marzipan and some meringues?" Jane isn't asking. She's begging. She has no money and they both know it.

Mrs. Dawkins blinks and Jane thinks she sees her lower lip quiver, but just as quickly the round woman hauls her apron up to mop her face. "Those were their favorites, weren't they?" she says, and Jane is glad she remembers.

Mrs. Dawkins stuffs a paper bag. "Every time you came in," she says. "when you three were little. You always thought of them first. Poor, sweet girls. Poor little things. Born like that."

Jane doesn't say anything.

"Guess you were lucky, weren't you?" Mrs. Dawkins hands her the bag, already wet with grease. She nods, confirming it to herself, the thing she's said a hundred times. "The lucky one. The first one out. The one not attached." Mrs. Dawkins stops talking, scrunches her bushy eyebrows together. "It's been a long time, sweets," she says. "A long time since you've seen them."

Sometimes there is more in what Mrs. Dawkins doesn't say.

Today, Jane doesn't know what that is. What words are missing.

"Good luck, sweets," Mrs. Dawkins says, finally.

Jane thinks she will need it.

***

Jane was seven when her sisters went missing. When they were stolen by the dreadful Perry Featherstone the first time the circus came to Aldermoor. That was nine years ago now.

Jane's father had sent her to the butcher. Jane remembers this exactly, because they could rarely afford meat. But that day she stepped over the blood-soaked gutter and braved the shop, shiny coins in hand. She carefully avoided looking at the half bodies of the pigs and cows, sawn down the middle, and the plucked fowl hanging from the rafters. She did, however, scoop a feather from the floor and tuck it into her straggly hair.

"Four sausages," she told the man with the gleaming muscled arms when he finally paid her attention. That's what Papa had said. *Get us some bags of mystery, Jane. Now that's a good girl. Run along.*

Jane stopped to see Mrs. Lydia Sophronia Dawkins before she went back upstairs.

Hello, bird girl, Mrs. Dawkins said when she saw the feather in Jane's hair. *Have you seen my sweet Jane?*

Jane liked that. *Bird girl.* It was better than *the lucky one, the fortunate sister.* She dawdled, filling her face with petit fours, laying them across the counter and pecking at them like a bird, while Mrs. Dawkins iced a cake with almond paste.

Jane took too long; she knows that now. But she liked the separateness from her sisters. The space to breathe. To be someone else.

She often wondered what it was like to be them, to never have space to yourself. To be attached to another person.

Jane liked the feeling—until she returned. Until she found her sisters were gone and so was the circus.

Her papa drank himself stupid that night and ate three of the sausages. He gave Jane the fourth, but Jane tossed it out the window to the cats below.

Jane could hear her Papa crying that night, sobbing through the plaster walls. She imagined he cried in the same manner the night Mama died, when her sisters split their mother apart while Jane lay, already swaddled, oblivious, in the baker's arms.

There was nothing to be done, Mrs. Dawkins had told Jane. *The doctor had to cut her open, you see. They all would've died, all of them. The doctor didn't know of course. Not until he pulled them out stuck together. But you, dear, you were such a silent little lamb. Never peeped a sound, almost like you knew enough to be quiet even then. I held you, you know. I was holding you when I first saw them. All alike, the three of you. All the same. Except they were conjoined, of course. A real shame.*

Jane didn't cry. Not then and not now. She only flicked the feather across her cheek in the moonlight, as soft as a kiss, and vowed to get her sisters back.

***

The circus draws the entire town, a splotch of glittering gold and bronze in the drab hues of Aldermoor. Fences have been erected all around the field and children clamor at them, eyes and mouths round and open. One young boy digs at the ground, tearing at soil. An attempt to gain his own admittance.

Jane hovers nearby, observing.

Already, a blimp flies overhead, sails blown wide against the blue sky, cages and barrels and tiny houses suspended from its underbelly. *Opening Day Tomorrow,* a trailing sign reads.

Hot air balloons from which hover strange women with tiny parasols, and men or boys with trumpets and bugles, are tethered in place. Other performers ride by on horses, practicing, balancing with hoops or poles of fire.

The circus will open tomorrow, but the show has already begun.

Already the townsfolk are searching past the automatons just inside the gates, the whirring and clicking and buzzing machines, the greeting lady with the skin of human flesh (is it real?) and the giant guards with their bronzed ghoul faces. Another automaton with clockwork all across its skull, bellows, *Welcome to Perry Featherstone's Peculiars. Something for everyone. Both man-made and natural.*

It's the natural peculiars everyone wants to see.

Yes, everyone loves the lion tamers and the trapeze artists and the human projectile from the canon. And who doesn't want a ride on a machine elephant or a bear or an ostrich? But no, Jane knows, with a cold piercing in her heart, that they mostly want to see the sideshow.

Jane knows this without a doubt. She remembers how everyone gawked at her sisters. In fear and awe and dread. She hasn't forgotten.

No one ever saw her.

The young boy with the nails full of dirt has succeeded. He's burrowed far enough down to shimmy his way under the fence. He only makes it ten steps, maybe twelve, before he's detained by an automaton. But it's enough.

"I saw one!" he yells to his comrades, kicking his feet against the machine man who holds him by his collar and tosses him back out. "What luck! It was the Three-Legged Courtesan!"

He's dumped on the ground outside again, and Jane watches as the gate slams with a decisive click. "Only peculiars allowed inside today," the bronzed-faced bodyguard recites. "Only peculiars."

The boy rolls over, brushes the dust from his face, and grins. "She really does have four breasts," he says.

Jane presses her lips together, the paper bag scrunched in her hand. *Only peculiars.*

Jane has waited a long time for this.

Oh, Mr. Featherstone, Jane imagines saying, *how do you feel about an avian-human hybrid?*

A bird girl? He'll muse. *How fascinating. How enchanting. Real wings growing on a girl. How difficult life must be for you. You must come with me. It'll be a good life. What else is there for you, really? What else?*

And Jane will only smile to herself, and not say the words in her head, just like Mrs. Lydia Sophronia Dawkins does sometimes. *Flying,* she will think. *That is what there is for me, Mr. Featherstone. Flying my sisters far away from you.*

***

When Jane was ten, a bird smacked into her window. She'd cleaned the glass that day, rubbing off all the finger marks she'd left on the pane. *That's why it flew into the window,* Jane thought. *It's my fault.* She ran downstairs and through the bakery and found the bird, a dove, dead on the cobblestone street.

She cupped it in her palms and brought it upstairs. She intended to ask Papa for a box to bury it in later. But until he came home, Jane inspected the bird from head to toe, marvelling at its wings, studying the shapes of the feathers and the pattern, how they all lay together intricately like a puzzle.

Jane began drawing that day, sketching out an elaborate frame, like the bones in the wings. A sketch that she would later take to an artisan, a surgical mechanist named Clem Palmer. Clem fashioned prosthetic limbs for people out of leather and polished willow wood and iron and india rubber. Clem used pulleys and levers and springs and trusses and made people new again, gave them back what they'd lost.

For Jane, he gave her what she never had.

A peculiarity.

***

Jane keeps her eyes on the circus out her attic window as she attaches the wings. The clasps are invisible, indiscernible from her skin. It'd taken many tries to get it right. Many years of her sweeping and darning, cleaning and cooking for Clem.

But the result is fantastic and worth both of their efforts.

Jane raises her arms, lets the wings unfold, the glorious golden feathers unfurling into place.

She'd never shown Papa or Mrs. Lydia Sophronia Dawkins. Jane has held onto this secret for a long time. And now it is her ticket into Perry Featherstone's Peculiars.

Jane dons a scandalously short plum dress over her corset and layers of cut petticoats, a dress she made specifically to fit, with cut-outs for the wings and gold embroidery to match. Papa would have had a spell if he'd seen it, but he's no longer here. Jane leaves her room and weaves through the attic to the other side, where a door allows her access to the roof.

Jane has practiced this before. Many times. While Mrs. Lydia Sophronia Dawkins kneaded dough with her feet, Jane soared off the roof of the bakery on Mulberry street. A bird girl in the dark of night. While the world dreamt, Jane flew.

Only once did Mrs. Dawkins say something the next morning. *Mr. Barnabas Keeler said he saw a human bird last night, flying like a witch against the moon. Can you believe such a thing? Oh, now don't be looking all pigeon-livered, Jane, you're my only bird girl, swear it on my heart. Perhaps if good ole Barnabas stayed home with his wife, well perhaps if he wasn't with that hedge-kreeper... and perhaps if he wasn't such a cock-eyed fool...*

Only once was something said. Just that one time. And never again.

Jane laid low after that. Waiting and waiting and waiting. The wings hidden under her sister's bed.

The day has grown bright, now. The sun is warming Jane's head, illuminating the strands of her pale hair. She's fashioned it into two buns, two knots, like the two sisters she wants to save. Over her head, she pulls a too-small knitted plum-colored hat, a remnant from long ago.

No one is looking at her; all eyes are turned toward the circus. Jane pulls the golden goggles over her eyes, a form of masquerade mask and protection all at once, and leaps.

***

Jane's sister's names are Madeline and Margaret. Maddie and Maggie. Mrs. Lydia Sophronia Dawkins says Jane's Mama named Jane but not the other two. Mama held Jane and snuggled her and said, *I'm calling her Jane,* before the pains started again.

Jane's Mama never held or snuggled Maddie and Maggie. She was gone by then.

Papa named the two who were fused at the hip, gave them matching names for life, like maybe they were the same person.

They weren't, of course. Maddie liked marzipan and pressing flowers and Maggie liked meringues and knitting coverings for anything in sight. They weren't the same at all.

Only their faces are the same, exactly like Jane's, three dolls made of the same mould. Sometimes Jane wishes she'd been given an M name too.

***

It's easier than Jane thinks it will be, flying into the circus. She soars by the back way of the cemetery, over her Mama's and Papa's graves, and glides in through the trees and over the fence where a golden hot air balloon hangs in the hazy sky.

She's spotted right away.

Whoa, what is that? Where did she come from? I ain't never seen a girl with wings!

Jane flaps about, coasting above, until she spies Perry Featherstone, the ringleader of it all. He stands off to the side by a striped tent wearing black boots and a tailcoat, hands clasped behind his back, top hat tipped skyward.

He sees her now. She's no longer invisible.

Jane descends, landing gracefully only a few feet away, not far from an automaton guarding the back entrance. "Only peculiars allowed inside today," the bronzed-faced bodyguard says, hand outstretched, latching onto her left wing. "Only peculiars."

Jane flinches, feigning feeling in her wing. The machine man pauses, unclenches his iron fist. He steps away, and Jane imagines if he could frown, if he could wrinkle his forehead in confusion, he would.

Perry Featherstone holds up a hand and Jane draws a breath.

He comes forward, twisting his moustache at the right corner. "Your name?" he asks, circling her.

"Jane."

"Have you a last name, Jane?"

"I do." She won't give it all away, not yet.

Perry Featherstone has a gleam in his eye. "Well, Jane with a last name, did you just fly into my circus without being invited?"

"Yes, sir. I thought—"

"You thought what?" Perry Featherstone is an intimidating man, more so than Jane imagined. But not because Jane feels threatened, but because she feels magnetised. Enticed in some way. Like Perry Featherstone knows something she doesn't.

Jane remembers what she planned to say. "Well, Mr. Featherstone, I thought you may have interest in an avian-human hybrid."

Perry Featherstone tentatively reaches out and grasps her wrist. The wing starts not far up from there, only a few inches. Jane quivers. She did not imagine this part. And yet his fingers are on the move, slowly stroking up further, touching her where the wings attach. *Did he do this to her sisters?* She wonders. *Did he fondle their hips and caress the smooth skin that attaches them to each other?*

Jane stands very still, tries not to flinch. Or maybe she should, maybe she should recoil and wince and act like she can't stand for her wings to be touched. She doesn't do this, though. She's frozen in place, the paper bag with the treats clutched firmly in her hand. She remains steady, lets him feel and finger and decide for himself.

When he wavers, scrunching his brows together and pursing his lips, Jane plays her trump card. She removes her goggles, revealing her face, and yanks off the knitted cap over her hair.

Perry Featherstone sucks in a breath. "Impossible," he says, and his eyes skitter over her and around her, as if searching for another half. "How?"

"My sisters were born stuck together," Jane says, before Perry Featherstone has a chance to think, "and I was born with wings." How could he not believe that? Not when he knows her sisters are the real deal? How could he doubt the third Windlass sister?

Perry Featherstone blinks, and Jane thinks, *yes, I think I've got him now.*

And then he says, "Incredible. A bird girl," just like he was supposed to. Almost as if he'd learned his lines in a play she'd written. "Real wings on a girl." His arm comes over her shoulders then, lightly, as if afraid to break her wings, so delicate, so sensitive. "You must tell me about your life," he says.

"Awful," Jane tells him. "So difficult after my sisters were gone. Everyone always poking fun. Always chirping and squawking at me... I have no one. No one." And it's barely a lie any longer. Not after Papa passed away last year. Jane truly has no family left.

"Of course," he says. "I understand. How difficult life must be for you. I'm sorry, so very sorry to have missed you. You must stay with us now. It'll be a good life. What else is there for you, really? What else?"

The very thing Jane has always imagined Perry Featherstone says. The thing that makes them stay.

***

Jane would like to have Perry Featherstone in the palm of her hand, but she doesn't. She sees the side-eye Perry continues to give her, sizing her up, scrutinizing her.

Luckily, he leads her directly to the peculiars, in a long house of sorts, all toasty golden-browns and coppers, spouting steam out of the chimney on the roof. Gears clack and pistons clank and when Perry Featherstone pulls the door open a whiff of reeking warm air washes over Jane.

There are bodies inside, too many for the small space really, and

Jane scans them as fast as she can, looking for Maddie and Maggie. The peculiars have gone quiet, all eyes on her and their ringmaster.

And then, from the dark back corner, Jane hears the gasps just as Perry Featherstone announces, "Please welcome Jane Windlass."

"Jane? Is it really you?" one of her sisters asks, and Jane focuses in the dim interior, and suddenly there they are, pushing toward her. They've changed so much, and yet how can Jane not know them? They have the same faces she sees in the mirror every day, only slightly chubbier, rounder.

"It is," Perry Featherstone bellows, as if he were already in the grand tent, announcing acts. "The returned sister. The long-lost sister of our famous Siamese twins."

Does Jane sense sarcasm in his voice?

"Triplets then," the three-legged courtesan purrs, perching on a chair, her third and tinier leg dangling between her two normal legs. "Well let them greet each other. Come on now, move, you dummies."

The sea of peculiars parts. The giant swings her long legs to the side and the fat lady presses herself as close as she can to the wall. A heavily tattooed woman grasps an armless woman around the waist and yanks her back. Only a few, up front, sit and stare. A lizard girl's mouth hangs open, her long tongue lolling from side to side, and the hairy maid strokes her beard.

Jane has imagined this moment a thousand times, but not like this, not with all these onlookers. She steps toward her sisters shyly, unsure. And scared. Terrified that they will say the wrong thing, that they will ask about her wings.

And sure enough, they stop short, only inches away from Jane, taking her in. And suddenly Jane knows how they've felt all these years, how it is to have people staring at you, but not even seeing you. Her sisters are looking at her wings, reaching out to brush their fingers over the feathers. They're not looking at her. After all these years, it's the wings they're noticing first.

And Perry is taking it all in.

"Jane," Maggie says finally, "what in the—"

"A moment alone," Jane blurts out, her knees shaking. "We need a moment alone. Please."

"Of course, you do," the three-legged courtesan says, forcing herself into their circle. "Come now, Perry, how could you? Letting the three have a reunion in a crowd like this? Be a dear and give them some space."

"Yes, of course," he agrees, twisting at his moustache again, his eyes roving over the four breasts of the courtesan. "My own tent, then. How's that, girls?"

Jane's skin crawls, but her sisters nod as if nothing is amiss.

Jane scans the peculiars again before she turns to follow Perry Featherstone and her sisters. She takes note of the dwarfs and the elastic skin lady and the lobster girl, her fingers fused into two claws, and the skeleton girl, the one who claims to live on air alone.

They're all women, Jane notes. *Perry Featherstone's peculiars are all women.*

***

Perry Featherstone's tent is lush with thick beds of feathers and draperies of silks and cottons. Maddie and Maggie settle onto a settee, and Perry Featherstone stands behind them, his hands atop each of their heads.

"Sit," he commands Jane, gesturing to a chair just across from her sisters. "I've sent for meat pies and pickled oysters and ginger beer and sweets. Though it looks as if you've brought something of your own."

Jane has almost forgotten the bag in her hand. She raises it now, pushes it at her sisters.

Maddie takes it from her and their fingers brush against each other. "Oh, Jane," she breathes, opening the bag. Then, she turns toward Maggie. "It's marzipan and meringues."

"Oh, Jane," Maggie repeats. "Dear, sweet Jane."

Their voices hold something akin to sympathy and Jane shifts her weight, uncomfortable.

"Won't you sit?" Perry Featherstone says, and Jane slides into the chair, somewhat awkwardly, trying unsuccessfully to get her wings to co-operate. Perry watches, eyes narrowed. "Ahh here is the food and drink, now." Perry Featherstone squeezes her sisters on their shoulders and rounds to Jane, cupping the back of her neck with his large hand. "I'll leave you three to catch up, shall I?"

"Yes, thank you." Jane's back is straight, rigid, the wings pinching.

She doesn't miss how Perry's fingers slide further down her spine, down to where the wings seemingly sprout from her back. He stops just before that, before he hits that point. Almost as if he's teasing himself. "I'll be back," he says, his voice gruff.

Jane has no doubt he will.

When he has gone, Jane rises. She flaps about the tent, peering through the cracks and into the nooks, making sure no one is around. When she is satisfied, she returns to her sisters, who are eyeing the tray of sweets that has been left. There are trifles and cakes and gingerbreads. And marzipan and meringues, bigger and better than the ones Mrs. Lydia Sophronia Dawkins makes.

The bag Jane brought is at Maggie's feet, forgotten.

"Jane, what have you done? How do you have those wings?" Maddie asks, her top tooth biting into her lower lip.

This is not the way Jane imagined this day, not at all. As if to try and gain back the version she wants, Jane throws herself at her sister's feet, clasping one of each of their hands as she kneels. "I've missed you," she says. "So much."

"Oh, we've missed you too, Jane," Maggie says, brushing a hand over Jane's head.

"Yes, so very much," Maddie agrees. She reaches out as well, caressing Jane's right wing. "But the wings, Jane... how?"

Jane waves the thought away; there will be time enough later to explain. For them to giggle long into the night about the time Jane sprouted wings. About the time she saved them. "We can sneak out tonight," she whispers. "Not back to the attic, not straight away of course, but we'll hide out. I know a place."

"Sneak out?" Maddie says.

"Back to Papa?" Maggie says, her voice rising.

"No, no." But how can Jane tell them that Papa is dead? She can't. Not like this. Jane paces, her wings heavy and cumbersome when not in flight. "These wings are strong. They can carry us all out of here. All three of us."

"Out of *here*?" Maddie crosses her arms and Jane pauses, realizing her sisters are looking back and forth at each other, shifting uncomfortably on the settee. "But Jane, we don't want to leave."

"*You don't want to leave?*" Jane can't have heard them right. "How can you *not* want to leave?"

Maddie pushes herself up, hauling Maggie with her. Maddie always was the more controlling of the two. "We like it here, Jane. We get paid really well." Maddie narrows her eyes. "Is that why you're here? Why you've come? Is that why you made those wings? You think you can be like us, be special? You want to take our spot?"

"What?" Jane says, flapping her wings. "No. That's not it. You've got it all wrong."

"You were always jealous of us," Maddie says. "I hate to say it, but it's the truth."

Jane looks wildly between them, but Maggie is nodding, agreeing with Maddie.

"Jealous?" Jane is seething, her insides boiling. "I've come to save you, and this is the thanks I get? What on earth could I be jealous of?" But even as the words tumble out, Jane's chest tightens. She recalls how she felt on her side of the room, alone in her single bed, while they were snuggled together in the double bed on the other side. She thinks of their matching names and her plain one. Of how she was sent alone on errands while her sisters played, hidden away in the attic. Dress-up and toy trains and talking dolls. Hours to press flowers and knit. Violets and daisies and knitted coverings for bricks and teapots and vases. And that blasted mannequin head, becoming whoever they wanted it to be that day. Oh, how their imaginations soared, while Jane fetched and did chores.

Jane deflates, shoulders slumped, wings hanging at her sides. "You get paid?" she asks Maddie.

"Lots. More than most people ever make in their whole lives."

Maggie adds, "It's not a bad life, Jane."

Jane still holds to a small thread of hope. "But... don't you miss your old life? Before you were stolen? Did you even miss me or... Papa?"

Both of their faces change then, harden into expressions of resentment.

"She doesn't know," Maddie says to Maggie, her chest heaving. "You tell her. I can't say it. I can't."

"What is it?" Jane asks. "What can't you say?"

Maggie takes a breath, drawing out the moment. Finally, she says, "Papa sold us, Jane. He *sold us.*"

Jane's knees buckle. She falls into the chair. Remembers her father's sobbing through the walls. She hears the guilt now, mingled with the sadness. "No, no, no."

"Oh yes," Maddie snaps, a hand on her hip, the one that isn't attached to Maggie. "He sent you for sausages, remember? Where do you think he got the money? Did you eat ours, too? After we were gone? Don't you remember, Jane?"

Jane remembers, alright. The sausages and then the new dress and shoes, the next day. Papa had sold her sisters and gotten her new clothes. Bought her off. Jane can only sit numbly, crumbling to pieces.

Her sisters lower themselves back onto the settee.

"Oh, forget it," Maddie says. "We weren't mad at you. It doesn't matter now. Not anymore."

"Everything matters." Jane's voice is barely a whisper. "It still matters."

There is a long silence and then Maggie takes a meringue from the tray Perry Featherstone has left. Only when she puts it in her mouth does she seem to remember the paper bag Jane brought. A flush mounts her neck, blooming crimson in her cheeks. "It's not so bad, here, really," she says. "We're used to people staring now. It wouldn't be any different out there."

"At least we're taken care of here," Maddie adds. "We have Perry."

Perry, Perry, Perry. Jane can see full well what Perry Featherstone has done to them. Used them and broken them and left them as shells of themselves. Made them think they were less, that this is all they are worth. The total sum of what they were allotted. Jane knows now the warning Mrs. Lydia Sophronia Dawkins didn't say this morning. Something to that effect, something about the passing of time. *They may be different now, Jane. Be prepared. They may have changed.*

"So, you won't come with me?" Jane asks. "You won't escape?"

Maddie shrugs. "Come on, Jane. What else is there for us, really? What else?"

Jane sees now, quite clearly, this is not just Perry Featherstone's doing. Papa played a role in this, too. He kept them cooped up, hidden in the dark, and the only light Perry has offered is the spotlight. It's all or nothing.

But Jane remembers the parts of her sisters they have forgotten. "Pressed flower cards," she says, her jaw set, "and knitted hats. That is what else."

At that, her sisters frown and let out small sighs, as if remembering something from long ago.

***

Perry Featherstone has cast a spell over her sisters, over all of the peculiars. Jane watches them, how their eyes light up every time he comes near, how their backs straighten and their chins rise.

They think he's saved them, but Jane knows better. They're only props to him, a means to an end.

And Perry has no interest in anyone that is not a peculiar. He sends for Jane that night, alone, and Jane knows it will be a test.

Sure enough, Perry is waiting for her at the canon. The fairgrounds are mostly dark now, quiet, the peculiars having turned in for the night. Maddie and Maggie are in a tent on the far side. There is a sleeping roll for Jane now, too, if she can prove herself. But Jane can't imagine keeping these wings on much longer. Already her skin burns where the wings latch in, biting and tugging something fierce, but she doesn't dare loosen them.

Perry caresses the large canon. "Usually we shoot someone out of this and they land in a net," he says, all quiet, like they are sharing a secret, "but imagine if the canon blasts, the person is shot into the air, and then, because they are *actually half-bird*"—and here, Perry's eyes light up—"the person takes flight."

Jane shivers in the light of the moon, wishes desperately for her warm attic bed. There is no safety net set up yet, nothing to catch her if she fails.

"Get in," Perry says.

There is no choice. Not really.

Jane climbs inside, shaking with terror. Her arms ache from the weight of the wings.

There is the sound of the steam engine being turned on and then the hiss of compressed air. Without warning, Jane feels the pressure against her feet, the catapult that launches her into the night.

For a few harrowing seconds, Jane forgets what to do. Frozen in fear, Jane gawks at the stars, almost feeling as if she's headed directly for them. But then her body turns to deadweight and she starts to fall. Momentum is lost. The feeling is unnerving and Jane scrambles, kicking her legs for a floor, for ground, that doesn't exist.

Then, she remembers. Flaps her arms. The wings stretch out and catch the air, and Jane flaps again, harder and faster. She will *not* fail. Once she's caught herself and steadied off, she glides in relieved circles overhead while Perry watches, astonished, though he's seen it before.

He is her prey now. Jane imagines nose-diving in, and wishes she'd had Clem fashion talons or a beak as well, something to rip Perry to shreds.

Instead, she circles until she's calm and then lands beside Perry, as graceful as a real bird.

She knows she's passed the test before Perry can say, "Amazing. Fantastic. Won't you stay with us, then?" He's practically drooling, like the children who covet the pickled eggs at the food booths.

"You paid for my sisters," Jane says, liking the way the power has shifted. "If you want me, you'll have to pay Papa for me, too."

"Of course," Perry says. "Tomorrow—"

"Tonight," Jane tells him. "Right now. Papa will be sleeping but you will leave the money with Mrs. Lydia Sophronia Dawkins in the bakery." Perry hesitates, and Jane adds, "I have to be home by midnight, Papa said. Unless you wanted me."

It works.

"I'll go tonight," Perry says. "I'm leaving now."

***

Jane flies home, skimming low through the back alleys. She lands on the roof just as someone in the street spots her, and throws herself into the attic. The rooms seem even smaller, lonelier, than ever before. Jane lights a lantern and casts her eyes about, letting her memories filter in.

She sees, in her mind's eye, her sisters hanging their heads out the peaked window, their blonde tresses whipping in the breeze as they watched Jane leave on errands everyday. Like princesses locked in a tower, they sniffed the air, let the sun warm their cheeks.

Of course they wouldn't want to come back, Jane thinks, finally understanding. *How silly of me, how ridiculous.*

And although they are siblings, Jane can see quite clearly now, that their childhood, their lives, their memories, are very different. Their stories are not the same at all.

Jane goes in the room the three of them shared once, so long ago, and sits on her bed. She can hear someone yelling from the street below, *A bird girl! A bird girl!*

All is lost, Jane thinks. *My sisters are under Perry's spell, and I am only me. I cannot join then, not really, because I am not peculiar.*

Only dull, ordinary, me.

Jane's pitiful thoughts are broken by crashing footsteps on the stairs, followed by a pounding on the main door.

"Jane!" Perry Featherstone calls. "I know you're in there. Open this door!"

Perry is huffing, Jane can hear it through the cracks. Before she can even think, he strikes the door again, rattling it on its hinges.

"Don't open it, sweets!" comes Mrs. Dawkin's voice, and immediately it turns to a whimper.

"Blasted woman," Perry says.

Jane hasn't heard Perry like this before, and she knows immediately what's happened. Mrs. Lydia Sophronia Dawkins has flapped her gums, said things she shouldn't have. Enlightened Perry to the truth.

"Get out, Jane!" Mrs. Dawkins calls, and Jane thinks maybe she should. But just as quickly she thinks, *what would be the point? What would that solve?*

Instead, Jane opens the door.

Immediately Perry swoops in, towering over her. "You're not peculiar at all," he sneers, waving the bag of gold in his hand. "And to think I almost paid for this." His free hand clamps down on her right wing, ripping.

Jane doesn't flinch. She stands tall and proud while Perry tears out feathers, plucking and snatching in handfuls. The more Jane doesn't respond, the more his madness grows.

Behind Perry, Mrs. Dawkins screeches. "Stop it, you brute! Stop!" But Perry continues, and Mrs. Dawkins runs from the room, squawking, "Help, help!" to the people in the streets below.

Perry's frantic slashing reaches further, tugging at the spots that attach to Jane's skin, and she backs away, into her bedroom.

Perry follows, still tearing at the wings. "What does it matter?" he says. "You can't feel it, can you? It's all false, a giant lie." He takes a good grip and the skin on Jane's wrists and spine tugs, splitting. The wings are not meant to be detached like this, but only with careful precision.

Jane *can* feel this.

Still, she doesn't say anything. She won't cry out, though her eyes water with tears.

"Did you think it would actually work?" Perry snatches at the middle of her back, rupturing the clasps, and Jane sinks to her knees. Her spine burns where the flesh is torn, and she can feel blood seeping. "Did you think you could fool Perry Featherstone?"

I did, Jane thinks. *I did fool you.*

Still, Perry doesn't stop. He pushes her backward, and her head whacks against the old plank floor. Jane is momentarily stunned; all she can see is Perry's eyes, wild, in the light of the lantern. And his face, bloated and red.

"You're nothing," Perry says. He is hacking at her wings now, stabbing at them with a knife he's procured. "You're not special at all."

Strangely, Jane thinks she can almost feel it, like a limb that's gone to sleep. The more he batters away, the freer Jane's arms become, and she reaches out in the dark, stretches her fingers toward her sister's bed, latches onto petals. Pressed flowers disintegrate between her fingers.

She only wanted them back.

Special. Unfortunate. Special. Unfortunate.

Jane doesn't know which is which sometimes.

"Not special at all," Perry repeats, as he finishes ruining her wings and severs the last ties. "You're just a girl," he spits out.

Just a girl.

Jane latches onto the knitting needles, filled with the most puzzling feeling. Her chest expands, filled with a warmth.

Surprisingly, Perry has said the truest thing. About Jane, and yet about all of his peculiars.

"How perfectly lovely of you to say," Jane says, sitting up, weightless now without the wings. "You finally got something right. We are all of us, *just girls.*"

Jane stabs the knitting needles into Perry's eyes, skewering both in one fell swoop.

***

The train leaves Aldermoor during the night a week later. Jane watches out the attic window as Perry Featherstone gropes his way about, blind, no longer as sure of himself or the world around him. Some of the peculiars remain yet, but many have gone.

Behind Jane, on the double bed, her sisters are giggling. With Perry changed, the spell is broken.

"What's so funny?" Jane asks, whirling about.

Maddie holds up the old mannequin head. She's knitted a black hat for it, to resemble Perry. Maggie has pressed flowers on for the eyes. They bring it over to the window and set it on the sill.

"Good bye, Perry," Maddie says.

"Good bye, Perry," Maggie says.

"Good riddance," Jane says.

"Now what?" Maddie asks.

"Now we go to bed. Tomorrow we're going to celebrate your homecoming by getting sausages and visiting Mrs. Lydia Sophronia Dawkins in the bakery."

"All of us?" Maggie asks.

"Yes, all of us," Jane says.

"They'll all stare," Maddie says. "They always do. It'll be no different than the show."

"Ahh, but it is," Jane says. "You'll only be living your lives. We'll

87

not promote them ogling you. The sickness is with them, not you. They are the unfortunates."

"Yes, but what if they still do?" Maddie asks, and Jane realizes it may take her sisters a long time to feel any different, to undo what Papa and Perry have done. Maybe even what Jane herself had a part in.

"Yes," Maggie agrees. "What if this, our joining, is all anyone ever sees?"

And it's possible. Some people will only see what's on the surface, Jane acknowledges. She swipes a knitting needle from Maggie, stabbing it in the air like a sword. "Then it's flowers for eyes," she says.

Sarah Van Goethem is a Canadian author who resides in southwestern Ontario. Her novels have been in PitchWars and longlisted for both The Bath Children's Novel Award and CANSCAIP'S Writing for Children Competition.

Sarah also writes short stories, some of the most recent being: "Accidents are Not Possible" for GRIMM, GRIT & GASOLINE, an anthology of decopunk fairytales, "The Healing" for GLASS AND GARDENS: SOLARPUNK WINTERS, (both by World Weaver Press), "Maggie of the Moss" in EARTH: GIANTS, GOLEMS, AND GARGOYLES (Tyche Books), and "Wind Song" for AIR: Sylphs, Spirits and Swan Maidens (Tyche Books).

Sarah is a nature lover, a wanderer of dark forests, and a gatherer of vintage. You can find her at auctions, thrift stores, and most definitely trespassing at anything abandoned. She is clever and cunning, and often outwits evil wizards by simply setting skulls, adorned in jewels and flowers, on window ledges.

Checkmate

Brian Trent

The black steamrotor chugged noisily beneath the maze of damp brick arches, cutting a frothy wake in the underground canal. Edward Oakshott stood rigidly at the bow, leaning against his silver cane. The dank stink of London's forgotten netherworld perspirated over the vessel's wood, the humidity visibly beading like a spate of glassy insect eyes on the many green lamplights they passed. Edward drummed his fingers against one clammy hand. His sense of direction, precise as his fashionable gold pocket-watch, reckoned they must be passing directly below the evening crowd at Charing Cross' Hungerford Market.

Yet he wondered at their boatman's skill in navigating these dark, labyrinthine channels. How often were customers ferried to Thoth's subterranean bazaar? Edward grinned in nervous anticipation and peered from beneath the rim of his hat at the constellation of green lamps marking the canal's many twists and turns.

"We shall be late if this continues," Sophia Westbury said behind him. Her folded parasol looked like a pale sword against her shoulder. "Really, Edward, was there no earlier date you could meet him? It had to wait until the very eve of war?"

"The party shall wait for me."

"It will be a scandal," Sophia said, though her bell-like voice belied the smile on her lips. Edward was *already* the scandal of the decade. Chessmen were synonymous with shadowy, secret shufflings in the night; living legends who could be your banker, teacher, butcher, parent, or carriage driver during times of peace. Edward's public antics had shocked Europe into a buzzing hive.

Sophia sighed and looped her arm 'round his. "What do you know about this Thoth? Any man who dwells like a spider beneath London, spinning mechanical webs beyond the Ministry's sight..." She shivered. "I feel like Faustus!"

"Henry sent a Bishop here last autumn, darling, the one who defended Cornwall. If Henry says Thoth is trustworthy, that is good enough for me."

At these words, the boat banked sharply through a new arch, throwing up a huge wake. Edward steadied himself with pressure to his cane, but cast a ghastly glare at their boatman in the ship's small cabin.

"Edward!"

The engines cut. They were adrift on a Stygian lake with a circle of distant green lamps in the distance enclosing them. Edward noticed Sophia lowering her parasol, one of her lacy gloved hands poised over the handle switch. For his part, he slipped a finger beneath his hat rim and lowered a cat-sight monocle over his left eye. Instantly the darkness blazed into a brilliant shade of blue. He spied a ring of brick columns plunging into the water, a vaulted ceiling, and several tunnels. The water lapped in gentle, uneven tides.

In the spectral blue of his monocle, Edward watched another vessel emerge from one of the tunnels. It was smaller and swifter than their steamrotor. It gave the appearance of an Italian gondola without rowers or visible engine of locomotion.

"A single man is at the helm," Edward reported, hand straying to the oversized steel revolver in his belt holster. "Something odd in his look."

Sophia scowled and readied her grip on the parasol. Who could trust any creature living in such a ghoulish netherworld? She had an aunt who loved scaring the family's children with gothic tales of revenants lurking beneath London's streets. If only the old woman knew how near to reality her fictions were!

"Hail him, Edward!" she whispered. "Let us hurry this nasty business!"

"No harm will come," he said calmly with a glance at his lover. The monocle turned her into a creature of stark contrasts; with a blink he saw her alternately as lovely Aphrodite of Victorian society garbed in the latest Parisian fashion, or a livid blue ice banshee… beautiful, slender, and deadly as a Chinese sword.

The figure on the strange boat called out to them. "Be you lost, sir?"

"Most certainly," Edward replied. "Hopelessly lost, unless you are the old Egyptian they call Thoth. The Thoth who toils in his unseen laboratory? Who emerges only to peddle his illegal wares?"

"The upper world delights in its stories, I see."

Edward heard the foreign cadence cladding each word like strange silk. The voice was baritone, oily and betraying a wheeze. "I am here at the behest of Henry Harding. He spoke of the aid you provided a Bishop from Cornwall. You saved his life."

The other vessel continued to drift soundlessly forward into the galaxy of phosphorous lamplight. Edward wondered what manner of machinery whirred beneath the vessel so gently as to leave the glassy canal surface undisturbed. Suddenly the ship stopped as if anchors had harpooned the canal floor. Edward gazed upon the shriveled face of Thoth. He felt his mouth go dry.

Half of Thoth's ancient face was like a withered tree, knobby, cracked, and with the rugged patina of a crocodile. The other half was a corroded metal mask, studded with screws and rivets. A rotating wheel of a half dozen false eyes was bolted into the steel near his aquiline nose. Leathery hoses protruded from Thoth's skull and snaked into a cumbersome backpack strapped about his waist.

Thoth breathed deeply, and the machinery of his backpack whined with the effort. "I was unaware of the Bishop's outcome. Anubis decides life and death, not me."

Sophia hissed her displeasure and snapped the parasol open, leveling it like a shield. The Egyptian's wheel of eyes blinked at the menacing tip in the center.

But Edward held up a hand. "Sophia, we must be cordial."

"He's a heathen sorcerer!" she whispered.

Edward called to the stranger, "I am a Knight."

Thoth rubbed a grizzled chin thoughtfully. "The world has known that for four years."

"London is being threatened by a Rook."

The Egyptian nodded again. Water poured from the ceiling, bursting in a short-lived stream out of gutters above.

Edward waited. "I do not wish to die just yet."

"No Knight has defeated a Rook in ten years."

"Precisely why I have come to see you."

"Anubis—"

"Yes, yes, yes." Edward felt his temperature rise. "Perhaps Anubis would consider a sacrifice of gold for his interred pharaohs? What will ten thousand guineas buy me? An electro-plated Book of the Dead? A feather of truth? *Or perhaps something that can aid a Knight in the battle of his life?*"

"What nation has declared against Britain?"

"Will my answer change your price-list?" Edward pounded the deck once with his cane. "What do you have for me?"

Thoth laughed shrilly. "To business it is, then! I only wonder if it is your death you fear, or losing face now that yours has become so public?"

Edward went flush. Truthfully, his public revelation was less audacity than unfortunate circumstance. Four years ago during a desperate battle with a German Knight, the melee had exploded out through the arena walls and over London streets. In full view of hundreds of upturned faces, Edward and his cursing opponent battled past church spires, marketplace roofs, and Hyde Park. Only then had Edward managed to deliver a crushing blow into the Knight's face. He remembered the way the man's eyes rolled white, and how he plummeted like a stone into the green park. The point of impact was subsequently honored by Her Majesty with a handsome placard.

Coming out publicly was a terribly natural thing to do after that. He descended on his rocket-pack straight into a crowd, found the nearest reporter, and said, "Edward Oakshott, Knight of Her Majesty's War Ministry, at your service!"

Society was shocked. Newspapers gave a swift cry urging Edward's disbarment from the Chesswar. Others didn't agree, and four years later it remained a contested subject, hotly debated in smoking room brawls and organized protests, for or against Oakshott, from London to Edinburgh and beyond.

To Thoth, Edward said, "What can I buy for ten thousand guineas?"

"Anubis," the boatman repeated. "Your lady thinks I invoke pagan gods when I speak of the Underworld Judge. This is not so. Anubis is what you may purchase, Sir Edward."

Hearing his name spoken by this ghoul brought a chill to Edward's spine. He pushed the monocle back under his hat rim. "And what is Anubis? A pet jackal to guard my estate?"

"A device you wear over your heart. It can jolt the dying back to life."

Sophia hissed again and began to protest, so Thoth wheezed angrily, "If my inventions offend certain sensibilities, then perhaps you have come to the wrong place! Anubis is worn over the heart! Touch its switch, and it injects tiny steel spiders into your body. They will revive you from a mortal wound."

"Spiders?"

"In point of fact they more closely resemble horseshoe crabs. Yet they weave and spin flesh, repairing damage as a spider may correct a sundered web. Tiny, tiny! More than four thousand folded up tight within the Anubis cocoon! Life from death, at the touch of a switch. A powerful advantage in a Chesswar duel, would you agree?"

"I would," Edward gasped, controlling his breathing. *Dear Lord! Has the ingenuity of our most marvelous age finally overthrown the tale of Lazarus?* His blood thrilled at the notion.

"The price is twenty thousand guineas," Thoth said. "And your oath before God to keep it secret! Place the money onto the dinghy beside you."

Edward realized that a miniscule float of wood, painted black as the water, had silently crept to the rail of his ship.

He tipped his hat. "Indeed, great Thoth. To the coffers of Osiris goes my gift!" He walked gingerly to a small hold and hoisted a lacquered mahogany box from within. Swiftly he opened it and removed two drawers of gold, did a quick tabulation of what remained, and closed the lid. For an instant he worried that the weight would sink the dinghy, and when he set the box upon it the water crept onto the planks in neat horizons. Yet it stayed buoyant. The dinghy twirled once in the water like a leaf and moved towards Thoth.

"Best wishes," Thoth called out, as he and the dinghy retreated into one of the tunnels.

Sophia looked ready to spit. "Edward! This—"

He hushed her as another dinghy moved on the water, bearing upon its deck the promised prize.

***

"Edward Oakshott, your arrival is almost too late to be fashionable!"

snapped the corpulent Mrs. Harding, wife of War Minister Henry Harding, the instant he stepped into luxurious Ministry Hall.

Edward hesitated for the firing squad of photographers, Sophia attached to his arm. He let his eyes move to the baroque wall clock in the instant before the flash. Those iron scythe-like hands were poised a few minutes from the ominous ring of 8-o'-clock.

Then the camera bulbs flashed noisily. "Mrs. Harding," Edward said congenially, "Good fashion relies on lost punctuality."

He moved past her into the widening maw of London's socialites, politicians, merchant kings, and foreign diplomats. Reporters threaded the crowd and surrounded him.

"Have you heard the latest from Nanjing?" one asked. "Minister Lin declared that you mock the art of war with your public antics! Do you have a response?"

"Yes. It surprises me Lin is so eager for a *second* war with Britain. Was losing Hong Kong not enough for the Emperor?"

The gatherers laughed uproariously, although a few politicians turned purple with consternation. Reporters hand-cranked their phonograph cylinders like dairy workers churning butter; Knight Oakshott was one of England's most quotable personalities, to the delight of newspapers and the chagrin of politicians.

"Mr. Oakshott," asked Gibson Bennett, a ferret even among journalists. His whiskered face, bespectacled eyes and pronounced nose made Edward think back to Thoth's secretive underground. How much would Bennett pay to expose *that* concealed British netherworld? "In the face of the latest Russian aggression across Europe and Turkey, do you think the old ways of war should be resumed? Armies, instead of sixteen elite soldiers for each country? Should the fate of so many people reside on the performance of so few?"

Edward's eyes flashed, and a photograph snapped that very second. Beautiful! he thought. He was already imagining the picture in tomorrow's edition: Saucy, possessed, a model of controlled aggression, enough to get ladies' pulses pounding. He suspected the edition would sell out within an hour.

"Ah yes," Edward said, measuring his words carefully. "It makes much more sense for all of London to be in the hands of falling bombs, bullets, and ballistae! Yes, let's trade in our Chessmen for a thousand-fold army of plunderers! Every political disagreement will once again result in cities destroyed! Risk the Parliament, the pyramids, and Paris because one monarch stubs his toe on another's footstool!"

The crowd erupted. Even the politicians smiled at this, and Edward saw Henry's mustachioed face in the crowd, nodding agreeably.

"A *civilized* age," Henry added, causing the crowd heads to whirl in his direction, "requires *civilized* warfare. The old ways are over with, done! Consider how much money, resource, and lives went into our spat with the American colonies. Nowadays an *official* declaration of hostilities would involve thirty-two combatants rather than thirty-two thousand."

"But Oakshott will be facing a Rook!" said a high voice from the crowd.

"The Rook has yet to declare its move," Edward said evenly. "He may choose to advance on Norwich instead. He may choose to sit tight."

The crowd turned its collective head again, this time to the baroque clock. The Rook was required to announce its next move by eight-o'-clock. If no declaration came, it would fall to Knight Oakshott to announce his move: Remain in London, attempt a strategic outflank to a neighboring prefecture, or jaunt straight to Coventry for a noble suicide against the Rook, an adjacent Pawn, and a newly invading Bishop. There might even be an enemy Queen among them; unlike all other units, Queen movements were as insidious and unseen as a viper in the shadows.

"Are you not petrified?"

Edward felt the sweat squeezed from his pores. He conjured a convincing smile. "Indeed I am. My heart is stone, my nerves are steel, and I will be a Knight to remember!" He tossed up his cane, and the crowd gasped as it twirled twice, only to be caught by Sophia. She laughed and suddenly Edward hopped over to her, knelt, his hat in his hands.

"Would you do the honors, my good lady?"

Sophia whispered. "You tempt the Fates, Edward."

He smiled, disguising an anxious swallow. A heavy bead of sweat crawled through his scalp and swelled like dew at his hairline. In less than twenty-four hours, he'd be sweating in battle with a Rook, dear Lord!

Silence filled the room like a toxic vapor among marble statues. Someone's nervous titter shattered the sickening quiet, and the crowd flinched.

"Sir Edward Oakshott," Sophia began, "Do you promise to protect Her Majesty's Empire as you have done so faithfully before?"

"I do, and most *humbly*!" There was a hearty outburst of laughter at this.

Life was choice and chance, he thought while waiting for Sophia to continue. He felt the sweat droplet growing heavy, tugged at by gravity. The Ministry floor was covered in a spray of inch-long gray and white tiles. He tried to guess which floor tile the sweat droplet might splatter against. More to the point, could he control the fall of the droplet, guarantee that it hit white? Was tomorrow's fight the same combination of choice and chance? Each Chessman had an established menu of technological enhancements agreed upon by international guidelines. Edward's success against four Spanish Pawns, a Portuguese Bishop, and even that legendary public duel with the German Knight owed to an alchemy of skill, knowledge, and chance.

And now Anubis was a factor.

"Do you commit yourself to this battle without reservation, and remain in it to whatever end?"

"I do!"

Thoth's device was heavy in his jacket pocket. He tried imagining the vast armies of sleeping silver spiders inside. He wondered what it would feel like to have them invade his body, scuttling through his veins and along the ropes of tendons, weaving scabs onto wounds and stitching up muscles. Then what? Do they stay in the body? Do they insidiously set the stage for him to become like the monstrous Thoth?

He found himself remembering a controversial cover illustration to *Quincy's Quarterly*, in which mechanical ladies were shopping for gears, wire, and replacement joints. Was *that* the future? Everything like a windup clock, hot blood replaced by greasy lubrications, and the soft timbre of Sophia's midnight confessions traded for hollow musical notes belched from a pipe organ?

Edward blinked at the gray and white tiles.

A Rook was a hulking horror clad in screws-and-bolts. It's designation during the First Chesswar Council in Frankfurt, 1798, caused three months of public debate (far more than any other Chessman caste), and the Yanks were especially vocal, swearing that that "Europe would let monsters fight her wars now!" Not as powerful as the all-powerful Queen, a Rook nonetheless provoked the most terror in public consciousness.

"Then our hopes rest with you, our Knight!" Sophia finished.

Edward grinned, eyes still transfixed by the row of floor tiles. His heart panged a strained note, and his fear rattled chains of self-control. *I choose the white tile.*

Sophia tapped him on both shoulders with the cane.

The last tap shook the droplet loose from his eyebrow. It fell like a glassy bead, splintered into a vaguely star-shaped pattern against the floor.

Gray.

The clock chimes rang, hollow and ghastly in the spacious room. Eight-o'-clock. Edward remained on his knees.

A teletype sprang to life, clacking madly.

Reporters surged toward the machine. The Ministry guards heaved to repel them and Henry leapt to it, grabbed the end of the leaflet and tore it free.

Henry read it for several lengthy seconds. Then he turned to the audience, found Edward, and announced in a clear high voice: "Rook advances on London."

***

The Old Street warehouse was perched on a narrow tower of colorless bricks like a country citadel. It was sandwiched in by several new government buildings which formed a kind of maze, so there was little chance of someone stumbling into its lonely alley. Should a careless carriage or wayward pedestrian see it, the warehouse appeared as just another unsightly example of crowded and careless development. Access was only possible from the ramp at its base which led to twin lifts grinding up the tower chute to the arena.

Inside, Edward and Harding walked abreast of the War Ministry's official witnesses, listening to a heavy downpour assail the corrugated steel walls. The spacious interior stank of damp sawdust and the smoky sweet odor of diesel. No windows interrupted the rusty walls. No doors. No escape.

Harding lowered his voice. "Is everything set?"

"As long as Thoth is no liar."

"He is not."

"These metal spiders, Henry. Do they—"

"Hush!"

They passed the observer's box, a cube of reinforced concrete and steel where the witnesses would wait and watch, making notes and crossing fingers at the mirror-bourn images piped in from the periscope growing out of its ceiling.

The Russians were already gathered at the far side of the arena, having arrived by airship to the Queen's palace and then shuttled off among a parade of decoys through London. Edward counted eight people. Behind them, just out of the cone of overhead lamplight, a hulking shadow lurked.

Edward's hand jerked towards his heart. His feet halted at a raised row of screws painted red. He regarded the invaders across the gulf of ten meters.

"Sir Edward Oakshott," Harding said, "Meet the Russian Rook."

***

The Rook resembled a large black cylindrical boiler on tripod legs set within a thick, grooved iron waistband; Edward marveled at the tracks which would allow easy limb rotations and readjustments. The legs' construction was exposed to plain sight, displaying a clockmaker's paradise of gears, rods, and pistons. Each terminated at a foot little more than a lead-colored squarish block.

The iron body was smooth except for a single porthole—a glass eye encircled by a black rim of rivets. Edward suddenly recalled the voice of his old Ministry instructor: "Shooting the hellish thing in the eye will seem the natural thing to do. You might even get lucky. But a Rook will protect its weak spot. Many Chessmen have died while trying to play Odysseus versus the bloody Cyclops."

There was no head. Instead, two grotesquely long arms sprouted from the top of the cylinder. They looked like pale branches of a muscular tree, and Edward felt his blood chill at the thought of the surgery necessary to rearrange a human body to fit this nightmarish reconfiguration. Rooks were different from other Chessmen. They didn't melt into normal life after they were made. What manner of man would elect this hellish existence... a freak living only for battle? Each arm was entwined by leather support hoses like black ivy garland, and each hand vanished into the sleeve of a weapon. The right arm hooked into a flame jet. The left was a kind of rifle. The bare elbows flexed and swiveled.

Edward pulled his pistol from his beltline. The Rook's arms froze in their hydra-like gyrations. Its porthole eye rotated to face him.

The Russian and British entourages quietly filed out of the arena and into the security of the witness box. Edward reassuringly touched the three circular ammunition wheels clipped to his jacket. Each wheel contained a unique set of projectile.

Harding shouted from his sanctuary: "The War Ministry of the British Empire declares—"

Edward plucked off the first of his three ammunition wheels and snapped it like a crest onto his revolver.

"—that the battle between Knight and Rook, on this 23rd day of April, in the Year of Our Lord 1843—"

He held his left arm rigid, balanced the revolver on its horizontal line, and used his wrist to activate a hidden switch. From his forearm a metallic shield unfurled in noisy extendable shutters. He withdrew the pistol before the last shutter clicked into place, and peered over the rim of the defensive shield at his opponent. He winked.

"—shall be recognized as an official proceeding in the engagement of war between the British and Russian Empires."

The Rook's glass eye turned red. Steam floated, wisp-like, from its seams.

A pistol shot rang out from the witness bunker.

The Rook sprang to life. Its right arm thrust forward the muzzle of a flame-jet, and suddenly Edward's shield was ablaze. He tilted the shield to redirect the incendiary flow, while also giving himself an opening for his pistol. Edward squeezed off two shots at the Rook's right arm as it turned towards him.

The slugs landed with meaty *thwacks* into the arm's flesh. The arm snapped back. Beneath the eye, a hatch squealed open and disgorged a nasty black oil cloud in Edward's direction. He hopped back two steps, discharging four more shots into the obscurity and hearing them flatten against the iron body.

Edward wasted no time in reloading the pistol. He snapped his shield arm down and his weapon arm up, a motion which pulled the tether to his concealed rocket pack. As he propelled up to the warehouse rafters on a plume of white steam, the Rook lunged through the oil cloud, all legs coming at him like a nightmarish spider. The left arm loosed two mushroom-shaped shells at high pressure speeds. They hit nothing. The eye rotated wildly, seeking its target.

From the rafters, Edward perched and loaded the next ammunition wheel. He took careful aim at the abomination's left arm and squeezed off three rapid shots.

The first slugs had been brass, but this next batch was acid. Only one found its target, but the Rook let loose a shriek like a chorus of tea kettles and unloaded a wild barrage of flame and shells into his general direction while its legs stomped about in a dance of agony. The rafter was shredded into a haze of metal particles, but Edward was already gone.

He had intended to land behind the Rook, but he watched that crimson eye track him unnervingly well. As he swooped in low for a landing the Rook was already rotating. Edward hastily changed tactics, his heart galloping at a frightful pace. The right flame arm was coming up to his face when he wrestled it, slapping himself against its solid, clammy flesh. He heard the flame shoot behind him and felt the backsplash of heat.

The Rook's strength was ungodly. Each pivot of the massive arm took Edward off his feet and slammed him down painfully. He thought crazily of being a slab of meat beneath a chef's mallet.

In desperation, Edward hooked his pistol over his head, aiming blind at the Rook's top, and fired four more times.

It wasn't merely the eye that was an Achilles' Heel. The Rook's top was a colorless dome beneath which the fleshy interior of this man-thing was hunched. The bullets flattened on impact, but dissolved away at the dome. Metal squealed and popped, opening the creature's vulnerable body to harm.

Then the left arm did the impossible. Edward had been warned about the superhuman flexibility of a Rook—that its human-looking arms were multi-jointed improvements on the mortal frame.

Bending *inversely*, the left arm hooked over the Rook and fired point-blank into Edward's head.

The impact was stunning. His hat—like his clothes—was designed to stop bullets, but dear God they hurt! Edward fired, aimlessly, and then he felt new hammer-strikes of bullets against his chest. He blew back from his enemy, the air driven from his lungs like a popped balloon.

Edward looked up from the floor and drew a startled breath, for he saw not one, but *three* Rooks. His head throbbed. He watched the trio of monstrosities rushing to him.

In a Dublin tavern in his reckless youth, he had once been involved in a fight with several sailors. One fellow had clubbed him upside the head with a bottle, and the resulting double-vision had lasted several minutes and created the mirage of fighting in a maelstrom of unwashed assailants.

But it hadn't looked like *this*.

Edward hastily drew down his monocle from beneath his cap, and squeezed his other eye shut. Two Rooks vanished, revealing the master of the illusion. In the center. It was pure Rook-trick, this manner of optical hallucination. Ah!

Edward exhaled as he pulled the trigger on his last acid round.

The shot plastered itself over the Cyclopean eye.

It was a masterful aim, and sent the Rook mad. Even as Edward tottered unsteadily to his feet, the Rook was unable to cope with being blinded. Edward hopped back, his fear burned away by success. Some of his old flair came back into his steps. He turned to the witness box, raised his monocle, and bowed low. Then he disengaged the empty ammunition wheel.

The Rook clearly felt its opponent was still lying prone, because it was expending its flames all across the floor. Heat vapors rose around it like the spirits of slain warriors, and in a bout of frustration it expelled another oil cloud. Edward snapped the last wheel onto his revolver and rested it on his shield arm. He searched the black and white fog, moving the barrel a millimeter back and forth, gauging the confusing dark shapes.

The infernal mists parted like a majestic curtain. The parted veil revealed the Rook's clunky geometry. Edward calmly took aim and squeezed three shots in deliberate, staccato beats. Incendiary bullets.

Something was wrong.

He knew his bullets must have hit his target, but there was no sound of the impact. Edward's sharp eyes caught sight of three bullet holes against the far wall. That couldn't be! Unless...

He reached up for his monocle again when his head snapped back. There was no pain at first, even when his head crashed into the floor. His cheek felt wet. Salty blood gushed down his throat.

When he came to his senses the Rook was already leaning over him, its false double gone. Its porthole eye had been melted away, and inside the ruined porthole Edward spied *another* eye, smaller and raw, set in a red face stapled with leather stitches and needles. There was tortured suffering and livid bloodthirst, but no inhumanity, in that blue gaze. It was a living hue, not the crystalline glassiness of sapphire or the lifeless veneer of cobalt. Edward could count the flecks in the iris if he wished. The pupil quivered, poised between expansion and contraction in the uneven luminosity. A tiny vein pulsated in the corner.

Edward's own vision was growing gray at the edges. His hand twitched toward Thoth's secret resurrection switch.

The blue eye watched Edward.

Press the switch and unleash the spiders into your body!

Edward's vision was fading fast, the blood in his throat a steady downpour that filled his stomach. *Hit the switch!* he thought. *Spring back to life!*

His fingers hesitated. He thought of the *Quincy's Quarterly* cover with the mechanical ladies shopping for spare parts. He remembered Thoth's frightful visage in the Stygian dark beneath Charing Cross.

The Rook's eye studied him with what seemed strange

sympathy. *Dear Lord, what a monstrosity the thing is! Did it have parents once? What sort of man had it been before volunteering for such alterations? And what may I become should my body become nest to Thoth's insectile army? I am a man with tools, not a tool fashioned in mockery of man!*

Edward gingerly touched the Anubis switch but did not press it. He imagined he could sense the spiders' urgency inside the device, humming with ugly need. *Let us build nests in you! Stitch egg-sacs into your muscles and red flesh, take position behind your eyes and into your brain, imprison your soul like a fly in eternal amber!*

An ugly lethargy burdened his arms. He imagined the ease of restoring life, winning London for London, and then one morning he would be like this abomination before him, a single eye trapped in a steel cage. Unexpected regret filled him as he thought of the thing's tea kettle shriek.

"Sophia," Edward whispered. He let his hand fall limp. He managed a feeble nod to his opponent as his vision faded into an omnipresent street fog.

***

"Victory goes to Rook!" the Russian Minister pronounced, emerging gleefully from the witness box.

Harding stared at Edward's corpse in open-mouthed despair, not caring who saw it. "He nearly won."

"Nearly does not a victory make. I congratulate you on a splendid fight, though the London marker now belongs to us."

Harding ignored him and walked past the Rook, hating its monstrosity even more than usual. He stared at Edward's bloody, shattered face.

"The London marker," the Russian repeated, raising his voice. "It was a brilliant match but your Knight lost, Sir Harding."

Harding stroked his mustache. "Yes, he did. But the marker will remain in my possession until the London battles are over."

"What? They *are* over! This is an outrage!"

Footsteps sounded behind them. Sophia entered the room, her face as tight as steel and full of venom as she perceived her lover's body on the floor. *Oh, Edward!*

Minister Harding bowed in anguish before her. "My Lady."

She returned the courtesy. "There is no need for telegraphs or senseless formalities here, would you agree?" She turned to the Russian Minister, and then let her gaze drill into the Rook. "Queen," she declared, "advances on Rook."

Within the melted porthole, a blue eye grew wide.

Brian Trent writes science fiction and fantasy, horror and fable. His contribution here, "Checkmate", is an original tale that draws folkloric inspiration from the chess game in *Through the Looking Glass*, as well as from the game of chess itself. Upon those checkered squares unfolds a unique story each time, with knights and queens, moving castles and the promise of success (or death) in every passing moment. Trent, an avid chess player himself, applies the strategic nature of the game and the specialized nature of its six "player classes" to a steampunk world that might have been. Trent's recent publications can be found in *Fantasy & Science Fiction* (March/April 2020, July/August 2020, and September/October 2020), Baen Books' *Weird World War III* anthology (October 2020), and more. His novel *Ten Thousand Thunders* was released last year from Flame Tree Press. You can catch up with Trent on his blog at www.briantrent.com.

NECROMANCY
Melissa Bobe

The stench rose sinister from the bottom of Bleecker Hill. It lived there, down where the river ended in muck, where they buried their children after the plague. It smelled like blood, left to rot out in the open air.

Natalie Jameson was the first afflicted. She went away to find work and adventure in the wider world, despite her mother's warnings. The town whispered in her wake, recounting how dreams of seeing the world's cities, riding trains and airships into the unknown, had utterly seduced the girl. And they would later tell how she had brought the plague with her when she returned.

Walking into town as the late summer sun set red, casting shadows lean and dark, Natalie appeared. The long plaits her mother had once braided for her each morning had been sliced away, short curls left peeking out beneath her aviator's cap. A silver hoop pierced her nose, shining to match its twin, looped over the center of her bottom lip. Her skirts, once pleated and long, were now short enough to reveal spindly legs laced into tall, heeled boots, tight stockings beneath leaving little to the imagination. And her torso revealed, through a tight-fitting tunic, a condition that the town absolutely would not tolerate.

Her mother's throat closed in panic upon seeing the girl, and so while she welcomed her daughter with a loving embrace, she immediately began plotting how to keep her from the eyes of their neighbors. She drugged Natalie's dinner, and locked her in the attic. She knew she had to get rid of the evidence that had rooted itself inside her daughter before any in the town might speak that most dangerous word: contagion. Such a thing could not be allowed to run its course. Like the other abominations of the wider, wicked world, it must be beaten out and forced away for good.

So the woman chained her daughter to the attic wall, cutting a crude hole at the base of the door through which food might be passed. She soaked bread in pennyroyal and licorice root, gave her only ale to drink. Though it was inevitable that the town would discover Natalie had returned, for the time being, her mother had to act as though she were alone. Only time would rid them of the damning thing inside of her daughter.

But Abigail Little had already told her own mother that she'd seen the Jameson girl making the climb from the bottom of the hill, walking through town until she'd reached her mother's house. And Abigail's mother told her neighbors, and they told their neighbors, and the town knew by the next evening.

They came by subtly at first, feeling some pity for this woman whose child had been so reckless as to venture outside the safety of the town. They offered herbs and more ale, sympathetic clicks of their tongue and assurances that she was doing the right thing.

But after a week passed, those murmurs of pity began to transform into panic. How had Natalie not been humbled back to her former self by now? Was the plague still within her? And how long before their daughters might be subject to the same disease?

Now, there were threats at the Jameson house: rocks thrown through windows at midnight, angry words called out during the day. The townsfolk demanded to see the girl, to take her to the prison if her mother couldn't properly rid her of this infection. The woman locked the door and refused to let them near her daughter, begging them to leave.

A week later, the butcher brought his sister to the town. She was a powerful apothecary, bitter-faced and aged. She addressed the townspeople, warning them, "The plague is a curse, and she who carries it will surely spread it if she is permitted to." She turned her cold, sharp eyes on the young girls gathered in the crowd. "The rest of you should beware: if you contract this plague, only ruin and death await you."

Abigail Little's eyes drifted towards the Jameson house as though she could not hear the crone's words at all. There was a light behind her gaze, a spark of knowledge and a craving simmering there, barely contained.

They broke down the door of the Jameson house at dawn. The townsfolk forced themselves upstairs, but when they found the girl, she was already dead. The corpse of an infant born much too soon lay in her arms, its face sticky with blood.

They left the burial to Natalie's mother, her punishment for allowing her daughter to leave in the first place. She buried both corpses in the mud at the base of the hill. The only witnesses were the rats that kept the town fearful of a hungry winter and one Abigail Little, who watched from behind a twisted oak, breathless with fascination.

Abigail took in the shape of Natalie Jameson, from her blue pierced lips to her booted feet, a girl like none she had ever seen before. It seemed that, even in death, there was something in her expression that had not been there before she'd left the town: a raised chin, a set jaw, beneath which there was a distinct lack of fear.

No fear, even in death.

Three days later, Abigail Little appeared walking the streets of the town with her hair cut short around her ears, a silver safety pin running through her left eyebrow, and a corset pulled tight above her short skirts, revealing the shape of her slender body.

The townspeople whispered to one another in a near-silent frenzy, their hushed tones vibrating like air charged with electricity before a coming storm.

Then, Abigail's dearest friends, Sally Mans and Mary Ridley, emerged from their homes in revealing dresses they had made by shredding and re-stitching more modest clothing. Sally had shorn her hair away so that the very bones of her skull were visible, and she'd placed on her head an old bowler hat that had belonged to her father when he was alive. Mary's ears sported rows of pins, and she'd donned a tailored jacket that her salesman brother had forgotten on his last visit from a nearby city.

The three girls walked the winding streets of the town, knowing smiles on their faces. Whispers followed in their wake, but they shared a single thought among them: *there is no curse, no plague in this town but the winter rats.*

The world was beckoning, and soon enough, they would find their way to the first airship into it.

***

Some ways away but not so far from the town as you might think, a young man sat in the woods, playing a pipe. A bird was drawn to the sound, a lovely and light melody that told of righteousness in the face of evil. The man wore a swallowtail coat made of patched strips of leather in every shade imaginable: umber, mustard, maroon, navy, viridian. His trousers revealed strong, youthful legs, at the base of which were traveler's boots, worn with years of wandering. His eyes were closed as he played, breathing circularly so that it seemed the tune might be without end.

Piper-the-First, so called as the eldest of seven sons, was the cleverest of his brothers. His eyes lifted suddenly, sensing an audience, and he regarded the bird, a young healthy hawk that had recently left its own brothers to build a home and future for itself. Finally taking a pause from his music, Piper spoke with the hawk, informing the creature that his lover had gone to visit her home and had not returned to him when he'd expected her. He had heard no word of her since.

The hawk flew off in the direction of Bleecker Hill. Within the hour, it returned with two rats from the town tucked carefully into its talons. Piper gently took the rats from the bird, setting them at his feet and greeting them with all of the gratitude he had offered the hawk upon its return. Though far from home, the rats were willing to help this man who seemed to have all of the cunning their own species boasted.

"I would like to know," he said to the rats, "what has befallen my Natalie."

And in hushed tones that only Piper could hear, the creatures spoke of the town and all that had happened there. Piper-the-First made for the camp that he and his brothers had set up earlier that day. They'd been wandering through the forest, offering their unique skills to the smaller towns that skirted the great stretches of woods. They planned to earn enough money for passage on an airship to warmer parts, where they would spend the winter. Natalie had intended to go with them; she had only taken leave of Piper to bid her mother a proper farewell.

Now, though, the brothers had a new destination to visit, and it lay just beyond Bleecker Hill.

***

Back in the town, Abigail, Sally, and Mary had vanished from the streets, but there were other girls showing signs of the plague. The town had gathered for a council meeting, fearing all of their daughters were at risk and concluding that drastic action must be taken.

The town prison had not been used for many years. Its walls were stone, its cells without windows, and each of those cells fitted with shackles that hung down from the ceiling on rusted chains. The only thing a prisoner could glimpse from this position, arms strung up and feet just grazing the dirt floor, was the forlorn sight of another inmate in the cell across the way.

The decision to imprison the girls had been unanimous. The only voice that hadn't joined in the resounding "Aye!" belonged to Natalie Jameson's mother. She had not spoken a word since the day she had buried her daughter's body.

Now the prison held Abigail Little and five others, strung up like so many poppets, their bodies pulling at the chains from above, their minds pushing against the insults hissed at them by their captors.

Later that week, when Piper-the-First and two of his brothers, Herald-the-Second and Drummer-the-Third, made their way slowly up Bleecker Hill, word of them spread like flames. All convened in the town square to see the strangers; among them was Abigail's own uncle, the prison jailer. The keys he had used to lock the shackles on the girls' wrists and the barred doors of their cells jingled dissonantly at his waist.

The sight of three handsome young men from the wider world was not a welcome one. Though they had arrived on foot and all they carried between them were a pipe, a trumpet, and a drum, their carriage and dress were enough to spark fear in the eyes that regarded them now. No town sons were these.

"I'm looking for Natalie Jameson." Piper did not hesitate to step forward and address the crowd. Behind him, Herald and Drummer looked steadfast at those who had gathered, unflinching as their elder brother.

"What do you want with my daughter?" To the surprise of many, it was Natalie's mother who broke the silence, speaking for the first time in weeks.

Piper removed his hat, giving the woman a nod of respect. He saw the mourning in her face, and he sensed beneath it something that made his sense of justice quiver. "Well met, Mother Jameson. Is Natalie well?"

"She is dead and buried." The woman's bitter voice cut the very air. "And do you know of the plague that took her from me, sir? You come here asking for my daughter and yet say nothing of how you seem to know her."

Piper paused, considering all he'd learned thus far before he spoke. His eyes remained downcast, so that none might glean what thoughts were spinning through his mind, whirring and clicking like so many gears in a clock or the cylinder of a cocked revolver.

"It is true that my brothers and I have come because we have heard this town is dealing with a plight of sorts," he finally began. "Are you not overrun with rats? We have cleansed other towns of pestilence, and thought perhaps our services might be welcomed."

A collective breath of relief cut the tension in the town square. One council member, a man who had advocated most strongly for the imprisonment of the girls, now stepped forward. "Indeed, we fear a winter of famine if we cannot banish the rats from our food stores and cupboards. If you would rid us of these filthy beasts, we would be in your debt."

Another more cautious council member added, "It won't be an easy task. Their numbers are formidable—whenever we kill one, it seems another four rise up to take their dead brother's place."

"Imagine that," Piper murmured to himself, a roguish note in the words that none of the townsfolk could hear. Raising his voice once more, he looked the two councilmen in the eye, and they found they could not comfortably meet the brightness of his gaze. "Fear not—we have known many situations even more dire than that which troubles this place. I believe we will be able to solve your problem, but we would require a week's food and lodging."

The innkeeper, grandfather of Sally Mans, spoke up now. "The inn is empty, with harvest season calling most travelers back to their homes in preparation for winter. I would be glad to offer you my best rooms on behalf of the town."

The brothers nodded their acceptance of this offer, not pausing to confer with one another. Had the town paid more attention to the detested pests in their food stores, they might have recognized a singular kind of synchronicity in the gesture, a habit of creatures so inseparable that they could be of one mind.

"You require nothing else?" the first councilman asked dubiously, an eyebrow raised in suspicion. "No tools to help you? No funds to be used for whatever means you'll apply to eliminate the beasts?"

"We come prepared with all we need," Piper assured him. "As it's late in the day, we will gratefully accept your hospitality. Let us take our leave with your innkeeper, so that we might settle in and assess the situation further."

The townspeople began to disperse. Natalie Jameson's mother was forgotten, as was the fact that the first thing Piper had asked was to know the whereabouts of her daughter. Her eyes trailed after the strangers as they made their way to the inn, a hollowness there that the brothers felt at their backs, though not one turned to acknowledge it.

***

That evening, Herald-the-Second went for a brief walk through the streets of the town in order to get a better sense of the place. He came upon the mother of Amy Little, Abigail's cousin, weeping on her doorstep.

"What has happened?" he asked. Herald had an open way about him that made even strangers feel they could confide in him.

"My daughter," the woman sobbed. "My daughter is gone."

"I can help you find her," he offered, resting a hand on the trumpet at his side, its brass shining under the light of the autumn moon.

But the woman shook her head, either unwilling or unable to say more. She stood and pushed in the front door of her home, closing it firmly behind her without another word to Herald.

When he arrived back at the inn, Herald told his brothers of what had transpired. "I don't know what this town is hiding," he concluded, "but I do fear for this missing girl, as Piper had rightly feared for Natalie."

Piper nodded. "We will bring the girl home, if we can, on the day we send the rats from the village."

"What of Natalie?" Drummer spoke now, stalwart and direct as was his way. "You must still seek answers there."

Piper offered a grim smile. "I plan to see her again, one way or another." He met Herald's eyes. "There is indeed something amiss with this town and its daughters—I do not believe these two are the only missing."

"What do we do then, brother?"

Piper considered a small rat that had made its way into the room and was cleaning itself on a windowsill, as comfortable in the company of the brothers as if it had been one of the family. "We listen, we learn, and we wait."

***

A week passed and the three brothers were seen often, making their way about the town, but what they were doing to deal with the rats was unclear to those who tried to trace their movements. They didn't speak much, as they weren't spoken to, but walked with soft steps and thoughtful expressions, their instruments always by their sides.

On the final day of that week, the townspeople woke to the sounds of music moving through the winding streets of their home. Some shivered in their beds, feeling a tug at their conscience that made them almost sick. Some sat bolt upright in terror, overcome with the sense that something was coming for them as they emerged from dreams of running from faceless pursuers. A few made their way to windows for a glimpse outside, seeking in the fog of early morning the source of the haunting tune.

Piper-the-First led his brothers through the streets, his pipe at his lips. For the moment, Herald and Drummer let their instruments rest; they were too powerful for this particular task. Behind the brothers, keeping pace with their steady strides, were the town rats, come from warm cupboards and food-filled basements into the misty morning, enchanted by the same sound that made the hair of the townspeople stand on edge.

The brothers led the rats down to the bottom of Bleecker Hill, but not before they passed by the town prison. And with keen ears that only musicians have, they were able to distinguish the faintest of sounds emanating from its stone walls: the sighs and moans of the town daughters who had been chained by their fathers, their uncles, their brothers, their would-be husbands. The sound of the pipe was, for these locked away girls, an expression of all the longing and need that had driven them from the stylings and destinies imposed upon them by the town. Its melody was as irresistible to them as it was to the multitude of rats dispersing at the bottom of the hill, bound for points unknown.

When the brothers came to stand at the base of the hill, Herald sounded one long note on his horn, intended to lead the rats on a good path so that they would not get lost along their way.

Drummer then turned to his brothers and asked, "You heard them in the prison?"

Piper and Herald nodded, but before they could speak further, there was movement in the muck that edged Bleecker Hill. Moved by the tone of the trumpet, a figure rose out of the filth, coming to stand on boots laced high, her corset caked with mud, her wrists starved and bloody with bracelets of cut flesh, the work of rusted manacles pulling at them until the rest of her had expired.

"I'll wager that's Amy Little," Piper remarked quietly, and Herald nodded.

Amy's eyes were wide and dilated beneath the cloud of recent death that had glazed them over. Her lips were parted, and she wavered uncertainly, unsure of what to do now that the string of music that had drawn her from her grave had been cut.

"I promised her mother I would lead her home," Herald said, "though I wonder if it is the right thing."

"Keep your word, brother," Drummer said, his mouth set in a hard line as he regarded the dead girl swaying before them.

"We are not done with this town," Piper added. "We will go back into the woods for the rest of our brothers and then make our return."

"A strange place, that locks up its children," Herald murmured sadly, bringing his trumpet to his lips once more.

"That locks up its daughters," Piper corrected him as the sad notes began to play.

Amy started up the hill, her feet dragging with a weight that only the dead can feel.

"We must not tarry," Piper told them. "I am not certain how much time the girls who are still imprisoned have left."

Without waiting for the townsfolk to spill into their streets, for the scream of Amy Little's mother at the sight of her daughter's walking corpse, the three brothers made for the woods, close on the tails of the many departing rats.

***

Abigail Little could barely see the shape of her uncle as he stood before her cell. She was weak with hunger, and her vision had begun to fail her that morning. Her grasp of what was real and what was imaginary seemed to fade with the day.

"What witchcraft have you done?" her uncle demanded, hatred in his voice.

She laughed faintly. "I don't know what you are speaking of, uncle, but there is little I could do from in here."

"Your cousin, Amy," he went on. "It is bad enough that she fell to the plague, as you will soon, my girl. But what magic have you cast to make my daughter appear at her mother's window two days since she expired?"

"The dead can't walk," Abigail replied, still laughing through her delirium. "Though I have heard they sometimes dance."

"You have no cause for merriment," her uncle spat. "Look at you—unclean from head to toe, dressed like a common slut. You'll end in filth like my daughter did."

"You make it so, uncle," she managed. "We would have belonged to the wider world by now, if not for you."

"No town girl belongs to any world. You belong to our sons, until you let the plague so degrade you. Then you belong to death."

"Death plays such sweet music," Abigail murmured. "He played it for me just this morning. Couldn't you hear it, uncle?"

The jailer stalked from the prison, having been among those who had woken with a start that day, fear making his heart pound in his chest as something deep within him told him that he and his convictions were in the wrong. He knew that the rats were gone and the three strangers had kept their word, but there was something that chilled him as he walked home, a sense that the departure of the rodents was not an end but a beginning, and one that he did not wish to encounter.

***

The three musicians, their faces grim with all that they had witnessed, were greeted by their younger brothers two days later.

"Brothers, what has befallen you since we last saw you?" asked Harper-the-Fifth worriedly, the most kind-hearted of the seven. "None of you look well."

The three gave an account of the town and its daughters, locked away so that no other girls might long to shed their childish frocks and their town's intentions for their future, some already dead and buried at the base of Bleecker Hill.

"What are you thinking, brother?" Fiddler-the-Fourth asked Piper, seeing the mechanisms turn behind his brother's eyes.

"I am thinking of justice."

"And rightly so," Drummer agreed. "But how?"

Piper didn't answer him, having fallen even more pensive. "And I am thinking, too, of Natalie."

"Will we raise her, as you did the other girl?" Harper wanted to know. He put a gentle hand on his brother's arm. "She won't be the same. It might grieve you to see her so."

The two youngest brothers, Singer-the-Sixth and Whistler-the-Seventh, were twins, and they had been silent while the others spoke. But now, the two of them stepped forward.

"We have a plan for justice," Singer said.

"And for Natalie," Whistler added. "So that she can rest more peacefully, along with the other girls who have died."

Piper considered the twins, knowing them to be exceptionally wise despite their youth, or perhaps because of it. "Tell us, brothers," he said finally. "Tell us the plot, and I will lead us all back with my pipe."

The seven departed at dawn the next day, once again headed for the town.

***

Natalie Jameson sat in the muck of Bleecker Hill. She had no clear thoughts, all her senses numbed by death. Her eyes were draped with the veil between worlds, and there was a stone upon her tongue.

Nearby stood Amy Little, who swayed as though listening for the next note of a melody only she could hear. She had come from her mother's house, finding the door locked and barred by her father. After circling the edges of the town for days, she had nowhere left to go but back to where her body had been.

From the mud and filth, Sally Mans, buried just the night before, reached up an uncertain hand, testing the air as though deciding whether to rise.

All three girls had their faces turned towards the woods, from which two distinct sounds could be heard. The first sound was music, strange and mirthful. It rode on a soft breeze out of the trees, fluctuating in strength as it rose and fell, coming like the waves of the sea.

The other sound was the patter of thousands of tiny feet, the rustle of whiskers and intermittent high-pitched squeaks accompanying the many small steps.

Both sounds were too faint and far away for the living to hear, but they traveled ever closer nevertheless.

The three dead girls continued to wait. Though they could not yet discern much, they knew one thing: the song would be upon them soon enough.

***

In the prison, Abigail Little hung by her wrists between life and death. She had already lost Sally and Amy, and in the cell across from hers, Mary wasn't far behind. But just as she was sure her uncle would be dropping her corpse on her mother's doorstep, a luscious sound came to rest on her tired ears.

The notes found their way through the stone walls of the prison, snaked themselves into the locks of the rusted shackles and barred cell doors. Moving slick as a skeleton key, the music clicked all of the locks open at once.

The girls emerged slowly from the prison. Their eyes were half-shut in ecstasy, their exhausted bodies nourished by the vital sound that drew their pulses and helped their hearts to beat. Though they had not slept or eaten in days, their feet were light. As they drifted towards the source of the sound, they found that they could move more easily and that their pain was fading away.

The music was playing at the base of the hill, and there, Abigail recognized the forms of her little cousin, her dear friend, and Natalie Jameson, the girl from whom she'd learned there might be more to this world than the prison of a tiny town.

And the dead girls were dancing.

They rose from the bottom of Bleecker Hill, and behind them were seven men, five with instruments at their hands and lips, two with their mouths open and whistling song emerging.

And behind the men were rats.

Abigail felt a strange expression pulling at her face. Only after she had raised an arm in greeting, to welcome this sea of music and pestilence to the town that had bred her to belong to others and never to herself, did she realize that she was smiling.

***

The brothers made their way up to the edge of the town, playing an eerily cheerful tune, pure and powerful enough for the dead to dance to. Piper-the-First led them and the rats that scurried at their heels; they were those that had left the town many days before, but they had called upon their whiskered cousins and friends from nearby villages, such that the horde they formed obscured the ground beneath them for a half-mile in all directions.

Many within the town froze in fear at the music they now heard rising all around them. Some trembled and whispered prayers; others locked their doors and windows frantically, hoping against hope that they might keep this powerful thing out, whatever it might be.

With a nod from Piper, the gathered rats fell upon the town like a great wave, filling every street such that none could even leave their homes. The only bodies that the creatures moved aside for were the town daughters, who danced from the prison of the town, from the prison of their homes, and went down to the bottom of Bleecker Hill to meet their recently departed friends.

Abigail Little caught Singer-the-Sixth by the hand, her bells of laughter accompanying the sonorous richness pouring from his handsome, smiling mouth. She pulled him into the dance, no intention of ever letting go of his hand, not even to bid her mother farewell as she left without a glance behind her.

And the seven brothers led them all dancing into the woods, towards the wider world, where Natalie, Sally, and Amy would have a peaceful place to rest by the sea, and where the others might forge their own fates. A lone hawk flew above them in the sky, enjoying the music and the warmth rising from the dance of so much frenzied freedom beneath his outstretched wings.

Melissa Bobe hasn't wandered quite as much as her Piper and his brothers, but her career has taken a few surprising turns. Over the past several years, she has taught college English, earned her doctoral degree (along with a few others), tried on some administrative roles, and now she happily works as a youth librarian. Writing has always been at the heart of her journey.

Melissa's novella *Sibyls* (2020) is available as both a paperback and an ebook. You can keep up with her writing adventures and her four adorable rescue cats on WordPress, Instagram, and Twitter @abookbumble.

Blood And Clockwork

Wendy Nikel

I woke with the king's blood on my hands.

***

It was Kender's idea, though I'd bring that secret to my grave rather than have him bear any guilt over his father's death.

A storm had kept the king's dignitaries from arriving as scheduled, granting Kender a rare morning of freedom. I was more than willing—as always—to throw aside my goggles and abandon my tools and gloves to spend a morning with him. My lungs could use a break from the fumes, anyway, and my mind might devise a solution for my morning's preoccupation after a bit of fresh air.

We slipped past the guards, escaped the castle, and rambled through the forest, giggling like children. When we reached the king's grove of sweet plums, Kender picked me the largest one and then settled beside me against the tree's trunk, letting the juice drip down his unshaven chin. His shoulder pressed against mine, and I thought—naïvely—that nothing could shatter the day's perfection.

"Father's worried about the Blueshirts again."

"Have there been more threats?" I asked, trying not to show a hint of my fear.

"More than ever. The head guard was found with his eyes gouged out and a warning tied to his neck. Father's so desperate he'd offer half his kingdom to anyone who could guarantee his safety." He tossed the plum's pit at a nearby tree. "The Duke of Carrigain's offered him one of their clockwork guards."

"Surely he's not considering it."

Kender shrugged. "Men are too weak. Powerless. Easily bribed and blackmailed. And since you've told him you won't make him one…"

"It's not that I won't; it's that I *can't*." I scowled. "Carrigain's models are flawed; I could disable them myself without breaking a nail."

Kender laughed. "Of course *you* could, Frances. I'd expect no less from the royal tinkerer."

"I'm not the only one who knows the trade."

"But you are the best."

My face warmed at his compliment. "Regardless, they're only machines. I refuse to offer my king a creation that could easily be sabotaged or used against him."

"What he really needs then," Kender said, "is a man built like a machine."

"A cyborg?"

"If that's what you'd call it. Someone fiercely loyal and cunning, with the strength and tirelessness of a machine." He leaned back against the tree trunk and closed his eyes. "It's impossible, of course, but no doubt you'll devise the next best thing. You've never let him down, you know."

"I know." My mind was already turning over one idea and then another. Alistair, the master tinkerer who'd taught me, had always said that every problem had a solution, if one only could find it. It was difficult to think here, though, with the taste of plums on my lips and Kender's gaze upon me. I sprang to my feet and wiped the grass off my skirts.

Kender caught my hand. "Where are you going?"

"To work."

"It's not even noon, Frances. Father won't expect me back for hours."

"So go on then," I laughed and waved him away. "Some of us have to earn our living around here."

"Hey, now! I'll have you know it's very hard work putting up with all those stuffy old men, listening to their carrying on about public policies and diplomacy and the cost of imports." He shuddered. "Can't I come with you? I promise not to touch a thing."

I laughed but shook my head. He'd provided the seed of the idea, but I had a feeling he wouldn't care much for what it grew into.

***

It took me weeks to make the preparations. All that while, I searched for some other way to test the final product, to no avail. I didn't trust anyone else at the palace, even more so after Kender confided in me his father's suspicions that there was a Blueshirt spy somewhere among the guards' ranks. I had to be certain that my concept would work, that there'd be no ill effects or miscalculations. If I was going to present the king with a surgically-mechanized guard, it had to be flawless.

I told Kender I was going to visit family. He ought to have been suspicious then, and perhaps he was, for he embraced me for longer than usual. Guilt ballooned within me, threatening to burst and expel the truth. Keeping a secret from Kender was a new experience for me. I despised it.

"You've got your dagger?"

"Of course." Kender had given it to me when I was sixteen after he overheard the palace stablemen talking lewdly about the kitchen maids.

"What makes you think they'd try anything with me?" I'd asked.

"You're far more appealing than any of the kitchen help."

That was the closest he'd ever gotten to voicing that which I so desperately wanted to hear. I've never blamed him for keeping his heart tucked away. We both knew that anything between us was destined to fail; his father intended for him to marry a certain nobleman's daughter. I'd once teased Kender into admitting that the young lady was lovely, but he'd amended the statement with the protest, "But what good is a pretty face on the head of a stranger?"

I'd taken those small marbles of hope, those shining bits of glass and glitter, and tucked them away deep within my heart. They'd been a comfort to me on those days when my own inferior station was too painful—when the king trotted me out to present my music boxes to the foreign ladies in their fine gowns and feathered hats or to demonstrate my latest steam-powered cannon to the men lounging upon the castle lawns.

The king meant well, but it was all I could do to keep from weeping that his greatest regard for me should be the same as that he had for the cook when she made a particularly fine meal or the breeding mare when she bore a strong colt.

"You'll return soon?" Kender pleaded now, still embracing me.

"Of course. Someone must design the commemorative ornament for the kingdom's anniversary celebration."

"You're worth far more to this kingdom than your clockworks, Frances."

I grasped that shimmering marble with all my might and tucked it away down deep. I'd spend the journey turning it over in my mind, examining it from all angles, holding it up to the light, knowing that, when the deed was done, it would lead me back here more surely than any compass.

***

I found Alastair ten miles south of the kingdom's border, in a tiny room above a shop with the simple word "TINKERER" painted over the doorframe. It was the third village I'd searched. In each, I held out a clockwork dove to anyone I met and asked if they knew where to find the man whose work bore the same marking.

The clock ticking in the shop's window read three a.m., but I pounded on the door, nonetheless. He was a light sleeper, and once he saw me, his curiosity would win out over any need for rest.

He peered out with beady, crow-like eyes and a grizzled beard that was grayer than when I'd seen him last—the night at the ball when his clockwork dancer went berserk, bursting into an inferno that sent shrapnel through the queen's neck. He'd been banished from the kingdom for life.

This was before the rise of the Blueshirts, so few believed his insistence that the work had been sabotaged. Me, I'd seen the miracles he could perform with metal and wire and glass—after all, he'd taught me all I knew. He'd never have presented something so flawed.

"The beloved monarch has thrown you out as well?" His voice was scratchy as a poorly oiled hinge.

"How would he know what time it was if I weren't around to wind his clocks?" I said, harkening back to the old days when Alastair would claim that's all I was good for. I'd been nothing but a homeless waif when he took me in and somehow convinced the king that I'd make a fine tinkerer someday.

"Look at those tiny fingers," he'd said. "Now's the time to train them, before they become good for nothing better than chopping carrots and stirring soup."

I met Kender that day, too. He was a scrawny boy with big eyes and untamable hair, who—upon spotting someone his own age— asked his mother if he might show me his pony. The king scowled, but the queen ruffled his hair and told him that he'd better first ask Alistair if he could spare me.

Alistair had looked about as pleased as the king, but when Kender took my hand and asked, "Please, Master Tinkerer, might you spare her? I'll never ask for any tin soldiers or wind-up bears again," I doubt a soul alive would have denied him.

"May I come in?" I asked now.

Alistair's expression was wary, and I wondered if I'd made a mistake in seeking him out. What choice did I have, though? No one else had the skills for the task.

"Come in then, Frances. This had better be important."

***

The procedure took days to complete. I wavered in and out of consciousness in an herb-induced haze, mindful only of the clink of Alistair's tools and the bewildering sensation of something shifting beneath my skin.

When I finally woke and looked upon my new form, I was amazed at how unchanged it appeared. Even the scars, marking where metal and wires had been inserted at each joint, were barely noticeable unless one knew where to look.

"That's it?" I asked, frowning at my seemingly unaltered reflection.

"Everything done to precisely your specifications." He wiped his hands on a towel which at one point may have been white but was now stained with rust-colored blood. "Your bones are unbreakable and your skin unable to be torn or cut by anything duller than a diamond. You ought to be able to lift a horse, and with that mechanism embedded in the back of your head, your body will not feel the effects of sleep deprivation for days at a time."

I touched the back of my neck and felt the clockwork beneath the skin. That was important. If need be, I could remain alert and vigilant through a long watch of the night, without growing weary or tired.

Assuming all functioned as it ought to, I could present myself to the king as proof that the procedure was both effective and relatively harmless, and then he could choose which others to offer it to. It was highly unusual to serve as my own test subject, but who else would have submitted to such an ordeal? And who else could be trusted?

For a moment, I allowed myself the indulgence of a daydream, imagining that, by this sacrifice of my own flesh, the king would somehow see that what I did was all, entirely, always for the good of the kingdom. For him. For Kender.

I ached to return to Kender and the palace so I set out immediately. The miles passed quickly with my newly strengthened body, and I found I could walk much more quickly than I had on the way there. I stopped beside the path to test my new strength. It was as I'd hoped; I could tear a full-grown tree from its roots with my bare hands and move a boulder three times my own size.

When darkness fell, I was still a ways from the palace. My body was free from aches or blisters, but my mind was weary and—upon approaching an inn—I decided that I would wait until I was at the palace before testing how long I could go without sleep. I devoured a bowl of stew and lay down between the threadbare blankets.

As I drifted off into a dream, the last thing I heard was a mechanized click that seemed to come from somewhere near the base of my skull.

***

The next morning, the inn was a den of whispers and suspicious, shifting eyes.

"A guest was strangled in his sleep," a sallow-faced serving girl replied when I asked.

"How awful. Have they discovered who did it?"

"No. The only clue was a bit of blue lace, like one might find on a lady's gown."

"Curious."

"If you ask me…" She leaned in more closely. "I suspect it was a lover's jealous husband. The dead man was large and powerful, you see; no woman could've done it on her own."

The comment sent a shiver up my spine, but I brushed it away. After all, I'd been in bed all night, and though my sleep had been rife with strange dreams, I'd woken well-rested.

But the unease followed me as I set out, like a restless spirit drifting behind me as I made my way to the palace.

***

I found the torn ribbon as I was preparing for bed.

For the next three days and nights, I sat up in my workshop, re-reading my notes and trying to determine what had gone wrong, where I'd miscalculated, how it'd all gone awry. Something had happened while I slept, something horrible, and the fact that I had no memory of it frightened me nearly as much as the awful crime itself.

I tried to disable the mechanism, but it was impossible; after all, I'd designed it to be so. In desperation, I tried to cut the device from my neck, but I couldn't leave a scratch upon it.

Kender visited my workshop whenever he could get away, though his concern grew at each passing day.

"You haven't changed your dress." His sudden appearance in the doorway startled me.

"Since when did you care about fashion?" I said rather snappily as I gathered up the designs and calculations I'd rather die than let him see.

"I care that you haven't slept. Your lamp was lit all evening. And the night before."

"How did you—?"

"I can see it from my window." He gestured up to the palace. "Why do you think I asked to move to the eastern wing when I was ten? Certainly not because I enjoy waking with the sun."

It was another brilliant marble of hope that he offered me, and I wanted nothing more than to hold it tightly. But I couldn't. Not while my very presence put him and his household in danger.

"I need to get back to work." When I looked up again, he was gone.

***

The king summoned me to his antechambers and sat me upon a sofa with a cup of piping-hot tea. I sipped it slowly and studied the patterns on the floor. It was becoming more difficult to fend off my fatigue, but so long as I kept busy, I was safe.

"I assume you wish to speak about the ornaments?" I braced myself for a scolding. The design for the anniversary's commemorative ornaments ought to have been completed days ago, yet my own experiment had preoccupied me. I was no closer to discovering the flaw in my calculations, and in the meantime, the king's design remained unfinished.

"Never mind that." He waved away my question. "Kender's been fraught with concern for you. I fear, at times, that he'll never be happy unless you are as well. It's a precarious position for a prince to be in. More tea?"

I didn't know how to respond, so I merely held out my cup.

"How are you feeling?" he asked as he poured.

"Tired." My eyes were as heavy as boulders, and even my new strength couldn't keep them open.

"You looked unwell." The king's voice sounded distant, soft. "Kender said you haven't slept in days, so I put a sleeping draught in your tea. Rest, and then we'll discuss whatever's bothering you."

My eyelids fell, and before hearing the mechanical *click* in the base of my skull I had just enough time to whisper, "Oh, my king. What have you done?"

***

The blood clung to my shaking hands as I covered the old man's face with a bedsheet. Any delusions I'd had about earning his favor vanished. My most desperate hopes now revolved around keeping myself out of prison and—more importantly—keeping Kender from discovering what I'd done. I could more easily bear the deepest dungeons than the thought of him knowing the truth.

I searched the room and choked back bile at each damning piece of evidence: The handle leading from the king's antechambers, torn from the door, leaving a gaping hole in the splintered wood. In the room beyond, the king's tea set, with settings laid for two. My dagger.

As I pried the weapon from where it'd stuck in his chest, I choked back grief and shame. The king been a merciful and wise ruler, and he'd raised his son to be a fine man and a gentle soul. Now that he was gone, Kender would be a just ruler, too. And no just ruler could allow murder to go unpunished. I took a final look around and prepared to flee.

The king's guards met me at the door, swords drawn.

I burst into genuine tears, which fortunately they misinterpreted. It didn't take them long to discover the body. They stood awkwardly apart from me and my blood-stained skirt, muttering sympathies about how awful it must've been for me to find him and cursing the wretched Blueshirts.

Kender had no such timidity. When he flew through the doors, he pulled me to himself, and my tears flowed freely at his compassion: that he'd comfort *me* when it was his father lying there dead.

He guided me to his own chambers and set me upon a chair by the fire. He wrapped me in a blanket that smelled of expensive soap, and he told me to stay there; he'd return as soon as he was able.

Before he left, he pressed his lips to my hair. It was a marble more precious and beautiful than all the rest, but this time, it shattered in my hands.

I still felt the blood on my fingers.

***

When Kender's footfalls disappeared down the hallway and the world returned to silence, I checked the door. Kender had told me that he'd lock it for my protection, and I hadn't had the heart to tell him that it was pointless, for the killer wasn't some rebellious Blueshirt wanting to overthrow the monarchy. The killer was locked in here with me, closer than anyone suspected, and perfectly capable of tearing down the door, if I wanted.

I didn't dare sit, lest I grow weary and sleep, so I paced the floor and tried to devise a way to escape from the one place I'd always felt at home. To run from the one person I never wanted to leave.

Kender returned bearing a silver tray heaped with hot broth and bread. When he asked if I'd slept, I lied. I hated the lies nearly as much as the secrets and the guilt. Nearly as much as the blood drying beneath my nails and staining the dagger in my pocket.

As I ate, Kender rose and paced the floor, following the same route my own feet had trod. I watched him, trying to memorize the fall of his gait, the waves of his hair, the shape of his face, so that when I made my excuses and disappeared into the night, I could keep his image with me.

He surprised me, though, by falling to his knees. "Marry me, Frances."

"Are you mad?" I tried to draw my hands away, but he held them tightly. "How can you even think of something like that now? And what about the arrangements your father made for you?"

"Never mind his arrangements; he cannot enforce them. What matters now is that I must take the throne and there isn't a person in this entire kingdom whom I trust… save one. I need you beside me, Frances, now more than ever. I can't do this without you. I need you. I love you."

He rose and crossed to the cupboard where his mother's jewels were kept. When he returned, he presented me not with a single, shining marble, but with a crown of rubies and sapphires, and one enormous diamond perched on top, each gem sparkling and singing out the words I'd so longed to hear. Their shimmer so blinded me, and their song so deafened me that I nearly said yes. I nearly forgot the blood crusting my skirt and the enemy that wore my slumbering skin.

I closed my eyes. I couldn't do what was necessary while staring into his eyes.

I meant to say no, but when the words crossed my lips, they sounded differently than I intended. "Give me three days."

His hands slipped from mine. I already felt the ripping, tearing sensation of him pulling away, confused and hurt and wounded. The crown tumbled from his hands, but before it could shatter upon the stone hearth, sending sharp slivers flying up to pierce my heart, I turned from the room and fled.

***

Each footstep called his name, urged me to return to him, to confess what I'd done. But fatigue weighed down my eyelids and worried my troubled mind. It took every bit of my strength to keep running through the lamp-lit streets, putting more and more distance between me and the palace.

I was nearly at the gates when two men blocked my path.

"Aren't you the king's tinkerer?"

"What's a young slip of a thing like you doing out here on the streets at night, all alone?"

"Perhaps you might be of use to us…"

I could've crushed them in bare hands, but I didn't. No one could know of my altered body. Not now, not ever. So when they grabbed me by the arms, I made a half-hearted effort to struggle. I was just about to slip from their grasp and run for the gates, when one of the men's sleeves fell askew and, upon his forearm, I caught a glimpse of a tattoo—the three blue Xes of the Blueshirts.

I froze. Blueshirts. In the city. Within a mile of the palace itself. And with the king gone, they'd target Kender next.

I fell limp, and they laughed at how easy I was to subdue, how quickly I gave up the fight, but in my mind, I imagined the horrible, painful punishment I'd serve to any who'd lay a finger upon the king's heir.

***

They led me through the narrow alleys of the city, down a rickety staircase and into the cellar of some dark building. They made no effort to blindfold me, so it was clear they didn't intend me to emerge from this hole in the earth. They'd soon learn their mistake.

A Blueshirt flag hung behind a table where the insurgents sat.

They looked up as we entered, and from the far end of the table, a figure hidden in shadows burst from his chair.

"Imbeciles! Of all the palace workers, you bring *her* here?" The voice was horribly, terribly, undeniably familiar.

Alistair.

Everything snapped into place like the perfectly measured teeth of a gear. No wonder I could find no flaws in my designs; there were none. *He'd* altered them, changing me into this monster.

"You! The king is dead because of you!" I flew from my attackers' grasp and upended the table with one hand. Wood shattered. Splinters flew. The other Blueshirts gaped and cowered. My old master, my old *friend*, quavered as my fingers snaked around his neck. I could've broken it as easily as flicking a crumb from the table. But no... Though the killer was within me, it was not *me*. I couldn't do it.

"The king is dead?" he choked out as I released him. A corner of his lips turned up in a hideous grin. "Hear that, comrades? The king is dead. Now is the perfect time to attack, when the palace is still in shock and the prince still overwhelmed with grief. Won't he be surprised at the role his little pet has played?"

My fingers itched to squeeze the breath from his lungs. The king had been right to banish him, yet I'd been correct, too; his clockwork disaster that had killed the queen hadn't been made in error at all. Its entire purpose had been to kill, just like the device he'd planted within me. I'd been a fool to assume that either malfunction was inadvertent.

But my anger at myself eclipsed other emotions. *Of course* the palace wouldn't have announced the king's death yet; they'd have kept it secret to avoid just such an attack as I'd now enabled. I was still reeling when one of my attackers spoke up.

"I knew we'd done well to bring her here."

"Goodness, no," Alistair said. "You fools don't realize the danger you've brought into our midst."

"She's just a girl. We'll lock her up in the cell and deal with her later."

Alistair and I glared at one another, for we both knew that no cell would hold me. Unfortunately, he'd also witnessed the reluctance in my eyes and felt the loosening of my grasp on his throat just moments before.

"Yes," he said. "Bring her to a cell and post a guard. Lonn, I'm sure your wife and dear, young children would prefer you remain behind as prison guard, rather than risking your life storming the palace. And perhaps if our prisoner is wise, she'll stay put so that no one else will come to harm."

The cell was damp and cold, but I knew what I must do. As the others bustled about in preparation, I laid my head down, steadied my breathing, and counted sheep. For even if I could not bear to kill a man and see the life leave his eyes, I knew that in my sleep, I had no such reservations.

My mind began to drift, and something behind my skull *click*ed.

***

I woke with blood on my hands. Again.

Around me, Blueshirts were bleeding, moaning, dying, dead. I was the cause of their anguish. I almost felt sorry for them, until I recalled the king's unseeing eyes and the burst of red upon his chest. The Blueshirts brought this upon themselves.

I searched their faces, but I ought to have known Alistair would have fled at the first indication of a fight, knowing that the monster he created could easily overpower him, too. Where he went, too, was no mystery. Clutching my dagger, I raced toward the palace.

When I arrived, the sun was just creeping over the horizon. The palace ought to have been bustling with the preparations for the day, but an eerie calm settled over it instead. I didn't encounter a single soul as I raced up to Kender's quarters. I only hoped I wasn't too late.

His mother's crown rested upon his table. The enormous diamond sparkled in the dim light and—with a start—I recalled

Alistair's words: *your skin unable to be torn or cut by anything duller than a diamond.* Here was the solution to my problem, and it'd been here, in Kender's quarters, all along.

I easily snapped the diamond from its facet, adding to the list of sins for which I hoped Kender would someday forgive me. Then, I positioned the diamond upon the back of my neck and braced myself.

The pain was sharp, and I dropped the diamond in my surprise. Warm liquid crept out of my neck and down the back of my dress as I tried to grasp the device with blood-slickened fingers. Dizziness threatened to overtake me, but I couldn't allow myself to faint.

A shadow from the darkened edges of my vision leapt upon me and pressed the diamond to my throat.

"I can't allow you to do that, you know," Alistair said. "There's still one more royal to dispose of."

Blood loss made me weak. I was losing my fight against unconsciousness. Only the unthinkable, unbearable thought of Kender dying at my hands kept me struggling against the pain. It gave me the strength I needed to turn upon Alistair. I pressed my fingers into my mentor's neck, even as he pressed the diamond deeper into my own.

"You wouldn't," he choked out. "Not while you're awake. You are not a killer."

But I was.

I'd killed a stranger who'd done me no wrong. I'd killed the king I'd vowed to serve. And I'd killed the insurgents who'd risen against him. The blood was already on my hands.

I had not been a killer, but Alistair had made me one.

I pressed harder, even as the diamond tore into me. I didn't let up as he gagged, his face turning blue. Instead, I watched as the spark of life left his eyes. His body jerked, then collapsed beneath me.

It was done.

With my last bit of strength, I reached behind my head and tore the infernal mechanism from my body. It shimmered in my hand: such a small thing that had nearly destroyed all that was dear to me. Blood trickled down my neck, the pain so intense that I didn't even feel the jolt as my body collapsed upon the carpeted floor. I didn't feel anything. Nothing at all.

Until somewhere in the dimness between consciousness and sleep, between life and the death I'd brought upon myself—the death I'd gladly accept, for his sake—Kender's arms found me. And as the gears implanted in me ground to their final halt, he cradled me close, whispering a multitude of tear-wracked words, each more precious than diamonds.

Wendy Nikel is a speculative fiction author with a degree in elementary education, a fondness for road trips, and a terrible habit of forgetting where she's left her cup of tea. She particularly enjoys writing stories about eerie places, twisted timelines, or (as in the case of the original fairy tale "Blood and Clockwork") the dangerous things that lurk in the shadows. Her time travel novella series, beginning with *The Continuum*, is available from World Weaver Press. For more info, visit wendynikel.com

Sappho and Erinna

Lex T. Lindsay

The bar is the sort of place made for someone like Evy Wiles. Tucked into the alley behind the train station, it's dirty and loud, the floor often vibrating from the movement of the steam locomotives entering and leaving St. Andrews.

Evy sits with her leather boots up on the table, a beer in her hand, the worn sleeves on her men's shirt rolled up to show the deep black lines of tattoos crawling up her pale arms. She glances at the clock next to the bar and watches its gear-shaped pendulum swing back and forth behind cracked glass.

The governor's man is late.

One table over, someone is loudly going on about the moral decay brought on by more women working outside of the home. By the time the gentleman in the too-nice suit arrives, Evy is quite literally elbows-deep in a bar fight. She's bleeding a little. Her opponent, sprawled unconscious atop the remnants of a chair, is bleeding a lot. Panting, Evy runs her fingers back through her short, dark hair to right it.

"This is the second time I've found you in such a state, Miss Wiles."

"This is the second time you've been late." Evy re-takes her seat, throwing her boots back up on the table. The governor's man, known only as J, sits across from her with his shiny black shoes firmly on the floor. J looks exactly the same as he had a week ago when they met in a different bar closer to the Governor's Mansion. Jet-black hair cut and styled in the fashion of the day, deeply tan skin, and sharp brown eyes.

"Your message said you have the solution to Governor Winston's family mystery." J tilts his head to the side, and Evy sneers. "Is it true, Miss Wiles? Did you succeed where the others have failed?"

"I've done what was asked of me."

"I hope for your sake that you have." J leans across the table. "Do tell, Miss Wiles."

Evy takes her feet down and leans in conspiratorially. "Shall we start at the beginning?"

***

Evy doesn't go to the Governor's Mansion in the dead of night. The dead of night is when creeping about is more suspicious, not less so. So she goes just around dinner, when men are still promenading with women in corsets and gowns with bustles. J lets her into a side door commonly used by staff.

"Governor Winston has offered you the study in the west wing to use until his daughters go to bed," J says, leading her through long hallways lined with flickering gas lamps encased in glass. He nods at them. "The latest invention. The glass keeps them from starting a fire or blackening the walls. The supports hide tubes used for ventilation."

"What will they think up next?" Evy asks absently, craning her neck to look up at a painting of a nude woman surrounded by blue fabric. Her body has been rendered in soft, feminine curves from her biceps to her belly and thighs. "Aren't you far more interesting than a lamp, darling?" she asks the woman, who reclines in a pose that could be rapture or rest while behind her, Cupid floats and some manner of Tom peeps in.

"Luca Giordano," J says. "The artist."

"Yes, but who is she?" Evy tilts her head.

"Venus."

"Naturally."

There is dinner waiting in the study. She eats in silence and takes pleasure in slipping a few valuable items into her pockets while she waits. Never know when gold or silver could be useful.

"The three Misses Winston have gone to bed, ma'am." There's a hesitancy before the servant says ma'am, her wrinkle-lined eyes falling first on Evy's vest, her leather-kneed trousers, and the inked vines and leaves wrapping around her arms.

"Thank you. I don't care much for coconut if you'd like the cake." Evy nods at her dinner plate.

"Do you need me to show you to their rooms?"

"No, I was very well-informed to their location but shall we pretend that you have while you work on that cake? A terrible thing to waste a good dessert."

Evy slips past the servant, reviewing J's directions. One turn to the left, two to the right, three doors.

"Miss?" the servant calls quietly, and Evy turns back around. In the light from the gas lamps, it's hard to tell if her skin is white or tan, if her eyes are a rich brown or a pleasant green. They're kind at any rate. She slips her hands into the pocket of her apron and steps closer, moonlight throwing into relief that her skin is indeed tan.

"Yes, love?" Evy asks.

"It true they're blackmailing you?" The g drops away from 'blackmailing,' a Southern lilt taking hold of her voice. "I heard talk."

"Perks of the job." Evy shrugs, her jaw going tight for a moment. "But it's true. I saw the original advertisement. It's not the sort of thing I'd take on willingly."

"The governor's not a good man, but those girls…" The servant takes a deep breath. "One of them will offer you a drink. If you drink it, it's lights out 'til morning."

"What's your name?" Evy asks.

"Natalia."

"Natalia, why would you tell me something like this?"

"They're good girls. So are you."

"How do you know?"

"Perks of the job." Natalia gives Evy a shrug of her own.

"Were you given yours in a similar fashion?"

"I'm here willingly. I have my own game to play," Natalia says. "Best of luck playing yours."

"And you." Evy gives her a lazy salute. "You really should have that cake."

"You know, I think I will. I have business in the study anyhow."

They part ways there, Natalia slipping into the room vacated by Evy, Evy moving down the hall once more.

The goal, as per J's instructions, is to get into the rooms of the governor's three daughters without them knowing she has done so. This will make it easier to achieve her actual mission: determining why staff have reported scuffed and dirty shoes some mornings, despite none of the sisters having left the mansion according to a slew of hired guards and employees.

Very mysterious indeed.

Evy fails in the first goal when she picks the lock of the suites and slithers inside only to find one of the three Misses Winston sitting casually in a chair by the fireplace. She turns toward Evy, and oh, oh dear.

Evy gasps, and it's not because she's been caught.

This would be the eldest Winston, Evy would presume—a woman around Evy's age mothered by the governor's late first wife, Radhika. Even in the firelight, the dark brown of her skin is visible, her black hair hanging in a single braid over her left shoulder. She's dressed in a nightgown, with a robe tied modestly over the top. Despite the loose clothing, some of her shape is still discernible. Fat around her middle and beneath the dimple of her chin, a darling little feature that someone should most definitely someday kiss.

"Venus, I presume," Evy says, switching gears to lean casually on the wall by the door. "Or perhaps Aphrodite?"

The daughter's lip quirks.

"Aditi Katherine Winston."

"Oh heavens, are we being that formal? Very well. Evette Elizabeth Wiles. I'd much prefer Evy."

"Would you like a drink, Miss Wiles?" Aditi looks down at the table where a pitcher sits next to a single glass.

"Will you be joining me?" Evy raises an eyebrow. Aditi presses her lips together and pours a glass, sliding it across the table and looking at Evy until she peels her body away from the wall and takes the seat opposite her. Evy picks it up and smells it. It smells sweet, like the iced tea they make down south. Evy toasts Aditi and brings it to her lips, then pulls it away.

"You know, I— Oh hell." Evy kicks the table, sending the pitcher spilling across it and dripping onto what is likely a very expensive rug. Aditi jumps to her feet and quickly unties her robe, dropping it to the floor while Evy liberates the contents of her glass down the side of the chair cushion, where it hopefully will not be discovered until at least the morning. Aditi is still on the floor when she finishes. The newly revealed night gown is floor-length with a high neck and long sleeves, but given her current position, Evy can see the bottom half of Aditi's shapely calves as well as the delicate bones of her ankles.

Evy swallows and forces her brain to catch up.

"I should help given that it's my fault."

"You should."

"It's just that I'm terribly..." Evy speaks slowly, then yawns, and Aditi's head pops up from the other side of the table. A few strands of hair have come loose from her braid. Evy's fingers twitch.

"You can rest over here if you like," Aditi says, letting her robe fall from her hands with a dull, wet thud. "It is quite comfortable, Miss Wiles."

"I…" Evy yawns again, her eyes drooping, the glass rolling out of her hand. Across from her, Aditi stands up. "S'far," Evy slurs.

"I suppose it is." A satisfied smile is the last thing Evy sees before she pretends to shut her eyes. Footsteps shuffle across the floor. A hand gently touches her shoulder, and Evy fears it may ruin the whole ruse for how fast it makes her heart hammer. Aditi gives her a gentle shake, then makes a satisfied noise. "Sleep well, Evette Elizabeth Wiles. Not that you deserve it, but I am at least a little sorry."

There are several minutes of rustling, of things being put right after Evy's little charade. Finally, a door on the opposite side of the room shuts with a quiet click and Evy dares to crack her eyes open. She is alone.

Opposite the entrance to the daughters' suite, there are four rooms. In one of them, Evy hears voices. She creeps toward them.

"And it's about time too. I thought you'd flirt all night."

"I was not flirting. Hurry up."

"No, Rose is right, you were flirting."

"Jane, if you don't mind." A beat. "Yes, that'll do. Shall we?"

Evy sinks into a careful squat to peer through the keyhole. All three of the sisters are dressed, not in the prim and proper wear of ladies of means, but in the ordinary dress of people like Evy. Corsets and blouses in earth tones and burgundy, large top hats with goggles wrapped around the rims. The youngest two daughters— undoubtedly mothered by the governor's late second wife, Yin Cho— have on bustle skirts over tan trousers, but Aditi has foregone the skirt altogether, her brown corset worn under a black half-coat, with tight black pants. Brown leather boots go nearly up to her knees.

Evy is going to faint.

At the foot of the bed, one of the younger women moves to pull back a rug and raise a trapdoor. Then, all three of them disappear down it, their voices fading as soon as the wood thuds shut. Through some mechanization, the rug slides back over the top of it.

"A million hired men and not one thought to lift a damned rug." Evy rolls her eyes, then picks the lock and slips inside. Kneeling on the floor, she pulls back the rug and presses her ear to the ground. Nothing. She takes her chances on opening it up.

At the bottom of a ladder, there is an earthen tunnel. That much she can tell by touch. She moves with her hands on either wall until she reaches a fork. Then, and only then, does she remove the tiny gas torch in her hip pouch and ignite it to life. She leaves it lit just long enough to find footprints in the earth, then kills it again. On it goes until she sees a light up ahead, orange slipping through the cracks around a door. Evy drops to look through its keyhole before pushing it open.

A store room.

"Girls, what are you up to?" Evy whispers, crawling over a few crates. None of them are labeled, but shelves on the wall hold beakers and flasks and things Evy couldn't name if someone held a pistol to her head. There is only one obvious path out. That door has no keyhole.

Evy looks around, lighting her torch up to see if there's a less conventional way to leave the room. She slowly shifts crates to peer behind them, then presses her ear to the door. Nothing. She could risk it. Even if she got caught, she knows where the sisters go. It's probably enough.

Above her, a board creaks and sends dust raining down. Evy looks up, then smiles. There is a single hole in the floor, likely made from a knot in the tree that bore it. From there, it's a simple matter of stacking boxes, then very carefully climbing to the top. Simple in theory anyhow. Evy has climbed a very many things in her life. Trellises. Ladders. Taller women. She is, inexplicably, nervous every single time, and this is no exception. It doesn't help that the crates wobble more the higher she goes, glass clinking within them whenever they do.

"I just think that mixing these two compounds could—"

"Explode, Jane. It could explode." A voice Evy doesn't recognize. Atop the very last box, she manages to stick her eye to the hole. She can't see much. Lights overhead that are much less orange than the standard gaslights. The edge of some kind of table. A foot coming down right over her peep hole.

Evy clenches her teeth together and says a very loud string of swears inside her head while she blinks dust and dirt away, her eye welling up and spilling drops down her cheek. She fists a hand in her hair, breathes deeply, internally swears some more.

"Oh come now, dear Georgie, aren't all great scientific discoveries made by trying things to see if they explode or not?" That'll be Rose, Evy supposes, rubbing her palm over her eyelid. The pain and irritation subsides enough for her to chance another look. She can just see the midnight skin of a hand before it reaches out and takes hold of another, much lighter in color.

"Debatable, but I do quite like my lab unexploded."

"It won't explode," Jane says. "Watch." The room above briefly glows a gentle yellow-green. Jane giggles and claps. "See, I told you. I told you! Now we're much closer to understanding the bioluminescence of fireflies. Well done, Jane. One Academy of Steam and Power Award to Jane Winston. And to George Mason of course. For his wonderful teaching and generous use of lab equipment and supplies."

"Getting to know any of you was a mistake," George says, but his thumb never stops moving back and forth over Rose's knuckles.

"No, it wasn't." Rose squeezes his hand tighter. "Now, uh, replicate the results? That's what comes next? Aditi, you're being very quiet about Jane's impending award."

"She's too busy thinking about her new girlfriend," Jane says, her voice accompanied by the soft tinkling of glass from above.

"Oh?" George asks.

"Father's latest hire to figure out our nighttime wanderings," Aditi says. "She'll be gone like all the others in a few days."

"Do you hear that?" Rose asks. "That little hint of disappointment in her voice? Don't you hear it, Jane?"

"Oh yes."

"I am not—" Aditi sighs. "One night down. Two to go. That… *tattooed rogue* spilled the tea everywhere though, so our Most Awarded Jane will need to mix up more sleeping draught before we go home."

Tattooed rogue. Evy has certainly been called worse by women who made her heart stop.

"Oh, 'tattooed rogue' now is it?" Jane asks. "Listen to her swoon. Pass me that beaker, Rosie."

"I am not swooning. I do not swoon."

"Sure, sure. You sound like Rosie the first night we met George. Only a matter of time before you start to insufferably pine for her. Taste this."

A scoff followed by a quiet hum of appreciation.

"Jane, no eating out of the lab equipment," George says. "But let me give it a try."

Below the action, Evy feels a sharp pain in her left knee, the thick padded patches on her trousers no longer enough protection for her current position. She shifts, then bites her lip when the whole stack of crates starts to wobble. Her right knee joins the left.

With her lip pulled between her teeth, she climbs down the stack. On the floor, so far from the action, it's quiet save the occasional laugh or exclamation that's loud enough to reach her. Evy reviews the information in her head, contemplates going back up, then ultimately puts the crates back to rights. She has enough. She knows everything she needs to know to make a report, to satisfy J and therefore Winston, and to get out of St. Andrews for good.

She glances at the hole, then heads back down the earthen tunnel. Back in the rooms, she removes her shoes and carefully cleans the mud off by using the back of the soaked chair cushion. They'll have to burn the damn thing at this rate. Or reupholster it at the very least.

Satisfied she's hidden her trail, Evy sinks down onto the cushion. This time, she really does fall asleep. In the morning, she finds breakfast on the table in front of her and a note in messy, looping letters.

Miss Wiles,
    I do hope you slept well!
Warmest wishes,
Aditi Katherine Winston

Evy tucks the note into her hip pouch, stuffs a piece of buttered toast in her mouth, and slips out of the mansion. Back in her rented quarters next to the airship station, she starts five different letters to J. She reads the note from Aditi twice as many times and swears she can hear the spark of Aditi's voice in every sarcastic word.

The air around her wobbles from the force of giant propeller blades while Evy reads through the letter yet again. She should finish her report, collect her agreed-upon price, and get out of town while she can.

But...

But.

Evy is more prepared the second night. She has rags stuffed in her hip pouch, a horn for better listening, and her own pair of goggles atop her head to avoid any more unfortunate shoe-eye incidents.

As predicted (and hoped), Aditi is waiting for her when she arrives. Somehow, even expecting it, it's worse the second time around. Instead of a braid, Aditi has her hair hanging in loose, long waves. Evy nearly collapses under the weight of her own wobbly knees.

"I see you have decided to try again," Aditi says.

"Yes well, I see your rug has made a full recovery and I simply cannot abide that." Evy winks and watches Aditi's mouth twitch, her brown eyes flashing bright.

"Did a rug do something terrible to you in childhood, Miss Wiles?"

"Well, actually a woman I once deeply loved left me over a rug," Evy says with mock forlorn. "Or was it that she took mine when we parted? Oh dear, now I can't even remember why rugs are my sworn enemies."

"You must not have loved her too much if you've already forgotten."

"I love every woman a little too much, darling." Evy says. "But perhaps I've forgotten the details of our parting because of how overwhelmingly deep my affections were. Of course, that supposes that I'm not making this whole thing up simply to see you laugh."

Aditi looks away and clears her throat.

"Well, Miss Wiles, was there or was there not a rug involved at some point in your relationship with a woman you once loved? That seems a good place to start if one were trying to figure it all out." Aditi looks at the pitcher on the table, and reaches for the glass, her thumb tracing the patterns painted onto its surface.

"I suppose with any luck, Miss Winston, we'll both someday find out."

Aditi's eyes snap to hers, and Evy wonders if Aditi can see it, the way Evy's pulse is fluttering wildly beneath the skin of her throat. She wishes very much that she could see Aditi's neck in return, that she could slip her fingers beneath the collar of her nightgown and feel her heartbeat thumping away at whatever speed it happens to be traveling.

Aditi takes a deep breath. "Tea, Miss Wiles?"

"Yes, it was wonderful last night."

Evy sits down and takes the glass, bringing it to her lips and pretending to sip.

"Will you tell me about the art above your fireplace, Miss Winston?" Evy asks. Aditi, as hoped, turns her whole body around to look at it, providing Evy with the perfect window to further ruin the chair.

"Sappho and Erinna in a Garden at Mytilene," Aditi says, standing up to walk over to it. "A reproduction of a painting by Simeon Solomon." She reaches up and touches the gilded frame, letting her fingers run down the edge. "I could tell you it was painted just a few years ago or how it came to be here. Or would you rather hear about why I love it so? See, I recognize the importance of Sappho as a historical figure to women like us. But ultimately, this painting could be any two people in love. Look at Sappho, how tightly she's embracing Erinna, not with her arms but with her whole body. The love on her face is so strong, if I stare long enough, my own heart aches with it."

A pause. Aditi looks back to Evy where she's pretending to yawn in her chair.

"You see, a lot of paintings of women are beautiful because women themselves are beautiful. But this one. They are not beautiful simply because they are women. They are beautiful because they are in love. Do you understand, Miss Wiles?"

Evy understands. She would very much like the opportunity to learn to understand it all over again very soon. But when Aditi starts to turn, she closes her eyes.

"Ah."

This time, before she goes, Aditi drapes a blanket over her and tucks it in around her body. She gently removes the goggles from Evy's head and sets them on the table.

"I do wish…" Aditi takes a deep breath, exhales, then goes.

There is more teasing in the other room while they change. Evy waits patiently, tells her heart to calm itself every time Aditi unconvincingly laughs off another accusation about being smitten.

She doesn't look through the keyhole this time, instead waiting for the room to go quiet.

On the other end of the tunnel, she stacks her crates back up high and carefully climbs up.

"She went on about Sappho for at least twenty minutes. If that isn't flirting for women who like other women, I dare say I don't know what is," Jane says.

"If at any time, either of you want to give it a rest, I would most appreciate it," Aditi says. "At the end of the day, she still took the job and I cannot… You saw Father's advertisement when this all started. You know what they all really want."

A long beat of silence. Through the hole, Evy watches another foot pass over, then catches a glimpse of a brown leather boot before its mate comes to a rest half on the hole, half not. She could reach up. She could ruin everything and…

And what, Evy? Touch a shoe? For the love of God, get a hold of yourself.

Evy's chest heaves beneath her vest like a tempest sea. She wills it to slow.

"So I've been thinking more about firefly bioluminescence and how replicating it could be put to use in lighting, particularly in personal torches," Jane says, but she never finishes the thought. Aditi moves, and just so happens to glance down at the floor, her eyes locking on Evy's where they've gone wide within Evy's goggles.

Fight, flight, or freeze.

Apparently Evy is going with the third. She inhales one sharp breath while Aditi stares down at her.

"Excuse me for a moment," Aditi says, and Evy can't move. Evy has run from shop clerks and police and disreputable men, but she can't seem to run now. The door to the upstairs flies open to Aditi with her hands on her wide hips, and for one brief moment, Evy is free to just admire her in her tight trousers and corset, in her little black jacket and high boots. And then the crates rock beneath her, wobbling to the right and then much too far to the left.

Evy manages to swear softly before everything comes crashing down, muscle memory somehow taking over to help her roll her body and avoid severe injury. She still ends up swiping a long piece of splintered wood somewhere, gashing open the sleeve of her shirt and, subsequently, her arm.

By the time it's all over, there are three more people standing behind Aditi, all of them looking at Evy with varying degrees of shock and apprehension. Aditi moves first, kneeling beside Evy with her brow furrowed and her jaw clenching tight.

"Are you dying, Miss Wiles?" she asks through her teeth.

"From this? No. From embarrassment? Quite possibly." Evy rips off her goggles. Her arm is on fire, and she's fairly sure there's a splinter embedded in her right buttock, but she's had worse. Maybe.

"Well-deserved, if you do." Aditi pulls a handkerchief from the pocket of her half jacket and gently presses it to Evy's arm. "You are a very good actress, Miss Wiles."

"So are you, love."

A staring contest. Evy turns away first, looking to the place where Aditi is gently holding her wounded bicep, applying firm pressure.

"I suppose you'll tell our father what you've learned and collect your winnings." Aditi's hand twitches. Evy looks back into her eyes, then at the precious dimple on her chin, then over at her sisters and the man who is presumably George. It's the first time Evy has properly looked at Jane and Rose. Jane is plump where Rose is thin, but they're both pale with dark hair and brown eyes. It's the first time Evy has seen George as well. He's short and skinny, with a hairless chin and eyes a shade darker than his skin. He's holding onto Rose tightly, as though she might float away if he lets go. In return she's gripping his arm with both hands, her knuckles white.

"It's more complicated than that, darling," Evy says softly.

"We've all seen the advertisement. We know what he was offering." Aditi loosens her grip, checking to see if the bleeding has stopped. Her hand tightens around Evy's arm once more. "Five thousand, a parcel of land, and one of his daughters. Quite a lot, isn't it?"

Evy reaches across her chest, wrapping her hand around Aditi's wrist.

"Two weeks ago, I was hired to steal information from the statehouse that would prove the governor and certain state senators are taking bribes and engaging in speculation, embezzlement, a host of illegal activities, really." Evy closes her eyes and takes a deep breath. Beneath her fingertips, she can feel Aditi's pulse dancing to a steady beat. "I was caught. And because I was caught by the kinds of people who do all of those things, they really had no desire to see me go to a public trial, where I might then share why I was trying to rob them, potentially leading to more eyes looking in their direction."

Aditi checks the wound again, then lets her hand fall away, Evy's fingertips trailing across her wrist when she does so. "I think you will avoid the hospital, Miss Wiles," she says softly.

"I was given one other option. To solve the mystery of the wayward daughters."

"I don't understand," Rose says. "Are you saying…"

"She had to do this or Father would've had her killed," Jane confirms, and Rose frowns deeply. George nuzzles against the side of Rose's head.

"It's not about the money or the land, darling," Evy says. "And if I'm to have any of you, well"—Evy reaches out and wraps her hand around Aditi's booted ankle—"where's the beauty in embracing Erinna if she does not love you?"

Above her, Aditi shakes, her face stony.

"Well," Jane says. "I think it might be a good idea for us all to go back upstairs now."

"What?"

"We have a problem." Jane turns toward the stairs. "And all the best solutions to problems are found in a lab, are they not?"

Aditi gets to her feet, looking down at Evy for several long seconds.

***

Evy finishes laying out the bare bones of the story, giving J many details while omitting many more. And then a lie.

"They asked me to withhold all of this, of course," Evy mutters.

"Tunnels?" J asks.

"Jane had a few hypotheses, naturally. Most of the other branches could be explained as emergency escapes based on where they end, but George's lab did time as a gambler's den, a brothel, and a doctor's office in the past. At any rate, the tunnels were clearly forgotten since they were created. The Misses Winston said they had to do quite a bit of cleaning to make them usable again."

"Well, Miss Wiles, you certainly did deliver." J sits back in his seat, shaking his head. "Tunnels. Countless money and resources, and the explanation is tunnels."

"If that's how you choose to look at it."

"And how do you choose to look at it, Miss Wiles?"

"I think the real explanation is love, J." Evy smiles. "You see, the youngest sister is in love with science. The middle sister is in love with the scientist."

"And the eldest?"

Evy smiles wider. She reaches for her beer and finishes it. "Loves her sisters dearly, of course."

J hums, then scoffs. "Well." He reaches into his coat pocket and pulls out a slip of paper, putting it on the table between them. "That's settled then. One ticket from St. Andrews to New York City, leaving—" J checks his watch. "You'd better hurry actually, Miss Wiles. And do know if you ever come back to St. Andrews, well, they'll never find you in the tunnels, will they?"

Evy scowls at him, then reaches for the ticket, tucking it into the inner pocket of her vest, her fingers touching a note written in a messy, looping scrawl. A snarky breakfast letter. Or is it really just another poem from Sappho? Perhaps both.

"Have a good afternoon, Mr. J," she says, standing up. "Can I ask one thing?"

"You can try."

"I understand there are certain expectations for the daughters of governors, but please be as gentle as possible in setting things to rights. We've all been made fools by love once or twice, haven't we?"

J tips his hat. "The girls will be dealt with as Governor Winston sees fit."

Grinding her teeth, Evy nods at him, then exits the bar.

The steam whistle is already blowing when she reaches the station. Evy steps aboard quickly, handing her ticket to the automaton next to the door. Heartbeat hammering in her throat, she moves down the aisle and between cars, not stopping until she reaches the very end, taking a seat next to a plump woman in a top hat and dark, round shades. Evy's chest is heaving, adrenaline spiking through her veins.

Beneath them, the pistons on the wheels start to pump. The train lurches forward. Slow at first, then picking up speed.

"Stop! Stop that train!" someone yells from outside of the window. The head next to hers swivels.

"It's him," Aditi says. "They know."

Evy reaches over and takes Aditi's hand. Outside, several men are running alongside the train, hitting it with their hands. Evy watches one reach for the handhold next to the door. He misses, then grabs hold, attempting to swing his body into the doorway. Aditi's hand gets tighter and tighter, until Evy's bones creak beneath her skin.

"Fall," Aditi whispers. "Please fall."

He doesn't, holding on and kicking wildly. Until he can't anymore. In the distance, a tunnel looms. A loud, relieved laugh bursts forth from Aditi's lungs. The man drops away, and both she and Evy exhale as though they've been holding their breath for several minutes.

When Evy turns her head, Aditi removes her sunglasses and gives her a wet-eyed smile before looking behind them to where Rose sits with her head on George's shoulder, his hand wrapped tightly around her wrist. Across from them, Jane has two seats to herself, her feet pulled up next to her, a newspaper spread across her lap. She looks up at Aditi and Evy and smiles.

"Best plan anyone has ever had," Jane says. "One Academy of Steam and Power Award for Plotting to Jane Winston."

"I'll say." Evy settles back in her seat, letting her head fall against the headrest.

"You really should peruse this most excellent article," Jane says, tossing the newspaper over to Evy. The headline on the front page reads, "Governor, Senators Implicated in Scandal" with the secondary headline below referring to hundreds of thousands in bribes and kickbacks.

"By Natalia Ferraez," Evy reads, a laugh bubbling up in her chest. Outside the windows, the hub of St. Andrews is already giving way to factories and mills. Soon they'll be in the countryside proper, moving on to somewhere new. The hand twined with hers feels so warm. She turns to Aditi again, reaching up to fit her thumb into the dimple in her chin.

And then, with no one except her sisters and George to see the impropriety of it all, Evy kisses it. And then her.

Lex T. Lindsay is a fat queer writer who can be found roaming the woods of Northeast Texas when she's not in her garden willing the tomatoes to ripen. Her interests include cats, tats, and fun hats. She read "The Twelve Dancing Princesses" and thought, "Well that kind of sucks for the princesses," and so "Sappho and Erinna" came to be. You can read more of her work in *Glass and Gardens: Solarpunk*

Winters (also by World Weaver Press), or follow her occasional tweets @LexTLindsay.

Divine Spark

Diana Hurlburt

On Mariah's fourteenth birthday, her mother woke her with a whisper that they were moving west, a gift just for her.

Huddled on her pallet, Mariah tried not to turn from her mother's arm. Wasn't that just like Ma, prophecies and delusions? The congregation was New York-bred, risen from the fiery district new and shining as the best of their mechanicals twenty years before. Whatever its roots, her mother's travel had never been directed by Mariah's wants, only by dire necessity and constant longing.

Ma murmured it again—*west*—and Mariah did shift, digging her elbow into the lumpy straw-tick to move away from her mother, to gaze through the window at a bruised dawn sky.

The news, when it came through proper channels, differed only in the particulars.

The messenger-bird's tin beak quivered, creaked open and ejected a familiar curled paper, then turned on its stilts and marched away from the door. Mariah read the missive twice, her finger tracking across each line. Reading wasn't her strong suit, despite her mother's pride in her own literacy, gleaned from the African Free School. Mariah's adept disliked this tendency, muttered about laziness and the necessity of literacy to their craft. Sometimes he cracked a measure across her knuckles as she read from a set of guidelines, to keep her hand from traveling down the page.

She didn't like the news, when the message's words rooted in her mind. She left the paper pinned on the wash-line where her mother would see it, and went to work.

"Movement is directed according to the Watchmaker's will," she recited, ear to the mechanical's chest as she plied a hammer to its jaw-hinge. "Their footsteps map the Earth in its fullness. We have only to follow, to build, to seek."

She was building, certainly. She was seeking.

The mechanical made no comment. She hadn't yet managed its powers of speech—wasn't sure that she could. It gazed at her with blank glass eyes, green and clear, mismatched as the rest of its body.

"I'd rather not," Mariah said. She straightened on her stool and set the hammer down, turning the mechanical's head. Its cheeks gleamed in slivers of early sun peeking through the shed's slats. "We have what we need here, and why—"

She touched the mechanical's face, her palm curving around ceramic. She'd tried to save the nicest bits from middens for her creation's visage. Two cheeks of blue-spattered white, a broken bowl. A rose-patterned teacup for lips, and bronze grating snatched from Kit's workshop between them. A high forehead formed of pottery, once white and now scorched, black-streaked but whole.

"Like clothing," she whispered. Mechanicals didn't need clothing, but hers would be fancy in its skin, ready for a party. She touched her apron's frayed hem. She had no clothing for parties; the Watchmaker's people dressed soberly. Her mother had dressed herself and Mariah in men's clothes, to keep them safer on the road. Mariah liked the movement that trousers permitted. She liked the Mariah that trousers created, stronger and not so mousy. Sometimes she wondered if all clothing could work such alchemy—if she might put on a hoopskirt and velvet dress and become beautiful, or wear Kit's apron and attain authority. Perhaps all those Mariahs lived in her somewhere... Perhaps, like the Watchmaker, she was in fact a *they*.

Sometimes, building her mechanical, she dreamed of rebuilding herself.

"When they say west," she asked the machine, "how far? Indian Territory?" It wasn't a phrase with meaning to Mariah, simply something people said. The hills north of Syracuse were rural but populated, familiar in their slopes and seasons. "The gospel must be carried to all people, but..."

But did Mariah have to be the one to do it? Wasn't it better that the congregation stayed here, and some proselytizing party went out, to Buffalo or Pittsburgh or wherever the Watchmaker saw fit?

"Maybe you'll be walking before then," she told the mechanical, and it turned its head, a slight tilt that thrilled in her veins.

"Reapers," Kit said when she arrived tardy to his workshop. "We're overdue two for the Wymouth farm. I've no plans to take abuse from that man again." His nose wrinkled above a bristling mustache. "We'll need their payment, if the congregation is to move by June."

Mariah rolled her sleeves to the elbow, to keep their linen from the thick blue heat necessary for forming reapers. Kit's directives bored through her as they began, his chidings and haphazard advice. Gossip ran an eternal round concerning at what point Kit might be ejected from the congregation, but he hadn't managed it yet. He was too good at the farm mechanicals, reapers and sowers, milkmaids. If his opinions bordered on heresy, Mariah knew the council depended on his skill such that they could ignore the rest of him.

"Heard tell of a death in town," Kit said. He lifted the second reaper's faceplate in tongs and plunged it into a water bucket, brown arms sweaty and gleaming. "You recall the Brewsters, Missy Mariah?

Off Spring Road?"

Mariah recalled Mr. Brewster's red face and redder beard… his wife shrinking behind him, staring at Kit mistrustfully when they'd delivered a reaper to the farm.

"Bring that here," Kit ordered, and spun the reaper on its frame to aim its left arm toward Mariah. She approached with a fan-shaped blade, then waited as he oiled the machine's wrist and elbow joints. "Word is it's a murder."

Mariah frowned, half-listening. The town's doings were no concern of hers. No town's business had been, not since her mother brought her north from New York City after another death. The congregation was its own town.

"Cut up," Kit said. He slotted the blade into place with a sharp click. "A mean way to go, eh? Comes of living too close, all cooped up." His own hands were a contrast to his mouth, Mariah thought, watching him apply liquid-hot iron beads to the reaper's scythe. Careful, deliberate, when his words ran to gossip, lambasting and opining. "People turning on their neighbors for pettiness." He shook his head, sweat dripping off tight black curls. "Cut up bad, he was."

Kit sat back on his stool, assessing the reaper. It was dormant, some of its parts still glowing. It wouldn't be activated until delivery to its employers; Mariah knew the proprietary key was somewhere on Kit's person, to be used only by the buyer. Her thoughts strayed from a man murdered to her own mechanical in its stuffy shed, waiting for her. She hadn't yet created its key.

She didn't know the key's shape, and her mechanical shouldn't have been able to move without one—to look at her, so it had seemed.

"Could be a good thing," Kit said. He stood, folding his arms across his heavy canvas apron. "Moving west. Could be it's time."

His brows furrowed together. Mariah braced herself for a lecture—for Kit's cutting assessment of their leaders, his sideways beliefs about the Watchmaker and what They wanted from Their adherents.

Instead he ran a rough fingertip along the reaper's scythe, his expression turning toward sorrow. He said again, "Could be it's time, Mariah. Sometimes it's not enough to let the river carry you."

The river had carried Kit, Mariah knew, north from bondage. That river had carried him and many others to a congregation where they could be safe… and there was another River upon which they all sailed, so the gospel went, a broad stream flowing from the Watchmaker's mouth. Her mother had set them upon it only recently, after much searching and heartache, but Mariah twisted in its currents, looking ahead for the shore, where a silent figure waited.

***

It pained Mariah to disassemble her mechanical, but, she told its blank face, it was necessary.

"We can't carry everything with us," she murmured, unscrewing its right shoulder joint. The arm dropped across her lap as the mechanical's weight changed, torso flopping forward into her arms. "You'll be safe. You'll be you, just in pieces. I'll build you again as I may."

She'd been so close, nearly complete. A few more days and the mechanical would've been ready—

Its china chin pressed Mariah's shoulder, and she let her head tip sideways. It was nice to hug someone, even someone who couldn't hug her back. The congregation was so cold sometimes, its children raised in common and its love of metal, its focus on texts she didn't always understand and political arguments about abolition and voting rights. She was lucky, she supposed, that they had come to the Watchmaker's people only three years before, that the council allowed her mother a small cabin and maintenance of her daughter. She didn't think she would've liked growing up with so many mothers and fathers as the other children had. Always someone telling you what to do. It was enough, her own mother and her adept, the gulf between their beliefs.

"I shouldn't be building you at all," Mariah told her mechanical as she separated head from neck. She held the cranium in both hands, admiring her work. That was not done; those who created mechanicals could be proud of their craft, but not admiring, because admiration meant beauty, and mechanicals were for function, not form. "I've barely begun my apprenticeship, and you—"

That was not done, either. Mechanicals weren't *you*. Even the ones who spoke didn't converse.

"You're beautiful," Mariah said, and guilt washed through her. No tin skins or exposed iron skeletons for her mechanical. It would be lovely in its patchwork state. "Art is separate, you see, to prevent us from idolatry. Art is painting and needlework and my mother's embroidery, and we don't keep it. Only…"

She was good at needlework, and with the watercolor kit that the woman of letters kept in her study. She'd listened to her mother read once, about Italy and the beautiful walls of villas. She'd dreamed of painting flowers and smiling lips onto their mechanicals. She could never speak such words to Kit, who had ferocious ideas about proper mechanicals. He didn't even like the whimsical creations, the messenger-birds and carousels made for children. He believed the mechanicals built with mind function to be possessed with the spirits of humans long-dead, rather than quickened by the Watchmaker's hand.

None of these tenets, which Kit argued over with Mariah's mother, with Sister Haycock and anyone who would listen, were more unseemly to the council's ear than what Mariah found herself attempting.

"It's blasphemous," she said, her voice low and blunted within the shed's shadowy warmth. "Man may not create a mechanical without knowing its function. I don't know what you're for. I only know I want—I want to know you."

She wrapped the mechanical's head carefully in burlap and tucked it into a large sack of cornmeal.

***

When the congregation trickled down the road into Syracuse, people gathered behind them.

Mariah had been gawked at before; every excursion into town, for trading or delivering goods, turned curious eyes toward her. Even before their arrival to the Watchmaker's people, life hadn't been so simple as a farm and family and chores. *Burned-Over*, people called the hills in which she'd been raised, and her mother thrived on that fire, leaping from revival camp to itinerant preacher as a flame moved from kindling to log. There was the cluster of Oneida communalists. There was the man in Rochester with his glowing plates of scripture and his seer stones. There was the council of the Watchmaker—their utilitarian devices, their far-leaning politics, their bold theology.

A stone whistled past Mariah's head and struck one of the reapers propped in the back of Kit's cart. "Idolaters!" someone yelled. Suddenly there were many voices calling, *idolaters* and *prideful sinners,* which Mariah had heard before, and *murderers,* which she had not.

"What did that woman mean?" she asked Kit when the congregation's carts and wagons kept moving with the determined pace of the lead councilwoman's wagon. "She called us murderers. Did she mean someone in particular? Was she—"

"Some people would lie to the face of God," Kit said. That was another quirk of his; rarely did Mariah hear the congregation speak of God. There was no God but the Watchmaker, the Bible of Mariah's younger years regarded as a historical text alongside the works of Socrates. One could tell Kit had come to it late, carrying with him an ancestral religion, or maybe that of his former owners. He glanced down at her from the cart's seat. "You keep to your work, Missy Mariah. Hop up there and shine those reapers another time. I won't hear the Wymouths begging the price down."

Mariah obeyed. She was grateful to have an adept at all, even one so strange as Kit—grateful the council had allowed her to begin apprenticeship, though she'd been five years past the age of baptism when she and her mother arrived in Syracuse. Perhaps part of it was that she seemed attuned to the work: that they saw her small skill with tinkering, gleaned from travels, and that her progress with design and construction had been quick. She climbed into the cart and applied a cloth to the reapers, rubbing their skins free of rusty discoloration. It was one more part of the work, and the Watchmaker valued work; it gave her hands something to do and her mind followed, a prayer according to the words of scripture.

Work let her ignore the parts and pieces packed in sacks and trunks, her dismembered mechanical waiting for life. It channeled her yearning into something useful. Yet it wasn't quite enough of a prayer to turn her eyes from the Brewster farm as they passed. Its landscape was too quiet for a spring morning and a clutter of metal lay heaped at the mouth of its lane.

***

The ground beneath Mariah's pallet didn't bother her. They'd camped so often along the road, she and her mother, before finally stumbling across an exhibition of the Watchmaker's craft at a revival meeting… before the ember of her mother's soul had been fired anew by possibility. Mariah hadn't been living in a settlement long enough to grow used to comfortable bedframes.

She lay atop her quilt and watched light change under the tent's rim, the small and private shifting of night. There was a magical hour between starry black and dawn where her mechanical lived—would live, might live, if no one caught her sneaking to the wagons to collect its scattered being.

Her eyes closed against tears, a sharp grief with tangled roots, and a hand slipped from under the quilt, fingers beseeching. Imagination was good, so the gospel went, sign of the divine spark, and a method of worship was to magnify that spark with making. But Mariah's imagination sometimes got the better of her and always had, from the time she was small and told her mother a fish-woman lived in

Kayaderosseras Creek.

Imagination teased her now, suggesting that a hand curled into hers, cool and comforting in the tent's darkness.

***

They reached Geneva, where the town fathers seemed displeased to see them.

"You stay put," Kit said, though Mariah had made no movements. Her mother was with the children and caretakers, and until the cart bumped to a stop Mariah had been content, pressed between a barrel of nails and two crates containing dummy skeletons, jointing together a foot. It was practice work necessary to apprentices; it didn't rouse Kit's suspicions, for he believed she would joint the foot and disassemble it again and move onto something else, the way the young ones amused themselves with painted tin puzzle-blocks. "Stay just there," he said, "no reason to draw attention," and Mariah frowned at the flexible iron phalanges.

She didn't like the snatches of conversation floating to her ears. Brother Hendricks of the council was arguing with a man, and Mariah thought it odd that Geneva's residents might turn them away from the market and general store. The Watchmaker's people had goods and skills to sell, and Geneva had food and supplies, and this was the run of things.

Kit hunched on the cart's seat, his ropy arms twisted tight. He glanced down at her between hat brim and shoulder. "News of a murder travels faster than wagons."

"I don't understand what Mr. Brewster has to do with us," Mariah said. She tested the foot's arch and range of motion. "Why should anyone think *we* killed him?"

The Watchmaker's people were pacifists, a congregation founded on tenets of abolition. They sought circumvention of slavery's violence, the first mechanicals created so that no man could find reason to own another. Their gospel spoke of war's wretchedness—specifically commanded against harm, against the building of devices of war, against hurting one's neighbors or facilitating hurt through the creation of certain mechanicals.

Certain mechanicals, Mariah mouthed. *Devices of war.* The text wasn't clear on what those were.

"A tool's got more than one use," Kit said. Here was another bit of his blasphemy: a tool by its scriptural definition had but one use. "There's folk we ought not to have traded with, maybe. There's those who'd take a mechanical and turn it whichever way they like."

Chills rose along Mariah's neck. The way Kit spoke sometimes, she believed he knew what she was building. Was she any better, her secret machinations and scuttling from discard barrel to cull heaps to steal even forgotten scraps? Was it a sin to take what Kit and the others taught her and use it for her own ends, especially when she herself didn't know those ends? Among the congregation's texts were stories from ancient days, of men who created machines out of greedy desire rather than righteousness. There was a story of a man bound by improper love for his creation, warning and commandment that a mechanical's function was not to be gazed upon.

The mechanical foot sat in her lap, the fabric between her knees dipping under its weight. It seemed perfect in both function and form.

"You said he was cut up," she told Kit. He gazed straight forward, eyes on the huddle of men and women near the caravan's front. "Mr. Brewster, all cut up. When we passed their farm, they'd thrown their reaper away. Just heaped it up by the fence like…"

It hurt her, the mess of parts by the Brewsters' lane. She'd stared too long, picking out hands and a faceplate, the belly-box where chaff ground up. The mechanicals weren't human, but they lived. There was a ritual to their creation and one for their disassembly, and to be cast out like bathwater was wrong.

"Folk don't like to believe their own hands might be used against them," Kit said. "White folk especially don't like to believe a weapon is effective in any hand but theirs."

Mariah tucked her head down, turning her cheek against the bonnet's stiffened fabric. She wished for ear-plugs, to stop the flow of *troublemaking* and *trading, that's all* and *unwelcome,* and the rest of the words, from the Watchmaker's people and Geneva's, that rang like hammering nails. She checked each of the metal foot's toes, painting a picture in her mind of what it would look like when attached to her mechanical. She could scavenge small china shards for its nails.

Beside her Kit hummed, singing words between breaths, bits of a hymn Mariah found frightening and tantalizing. It told the story of the gospel and what men were meant to do with it, how the Watchmaker might be brought into the world anew on the strength of the congregation's hands. This, Mariah knew, was but one reason the people in Syracuse and elsewhere called them idolaters. The Christian Bible spoke against deities created by human hands, but the congregation knew the connection between people and their tools was godly. They were building small temples, in preparation for the day that one such temple might be occupied by holy presence.

"And on the final day," Kit sang, "through craft and divine mold—"

He slipped a hand through the wagon's slats to pet Mariah's braids. She smiled, singing the closing line with him. "The Maker returns on clouds so fair, Their promises to unfold."

Kit kept humming, but Mariah gazed at her lap. She held the foot between her palms and thought of her own feet in their boots, callused and tired, of the tracks the congregation left behind them: prints in earth, wheel-tracks and shoe-soles, bare children's feet, and the angular, deep marks of mechanicals.

There was a mechanical's print in the dirt beside the cart here, though no machine had walked with Kit's gear.

***

It struck Mariah strange that the council held a revival meeting, when this town seemed set against them.

She watched through a slit in the main tent's canvas as Brother Sainte-Marie displayed the smallest mechanicals. Machine parts lay within her own reach, her mechanical's ribcage and spine. The meeting was good, even if some of the congregation felt it unsafe; those adults not presenting or testifying were with the children, and the young people were all rapt, staring at the dais or…

Mariah's hands paused on a curl of wire. Boys and girls her age lived among the Watchmaker's people, though not many. They'd all found the townspeople around Syracuse fascinating. The fuller's apprentice had twice been disciplined for sneaking away with a Fayetteville boy, and Sarah, the girl closest in age to Mariah, had giggled to her over a young man itinerant as they, who sold Bibles of strange translation and religious artifacts. She'd dreamed of traveling with him instead of the congregation.

Now, as curious Geneva residents crowded into a field to gawk at the mechanicals, Mariah knew Joseph and Matilda and Georgie and maybe even Sarah were gawking back at the boys and girls among the spectators. They were smoothing their plain clothing, wishing for frilled bonnets and embroidered suspenders and shiny boots. They were wondering what it felt like, to live in town and attend church on Sundays and go courting.

Mariah bent her head, winding the wire along the mechanical's spinal cord. The work gave her more pleasure than any fumbled kisses Georgie Hughes had bestowed on her last summer. No matter that her mechanical was yet in pieces—each portion she worked on, creating and fine-tuning, lay in wait. She'd work as she could, a fibula here and a hip-joint there, and when it came time all would be assembled into perfect function. She'd have something to show Kit, and Brother Hendricks and her mother, and none of them would be able to tell her no. Once a mechanical was made, it couldn't be unmade without cause.

"The mechanical is created as a helpmeet for mankind," she recited with Brother Sainte-Marie on the dais, her voice lost beneath his authoritative boom and the crowd's scattered shouts. She pressed her hand to the iron sternum and felt her own heartbeat throb, a pulse of longing and excitement. "The universe is a sphere of mechanical perfection. We carry out the Watchmaker's work with our own hands."

It was comforting... not quite a prayer, or a testimony, but the current of belief that ran through Mariah's life, undergirding her efforts. "Proof," she said to the ribs she was polishing. "I'm only trying to live the gospel."

The mechanical gave no answer—its head still rested in the sack of cornmeal where she'd stowed it, hidden away in a supply wagon—but the breastbone rose, pressing into her palm as though the ribcage had drawn breath.

Mariah kept still. She closed her eyes and imagined the torso within her arms in its proper place—each metal limb and wire ligament joined, the cobbled-together skeleton cloaked in ceramic and paint, patchcoat but lovely, glowing. She whispered the words she would carve into a strip of hammered silver, to be secured inside this ribcage in place of a beating heart. It was the wrong way around, the steps out of order as every part of this enterprise had been scattered, misplaced. She had no key to turn within the mechanical's chest, but she knew the words to quicken it.

She didn't know its function, only that it would be beautiful. Perhaps the old stories were wrong and that was function enough.

Her lips opened again, and her prayer was drowned in a sudden riot of cries and clashing metal.

***

A Millerite camp outside Fayetteville had been stormed, when Mariah was eight, after which her mother bundled her up and moved on, sheltering with the Oneida commune. Always some cause for their movement—scorn from the settled towns, a doctrine with which her mother did not agree, danger from those who looked too closely at even a freeborn African woman and her girl.

Mariah's heart wrenched as she ran, the mechanical's torso clasped in her arms. She didn't want to leave the Watchmaker's people. Whatever tonight brought, it mustn't be allowed to drive her mother away from the people who—though they were still strange—had given Mariah tools, reassurances, a way of being. Why couldn't the towns let them be? They were only passing through, speaking the gospel as did so many others, Baptists and the Seventh Day's adherents. Once, in Minoa, she'd watched townspeople break a milkmaid and scatter its parts, jeering and praying.

There were many more here tonight than had been in Minoa's woods.

Someone snatched at her and Mariah tripped, flailing sideways, tools dropping from her apron's pockets. "Come here, girl," Kit said, hoisting her as though she and the machine parts together weighed nothing. "Where've you been? Your ma?"

"I don't—she was with Sister Mortensen," Mariah gasped. Metal ribs pressed into hers, cutting and angular. "They were preparing a milkmaid for display, but—"

"We'll find her." Kit wasn't running, but he moved quickly among the tents, hunched low. "What mess have you got? I might as well be toting a reaper. You been stealing pies from Brother Haycock, Missy Mariah?"

"I was—" Mariah began, but Kit came up short, stumbling over a stake, and the mechanical's torso bounced from her grip.

"What's all this?" someone said. Kit set her down, the hand on her shoulder edging her behind him. A white man stood in front of them, blocking the path to the wagons and mules. He smiled, at Mariah and then at Kit, no expression of welcome. "You runaways, thinking to hide here and there. Stealing work from honest Christians."

"We've stolen nothing," Kit said.

The man squinted against torchlight. "There's those who'd see the return of their property, boy. You think your false gods will save you?"

Mariah's head spun. She'd feared for the congregation's livelihood and gospel, and forgotten to fear for its people. Who was this man, who'd apparently not heard that New York was a free state—final emancipation celebrated barely three years before? He'd have a time carrying away any of the African folk in the congregation, but this night… the mess and hysteria… She couldn't lose Kit. How could she protect him? She, fourteen years old and useless, soft and daydreaming, shirking duties.

Perhaps her mechanical was a sin after all, and she'd brought this down on the congregation.

The man reached for Kit, and Mariah screamed. "Ma! Brother Hendricks—"

"That'll do you no good, little miss," the man said. "God will see his work done tonight."

Kit wasn't resisting, Mariah saw with horror—Kit, who'd argue with a fence post, whose strong arms could lever the largest of the reapers into a wagon. She kept her hand in his. Her boots tripped over the jutting ribs of her mechanical as the man shoved Kit.

"Get along there, both of you. Always a market for healthy slaves—"

Mariah's eyes blurred. Through filmy tears a light grew, casting sharp shadows from the tents. She believed it torchlight, more strangers descending on them, but it was softer, steady and pale instead of flickering-orange. A shape rose within the light, tall and sturdy—*Ma*, Mariah thought, but no, too tall for any human woman. It moved without movement; it appeared and disappeared, the light growing stronger; step by step it solidified, its outline drawn dark and glinting.

It assembled itself before Mariah's eyes, light firming into the familiar shape of an iron skeleton. A colorful skin covered its limbs. Astonished, she watched blue-painted cheeks swell, and a tin breastplate appeared, star-punched like the lanterns the congregation made for winter. Its legs moved seamlessly, mosaics of white ceramic and reddish pottery, and a hand reached out.

Mariah felt fingers brush hers, as fingers had twisted through her own in the dark, not so long ago. Her legs cramped like she'd been running for a long time and finally stopped. Breath filled her lungs and her heart thrummed, ecstasy driving away fear.

"What in hellfire?" the strange man yelped. He threw an arm across his eyes, blocking the light. "Our Father which art in Heaven—"

His prayer descended into whimpering when the mechanical drew close. Its arms encircled Kit as his own wrapped around Mariah, and the stranger staggered away. He dropped to his knees with a jolt that reminded Mariah of a mule she'd seen once, hamstrung in a field accident. He fell away in her sight, shrinking, an insect on the grass scrabbling toward a tent as more people swarmed close.

She wasn't sure if they flew, she and Kit and the mechanical, or if it was only the sudden lightness in her mind: the repetition of her prayer, the words not yet written inside the mechanical's chest but inscribed, indelible and undying, within their two hearts.

Diana Hurlburt is a librarian, writer, and Floridian in upstate New York. Selections of her short work can be found at *Memoir Mixtapes, Luna Station Quarterly, Saw Palm,* and *phoebe,* in the World Weaver Press anthology *Equus,* and forthcoming from Sword & Kettle Press's mini-chapbook series. A lifelong fan of Greek myths, she drew on the story of Pygmalion and Galatea for "Divine Spark." When not remixing New York religious history with Ovid's tales, she's chugging cold brew, reading romance, and watching fast horses.

The Balance of Memory

Reese Hogan

Papa's story always started the same way. *My child had a horrible accident.* Except story wasn't the right word. Henrik said the word should be *excuse.* Gerta said it was an *apology. This is why. I'm sorry but.* Neither Henrik nor Gerta much liked being explained to anyone, much less Papa's women. It was one of the few things they had in common.

The latest one's name was Marjorie. They hadn't met her yet. But they pressed against the door of their bedroom and listened through its rusted steel, right where the gear in the middle left a gap the size of Gerta's pinkie.

"My child had a horrible accident," said Papa. "I won't go into details. The important part is that I tried to reconstruct the body afterwards. Laid out the parts, hoping there was enough left to—"

"I rather think you *should* go into details," the woman named Marjorie broke in. "Seeing as how that would inform which 'parts' you'd need to rebuild, which in turn, informs whether it was a good expenditure of your time."

Henrik turned toward Gerta. The black goggles that had taken the place of his eyes reflected her own face back at her. One of the steel teeth in her exposed jawbone had come loose again, and dangled like a broken gear. She shoved it back in with her thumb.

"What's expenditure?" Henrik whispered.

"Like how much you spend on something," Gerta murmured. "Now, quiet, I want to hear this." She brushed her red hair back from her mechanical ear so it fit against the door better.

"There was an accident in my lab," Papa was saying. "My wife was killed instantly. My child was… close. I did everything I could to save them. But things were bad. There was a heartbeat, but so faint. Brain activity, but so slow. I couldn't afford automatons for rewiring, or the proper solder for organic tissue. So I made do with what I had. But that's not what pulled my baby through in the end."

"Baby?" Marjorie echoed. "I'd pictured this as an older child."

"Eleven," Papa said. "But baby. Always my baby."

"Always my *experiment,* more like," Henrik muttered.

Gerta scowled at him. "Not now, Henrik."

Henrik's perfectly human lips turned up in a sneer. He didn't answer.

"I took a break at one point," Papa said. "I was despairing. For both of my family members to be snatched away so cruelly…" His voice faltered. "But the fates made it up to me. For when I returned to my lab, I found not one, but two, children waiting for me, alive and well. And though neither one *looked* like the baby I'd almost lost, they were *both* my child. I think the singularity of consciousness took hold, and my child rebuilt themselves in their own image. As they'd always imagined they might be."

"How do you mean?" Marjorie's voice was a bit smaller, as she tried to comprehend this strange fact that sent most people running.

"Two bodies," said Papa. "One person."

"When you say singularity of consciousness, are you implying the mechanical portion of your… child… gained sentience?"

"I am implying only that something miraculous happened inside my child's soul that night. It's not something I built. But it's not something of the Creator, either. It's something in between; something straight from the beauty of their mind."

There was a long pause. Then Marjorie said, "Is it okay if I think of them as two people?"

"No," whispered Henrik.

"Yes," said Gerta, quirking her metal jaw into a smirk.

"Mother wouldn't have approved," he said. "Of her *or* Papa's intentions for her."

"You mean as a new body for Mother's dead soul?" Gerta rolled her eyes. "It didn't work the last sixteen times, and it won't work this one. We've nothing to worry about."

"Who's worrying?" he said softly. "I'm just wondering what she'd think of being another of Papa's experiments."

"Does it matter?" Gerta bent toward the gap behind the gear to try to catch a glimpse of this new woman.

"Do you think she likes skipping stones at the pond?" Henrik said.

"Maybe," said Gerta.

"I suppose there are stranger things," she heard Marjorie say, in response to some unheard question. "I did live through the wind-up toaster craze, after all."

Gerta almost smiled. But then Marjorie added, "Well, if they really are only one person, they only need the rations of one person. Right?"

Gerta looked at Henrik, and Henrik stared back. On the other side of the door, Papa said, "You don't need to worry about that. Food isn't what they survive on."

***

When Henrik and Gerta were One, they were haunted by a nearly incessant fear that everything they loved could be taken away. Family members could be killed. Houses could burn down. Toys could be destroyed, rations could be withheld, music could go silent, freedom itself could be snatched in the blink of an eye. But they eventually came to realize that, even if that dark place materialized, there was one thing they could count on to always be there. That was the day One became two; when the sheer childhood fear of losing everything else became more than they could bear. *You can't take me away from myself,* One had thought, fear hardening into an impenetrable sense of security. To this day, Henrik and Gerta distinctly remembered those words.

Less than a year later, their small family was ripped apart, and they learned they were wrong about all of it. They could be separated. And not everything they'd lost was gone forever.

It just didn't exist the way they remembered it.

"Have you noticed," said Gerta, "that there aren't as many ghosts as there used to be?"

She and Henrik sat cross-legged on the floor of Papa's laboratory. Gerta was tightening her steel tooth, using Henrik's goggles as a looking glass. The organic fingers beneath her gloves ached as she turned the screwdriver.

"It's because it's all fixable now," said Henrik, "same as we were. Folks don't die anymore, not the way they used to."

"They must, though," said Gerta, giving the screw a final twist. "Papa's a genius; not everyone out there has someone like him. Why, I have a ticking heart made of no more than a spool of wire and a pocketwatch!"

"We got that *before* the accident," Henrik reminded her.

"No, we didn't," said Gerta.

Henrik frowned. "Yes, we did. Papa asked us to help out with that experiment, after we got back from the pond. It was the same day we made a trail of breadcrumbs around the pond and birds ate them all, remember? Then we got back and Papa cut our chest open and—"

She waved a hand dismissively. "It's not possible you could have a memory from before that I don't, Henrik. You're misremembering."

Henrik looked at her suspiciously, this half that existed only in shadow and light beyond his goggles, and wondered if she *really* couldn't remember. It was possible; although they shared thoughts they'd had before, when they were One, now they were a tipping seesaw where feelings and emotions balanced out by dumping it all on one side or the other. At least that's how Gerta had explained it to him once. Maybe memories were part of that balance, too.

Gerta was looking at him thoughtfully. "I do remember the breadcrumbs, though. But we didn't leave them around the pond. We left them in a trail to get back home, because Mother left us alone out there."

"What?" Henrik said sharply. "No! She would never!"

"She did. She said we were eating all the food, then sent us out there with just a loaf of bread. And birds ate a lot of crumbs, yeah, but we found our way home anyhow. Papa was livid when we told him."

She gathered her layered skirts and came to her feet. Henrik pushed himself up as well, adjusting the suspenders over his shirt with a snap of his wrists. They clanked hard on the metal chest beneath.

"I don't believe it," he said shortly. "That Mother did that *or* that he cared. If he'd had to choose a side, it would've been her."

Gerta bit her lip. Henrik wasn't lying. Which meant he had to be wrong. And fragmented memories had no part in their life; without those memories, their days of a normal human life would fade, and where would they be then?

She shoved it from her mind and turned, making her way back through the lab. Henrik followed. The knee of his organic leg ached, making him unsteady. He focused instead on the tools cluttering the tables—brass telescopes and aero clocks and heavy iron cameras and burnt-out gaslamps—from a one-time dream of exploration that had never happened. Now Papa was close to losing the lab. Finding a new body to house Mother's ghost was more important to him than food on the table. In the end, Marjorie would end up like all the others: an empty body without its ghost, and incapable of taking another's. What did Papa do with all those ghosts he pushed out of their shells? He'd given some to Henrik and Gerta, but not enough. Not enough by far.

Gerta's mechanical ears picked up a footfall on the stairwell. She grabbed Henrik's wrist, feeling the human joints of her fingers grind painfully as she did so. Henrik paused, glancing back. Then Marjorie's voice drifted down in a soft murmur not meant to carry.

"What would it look like?"

They hadn't met her yet, hadn't so much as been in the same room with her. But the air wafting down ahead of her, bringing with it the scents of cedar and rose, was strong enough to freeze Henrik and Gerta where they stood. They breathed it in through the steam and iron smell of the lab.

"I'm telling you," said Marjorie, "he has this bizarre tale about a kid dying and turning into two people. Don't you think that could be connected?"

She finally came into sight. She wore trousers with heeled boots, and a leather corset that left her shoulders bare. Poking through her waves of dark hair was a contraption of some kind, a moving gear visible within. Right at the position of her ear; was it this she was talking into? For there was no sign of Papa.

Marjorie headed straight to Papa's tables and started opening containers and unscrewing bottles, letting out hisses of steam and gases. Henrik's and Gerta's gazes met, horrified. If Papa knew she was doing this, he'd kill her! Gerta nodded toward the ceiling, wondering if they should try to sneak past Marjorie and tell Papa. But Henrik's eyes went to the mist and steam suddenly drifting through the air before them, and there was no need to communicate this thought: *she was letting out ghosts.* And not just one or two, but a scattering thick enough to make the air crackle with their life energy.

Henrik and Gerta sighed, releasing the same breath into the same room.

Papa had rules about consuming the dead under his roof. But it had been too long since they'd had sustenance—days and days now—and there were enough here that he shouldn't miss any for his experiments.

Gerta reached her hand out, the one with the aching joints that ground together, and curled her fingers around the shining mist. Like sticky spiderwebs, they clung to her gloves. Through the view of Henrik's goggles, they left a black sheen across the fabric. He gathered it in too, the dark strands stretching like cobwebs of filth. He tried not to think about who these ghosts had been, and instead concentrated on what they would become. Life. Energy. Another day.

"What I'm *saying*," Marjorie continued, oblivious of the scattering ghosts, "is that if he really does have the technology to grant immortality, he may have already used it. What if it's not here?"

Gerta cupped the strands in her gloved hands. Several of the tendrils groped toward her, as if trying to find something. Next to her, Henrik wrapped the black filaments around his fingers. They dug barbs into the human bits of his hands, twisting as if they were fighting him. Pain lanced through his hands, compounding the already aching joints of his wrists.

As one, they brought their cupped hands to their mouths. Gerta tipped the ghosts toward her steel jaw. Henrik scrunched up his face with disgust and pain, bracing himself as he bit down. As Gerta's teeth sank into the tendrils of mist, Marjorie turned and saw her. She let out a shriek, stumbling against a table. Pounding footsteps suddenly sounded overhead, running toward the lab. Gerta cried out as the ghosts fled like a spilled can of bolts. One left a slash of blood across Henrik's hand as it disappeared.

***

The rocks of the beach bordering the pond slammed against Gerta's back as she stumbled backward, unable to catch herself. Henrik landed hard on his knees and palms. Pain shot through hands that hadn't healed. Papa stood in front of his Land Voyager, staring down at them furiously, his magnifying lenses shoved up on his balding head and his tie hanging crooked.

"What have I told you about *never* doing that under my roof?" he shouted.

Marjorie stood next to him, pale as death, hands clutching the earpiece she'd been using earlier at her chest. "Those kids aren't human!" she said. "They have death in their eyes. I was *scared*, Thomas."

Gerta glanced at Henrik as he struggled to his feet. She was pretty sure Marjorie couldn't see the gossamer threads still clinging to Henrik's lips, so what could *death in their eyes* even mean? What eyes?

"She was robbing your lab, Papa!" said Henrik, pleading.

"Then you should have come to *me*," Papa said, eyes flashing. "You have no idea what you've done. You almost cost me everything!"

He got back in the vehicle, slamming the door behind him. Marjorie followed, studying them through the viewing glass. Gerta glared resentfully at the Land Voyager as it drove away, Papa's homemade gear shaft cranking noisily the whole way. Gravel clung to her layered skirts as she stood. Twisted black fibers stretched across her steel teeth.

"What did I tell you?" said Henrik bitterly. "It's not his kid that's important to him. It's finding a new body for Mother's ghost. He doesn't care a *whit* about us." He picked up a rock and sent it skittering across the pond. It skimmed fifteen hops before hitting the opposite side, leaving only pale rings in the water. Henrik's wrist sparked with pain.

"Once his experiment with her fails, he'll be back," said Gerta. "He's not gonna leave us here."

"What about all those ghosts he was keeping in his lab?" Henrik argued. "Ghosts he could have been giving *us* to keep us alive. But he didn't. He doesn't care about us! He'd rather hold onto them to test in new bodies. It's *always* about Mother, even though Mother is dead and we're still here."

"Is that what you think those ghosts were for?" said Gerta. "The only one I know for sure he keeps somewhere is…"

She trailed off, staring at the ripples on the pond. A cool breeze lifted her hair from her forehead, bringing with it the scent of fish.

"…is Mother's," she whispered.

Henrik turned, mouth half-open. "Wait. You're not saying we…"

"Marjorie was opening jars down there. Containers. Papa has to keep Mother's ghost *somewhere*, right? This must be why he told us never to consume ghosts under his roof!"

Henrik paled. "No. We wouldn't have done that. We would have known!"

"You heard what he said. *You almost cost me everything.*"

Henrik sank to the rocky beach, picking up a flat stone and clutching it in his hands. He felt like he was about to cry, though he didn't think it was possible without eyes.

"But we didn't consume her," said Gerta softly. "And once Papa catches Mother's ghost again… once he expels Marjorie's ghost and tries to put Mother's in… when he finishes this latest try, he'll come back for us. I know he will."

"Yeah," said Henrik hollowly. "So he can just cast us aside again the *next* time we come between him and Mother."

Gerta sat beside Henrik, pulling her knees to her chest. Her fingers throbbed with a persistent ache now, as if they were barely hanging on. She didn't dare pull off her glove to see how badly they'd started to rot beneath. She noticed Henrik similarly kept his cuffs pulled over the wrists under his partly-bionic hands. His cheekbones and chin still looked healthy enough—just a little gray—but the fine cobweb threads sticking to his jaw suggested he'd gotten just enough to stave the deterioration off his face. For now.

"Henrik?" she said.

His goggles swung in her direction, his flat rock still clutched before him. "Yeah?"

"What Marjorie said, about us having death in our eyes… do you think it's true? Are we dead?"

"I think so, yeah," he said.

Gerta's stomach clenched to hear him say it so casually. "But I thought it was the opposite! That we would live forever, like everyone else nowadays."

Henrik smiled humorlessly. "I often wonder if we're even real."

She thought maybe the balance had shifted again—Henrik normally wasn't the half who wondered these things—but then she realized he'd always seen ghosts as corruption and death as a kind of betrayal.

She put her hand on his, so they held the stone together. "Papa *will* come back," she repeated, staring into the black glass of his goggles. "And we are not dead."

"There are no ghosts around here," answered Henrik. "We've stripped this place clean. It's only a matter of time now."

"No. There's one place that *must* still have ghosts. The Gracie Wood Cemetery."

He jerked back. "I'm not goin' to Boneyard Boulevard."

"Stop calling it that. It's just a place like any other."

His jaw clenched. He took several moments to answer. "Fine. I guess it beats killing people."

She stared. "You did not just say that."

"You mean you've never thought about it? As a way to get ghosts?"

"No! Of course not!" Is this what Marjorie had meant? *Death in their eyes?*

"What would it matter?" said Henrik quietly. "Everyone leaves us in the end anyway. Papa was nothing new."

Gerta shook her head. "It matters."

"Why?"

"I… I don't know." She stood, shaken, and Henrik stood with her. Their hands were still wrapped around the same flat stone, and for a moment, they were One again, standing on the beach of the pond, and Mother and Papa were beside them sharing a kiss under a parasol. Then Henrik pulled his hand out to the side and threw. Gerta counted the skips of the stone through a blur of tears: sixteen, nineteen, twenty-one. More than One had ever been able to do.

Would they have worked up to that someday without splitting? Or were the cracks always there, destined to break apart even the one thing that should have stayed together until the end?

***

The sun was nearing the treetops by the time they reached the graveyard. Gerta and Henrik held hands, their grasps loose so as not to hurt their crumbling flesh. A low wind sent the smells of moist dirt and mulch across the grounds. The sign for the Gracie Wood Cemetery was black and tarnished, easily a hundred years old, but the rivets tacking it to the stone archway were bright silver and modern— replaced since Papa had stolen them almost a year earlier to fix his broken child.

A hush fell over them as they entered. Gerta watched for the telltale white mist of a nearby ghost, while Henrik scanned the life-sized statues of saints and gargoyles nervously, his hand squeezing Gerta's tighter. After a second, she winced and shook him off, and he mumbled an apology.

"Relax, will you?" she said. "We find a few ghosts in here, and it'll save our lives."

"I just... remember ghosts here. From before, I mean. Before we were looking for them. I didn't like this place."

"Impossible," said Gerta. "I would've remembered something like that."

Henrik started to answer, but then he slowed to a stop, staring overhead. The sky was slowly being obscured by tendrils of black, reaching and curling like some deep-sea creature. Just seeing the spirits sent his human joints pulsing in a freshly aching agony. He groaned, stumbling, and barely caught himself on a wrist that sent fire shooting up his arm, until it blessedly ended at his mechanical shoulder. Gerta grimaced, tucking her hands under her armpits.

"How do we get 'em down here?" Henrik said through gritted teeth.

"I don't know." Gerta looked deeper into the cemetery. "But they're stretching up that way, toward the hill."

"Let's go, then."

They staggered forward, cutting away from the path and climbing over ancient stones and rotted stairways, following the path of ghosts like a river in the sky. Gerta could see it easier, as a white mist against the late-afternoon sky, but Henrik could follow it almost by feel alone. As they walked, the balance shifted. The dread in Henrik's human heart paled in comparison to his hunger, and he pushed himself faster until Gerta struggled to keep up. Gerta, meanwhile, so determined to give them another day of sustenance and life, noted how strange it was that these spirits were so high and... and *linear*, for lack of a better word. A trail. A chain. A *lure*.

"They're leading us somewhere," she whispered.

But Henrik didn't hear. He was already nearing the grand mausoleum at the center of the cemetery, built straight back into the hill they were climbing. Pillars framed the double iron doors, and ivy cascaded from the peaked roof around its marble façade. It was here that the river of ghosts led, spilling over the two-story roof like mist from a waterfall, making the mausoleum look even eerier and more ethereal than usual. Henrik paused and gaped up at them, his breath coming fast.

Gerta finally caught up to him, gasping at the pain in her ankles. "Wait! There's something strange going on here, Henrik."

Henrik climbed onto a pillar and reached upward, stretching his fingers toward those drifting threads. "What d'you mean, strange?"

"Like the fact that they seemed to *lead* us here!"

He shook his head. "No. Ghosts aren't as clever as all that. More likely they're escaping out of this... this vault. Or tomb. Whatever it is."

He had a point. Ghosts *weren't* clever. Just desperate and scared like everyone else. But they also shouldn't be escaping mausoleums; these things were airtight, and any ghosts they might have were—

The front door of the majestic building creaked as it opened. Henrik looked down in surprise. It was only a crack, with nothing but a sliver of darkness beyond, but it was definitely open.

"I know what you are," a voice whispered from inside.

Fear seized Gerta's metal heart. But Henrik burned with curiosity, and climbed gingerly from the pillar's base to approach the open door. "And what is that?"

"A split soul," the voice rasped. "You're not the first I've seen."

Henrik's breath caught. "There are others?"

"You think I house the ghosts here for my own wellbeing?" A ragged laugh. "No. It's because I know how it is out there. How immortality is taking over humanity with its technology and machines. People like you and I need a safe place to find sustenance and acceptance."

"You and I?" Henrik repeated, his voice breathless with awe.

"Come in here. I'll show you."

Henrik started forward. Gerta held a hand out, feeling like it would break her brittle fingers. "No!"

Henrik paused, hand on the doorjamb. "What's wrong? Aren't you coming?"

"I don't trust this," said Gerta. "All those ghosts…"

He let out a slight laugh. "Ghosts don't talk, Gerta. Whatever this is, it's human. Like us."

"I thought you didn't think we *were* human," she said.

His brow furrowed over his goggles. "Together we are."

"Then we shouldn't be apart!"

"Tell you what," he said. "You can wait out here, and I'll get a ghost and bring it out. You don't have to step foot inside."

"But—" The rest of her protest was cut off abruptly as the mausoleum door closed behind him with a thump.

Gerta was left standing atop the hill, cold wind whipping her hair in her face and the white film of ghosts far overhead. She let out a hiss of anxiety through her metal teeth and walked closer to the door, hoping to hear something inside. But it was as quiet as... well, as a tomb. She looked down over the gravestones toward the cemetery gate, hoping to see Papa's Land Voyager driving in, or the lights of some other savior. There was nothing. So she turned back to the door, laying her gloved hand against its steel filigree. She could feel that fear climbing higher and higher in her throat, until it felt it would choke her.

But then she remembered the tipping scales. If the balance of fear was tipped so far toward her right now, that must mean Henrik felt no fear at all. Which could hardly mean he was in danger. Right? Was he consuming his fill of ghosts while she stood out here in the cold, her fingers aching with unbearable pain? Could the person who'd called out to them *really* be another split soul? Did they have another half in there with them? She closed her eyes, willing Henrik to somehow send the answers straight into her mind. But of course that wasn't possible. They weren't One anymore.

She put her hand on the twisted handle and pulled. When nothing but silence greeted her, she pulled the door open farther. She saw only a long dark hallway. Light flickered at the far end, as if from a torch.

"Henrik?" she called.

His voice came back immediately. "Straight back, Gerta!"

Reassured, she stepped into the tomb and let the door shut softly behind her. If possible, it was even colder in here, the air uncomfortably dank and musty. As she neared the back, she made out a pair of torches illuminating shelves filled with coffins on either side. More coffins had been left open on the floor, scattered around the pair of people within. One of them was Henrik. His hands were cupped before him, holding a nebulous cloud of bright white, almost burning with life energy. He looked up at her, face flushed and vibrant, and smiled through lips stretched with wispy fibers.

The other occupant turned to face Gerta. An overlarge cowl obscured the face beneath.

"She's like us, Gerta!" said Henrik eagerly. "She says she has another half out there, one who—"

The cowled figure put an arm out, hand landing squarely on Henrik's chest, and shoved. Henrik's hands flew out in shock. The backs of his legs buckled as they bumped something, and he fell. He only realized what had happened when his back hit hard enough to knock his air out and his arm spasmed to the side. His elbow hit a wall. He screamed and started to push himself up, but a hinged lid came down and slammed shut over his head, sealing him into blackness. His scream bounced back at him from half a foot away.

Gerta watched in horror as the cowled figure latched the coffin lid with Henrik inside. "What are you doing?" she cried.

The person straightened and tossed back the hood, and Gerta found herself staring at Marjorie. The woman's smile was brittle.

"Your father's ghosts worked like a charm, didn't they, child?"

Gerta's eyes tracked up past the ceiling, toward where the ghosts hovered above the mausoleum. "*You* brought them here?"

"I can't believe your father thought *I* would be one of his experiments. I trapped him in the cage he once used for you, then took his ghosts and came here. I left his wife's with him. For the sake of mercy, I suppose."

Cage? The idea felt familiar, somehow, but it wasn't something Gerta wished to contemplate right now. The ghosts. They were what mattered. "You can see the ghosts, too?" she said.

"It comes from spending months studying what you are," said Marjorie. "For example, I know your father used a special tool of immortality on you, and I even know what it was. Cursed rivets from the cemetery. Right?"

Gerta could hear Henrik's screams inside the closed coffin, mounting closer and closer to full-blown panic. She couldn't stop picturing him falling into that coffin. It was too close to a moment that had very nearly happened to another child, not all that long ago.

"If I'm to use these rivets myself," Marjorie continued, "I'd like to be the *only* immortal one, rather than sharing it with some other… *unnatural*… being. In other words, I need to know whether I can kill the counterpart if they are created."

"You mean like killing Henrik?" Gerta said, her voice cracking.

Marjorie's red lips turned up in a smile. "And seeing whether *you* survive. Yes, dear. Exactly like that."

She turned toward the wall beside the coffin. When her back turned, Gerta rushed to the coffin and grabbed the lid, pulling with all her might. The movement sent a sharp shock of pain through her shoulders and fingers. She gasped at the intensity of it.

"Let me out!" Henrik begged, banging on the walls. His voice was barely audible through the thick wood. "Gerta, help me!"

The lid wouldn't budge. There was a lock holding the latch closed. She hadn't even seen Marjorie slip it on. Gerta looked up in time to see Marjorie twist a knob on the wall. Her eyes widened as she saw a hose snaking from the bottom of the knob and across the floor, then disappearing into a hole in Henrik's coffin.

The rushing sound hit Henrik's ears even over his screams, and he paused for a second, hiccupping with fear. A bone-numbing cold was seeping beneath him, spreading along his back and legs. *It's water,* he realized with a chill. He screamed again, but it came out as more of a choking sob. He beat at the lid, slamming his palms and feet against it, feeling the ice-cold water creeping over his shoulders and lapping at his stomach.

Gerta bolted over to the hose to yank it out, but Marjorie shoved her away and Gerta's ankles gave out on her, too weak from lack of nourishment to support her.

"How could you do this to an eleven year-old boy?" she said, struggling back to her knees.

Marjorie's lip curled. "He's not a boy, any more than you're a girl.

You're an experiment of your father's. Something was lost when you split into two, and the balance can only be restored by destroying the anomaly he created."

"That's not true!" Gerta said. "We split long before our bodies did, but it didn't stop us being human. We'll *always* be human, as long as…" Her voice trailed off as she remembered hers and Henrik's words just before he'd entered the mausoleum.

I thought you didn't think we were human.

…Together we are.

She could still hear Henrik inside the coffin, crying in terror. But her own fear was gradually falling away, leaving her with an eerie calm. And her skin… it was no longer cold and clammy, the way the tomb was, but heating up like a fever burned beneath it. It was the balance, she realized, tipping toward Henrik as the cold water and fear pulled both away from her. *I can use this*, she thought. *I can tip something back to my other half.*

The water had covered Henrik's neck now, and was lapping over his chin and mouth. He kept shoving at that lid, futilely, as the water started closing over his head. He tried to take a deep breath. To hold it. It wouldn't matter. This was it…

But outside the coffin, Gerta also took a deep breath. She pulled in all the air she could, past her steel jaws and into her metal lungs… and then she held it there. Her body didn't need the air. But by holding it in her own chest, she sent it back to Henrik, who desperately did.

And then she sat back, letting her muscles go limp, letting her weakness consume her so she could tip the strength back to Henrik. For just a moment, she let him hold all that made them human. And then she gave him everything that made them *inhuman* as well.

The lock strained at the coffin's latch as Henrik fought. Water seeped out from beneath the lid, spilling in rivulets down the side. Marjorie was watching Gerta, an uneasy look on her face as she seemed to realize that killing Henrik *would* in fact kill Gerta, too. So she wasn't watching when the lock snapped and the coffin's lid burst open. Henrik grabbed the sides and pulled himself from the water, his teeth bared in anger. Gerta felt a stab of fear when she saw him—was it the balance tipping back? Or something more?—then Henrik was leaping out of the coffin. Marjorie barely had time to cry out before he grabbed the back of her neck and shoved her head into the water-filled coffin. Still imbued with the inhuman strength Gerta had loaned him, he held her under while she struggled.

Gerta raised her head, trying to pull the shared strength back from him. "Henrik! Stop!"

His face snapped toward her, goggles streaming with water. "She locked me in a *box*, Gerta!" he said, his voice shaking with anger and fear. "It was like I was in Papa's cage all over again, screaming to be let out while he waited on some end result to write in his notebook. It was like I wasn't *human* to him!"

"No, it was *Mother* who didn't see me as human," Gerta said. "It was her who would leave me miles from home, or deny me supper!"

Henrik stared. His hold on Marjorie seemed to loosen, just slightly. "But whose memories are real?" he said.

Gerta couldn't tear her eyes from Marjorie's weakening struggles. She remembered the day of the accident, lying broken and dying in the lab—*You can't take me away from myself*—and her certainty afterward that everything would be okay as long as she and Henrik had each other. But those memories… those memories said differently.

She put a hand over her metal heart, feeling it tick a steady rhythm despite the ache that seemed it would tear her in two. "Maybe they're all real," she said, feeling sick.

Henrik turned back to Marjorie, and Gerta didn't have the heart to call him away again. It was a long time before Henrik's arm finally went slack. Marjorie slumped, head still in the water, body draped over the coffin's side. When Henrik stepped back, black webs stretched from his hands to her body. He gathered in her ghost until it was a mass of filth and fibers filling his arms, then he came over and knelt by Gerta.

She hesitated before reaching out and taking the life-giving substance. But it wasn't her own conscience that kept her from consuming it. It was a voice shouting from the door of the mausoleum.

"Gerta! Henrik! There you are!"

Henrik's head rose. Papa came into sight, out of breath and eyes fervent behind his spectacles. He held a jar in the crook of his arm. The nebulous shape of a ghost was visible within.

"You found her," Papa got out, looking toward the body slumped over the coffin's edge.

"She found us," Gerta said. She sat up straighter, still holding Marjorie's ghost in both gloved hands.

"I came here as fast as I could once I freed myself," Papa said.

Gerta's and Henrik's eyes met. It didn't escape either of them that Papa didn't once look away from Marjorie's body to make sure they were okay. He had interest in only one thing, and it was clutched to his body in a jar.

Gerta and Henrik stood. Gerta walked over to Marjorie's body, putting herself in Papa's line of sight.

"We already pulled her ghost from her body," she said, holding up the misty cloud of white.

"All we need is Mother's to replace it," said Henrik, joining her.

Papa's gaze finally landed on them. He brought the jar to his chest, clinging to it like a life preserver. "I came so close to losing her..."

"So did we," said Gerta. "We didn't mean to... to do what we did. In the lab."

"We didn't," Henrik echoed.

Papa shook his head, looking back toward Marjorie. "I need to bring her back to the laboratory—"

"No, you don't," said Gerta. "We know what to do."

Papa looked back uncertainly. "You do?"

"We've learned a few things about ghosts ourselves over the years," said Henrik.

"Especially while we were watching from the cage," said Gerta. Her voice trailed up at the end like a question. Like an invitation to deny it.

But Papa's eyes sparked in hope. "Tell me! What do I do?"

"Give her to us," said Henrik, holding out his half-bionic hands.

Papa barely hesitated before unscrewing the jar. He passed the whole thing to Henrik, who held it in his hands and looked down into it. The ghost within was a well of darkness and grit. It was the most substantial thing he'd seen since he died. It was his mother, and she was dead. Nothing would ever change that.

Gerta looked at Henrik, tears welling in her green eyes. "It wasn't the accident that split us apart," she whispered. "It was something before that."

"It was the fear of losing everything," said Henrik.

"It was the need for someone who wouldn't *betray* us," said Gerta.

"What?" Papa said, looking between them. "What are you saying?"

Henrik reached into the jar and collected Mother's ghost. He felt the grains of filth sliding between his fingers, like dirt from a grave. He'd always hated this part. It reminded him how far he'd come from being human.

He took a bite.

Papa gasped, lunging toward him. Gerta shoved Marjorie's ghost out, throwing it at Papa like a weapon. A black and white mass of mist and fiber and grit slammed into his face. She wasn't sure he'd even feel it, but he stumbled back, screaming. Gerta took a handful of Mother's ghost. She grimaced, but she didn't have a choice. She had to know.

And they remembered.

Henrik remembered a belt strap against his back when he'd snuck a cookie after dinner. Gerta remembered the cage. Henrik remembered board games with Papa, and summer days in the hay loft. Gerta remembered a dance with both parents on a dark winter night. But she also remembered the pain of her chest being cut open, and the metal heart that was put it in its place. Henrik remembered Mother watching the whole thing. And he remembered his eyes. They'd been brown. Like Papa's. All before the accident. The split of their body had happened afterward... but the split of their mind had happened long before.

They remembered.

"Emory, *stop*!" Papa shouted.

Henrik and Gerta froze. What was left of Mother fell from their hands, drifting in tendrils to the floor. Without looking, their hands found one another's and their grips tightened, as if that single word might tear them apart again.

Papa fell to his knees, hands grasping for what remained of Mother's ghost. Disconcertingly, he seemed to be sobbing as he muttered under his breath. "I can still fix this. And Emory... I can fix Emory... this should never have happened... what went wrong? Where did I go wrong?"

Henrik and Gerta considered their partly-bionic bodies and their reliance on ghosts for survival, and they shared a single thought, in the privacy of their minds: *What does he mean by fix? What will we become next?*

Gerta heard Henrik's voice—not out loud, but in her head. "It's okay. It's okay to walk away from this. Our memories are whole again. There is nothing else we need."

He was right. Gerta didn't feel Henrik's hand anymore, and Henrik didn't feel Gerta's presence, but somehow, as one, they turned and walked toward the mausoleum door. They ignored Papa's calls. They ignored his pain. They had a single future, and they knew now that it wasn't too late. They could become something new. They could be human again.

The crisp evening air touched their organic skin as they left the tomb. They disappeared through the cemetery gate in the last rays of sunlight—two beings with only one shadow.

Reese Hogan is a nonbinary science fiction author from New Mexico. They have published three novels, and the latest, *Shrouded Loyalties* from Angry Robot, was a Best SFF of August 2019 pick by both Amazon and Barnes & Noble. When Reese first began a retelling of Hansel & Gretel, they were struck by the traumatic childhood the siblings must have faced even before they were abandoned in the woods. This led to an exploration of coping mechanisms, repression, and the need for companionship, and a few weeks later, "The Balance of Memory" was born. It is Reese's first traditionally published short story. Read more at ReeseHogan.com or follow them on Twitter @ReeseHogan1.

The Giant and the Unicorn

Alethea Kontis

In the beginning, the Toymaker fashioned the Box. In the second year, he scattered his power throughout the Box and made the heavens and the stars. In the third year he cast the cogs and the wheels, the grasses and the trees. In the fourth year he formed the animals: the bear, the fox, the dragon, the griffin, the monkey, and the unicorn. In the fifth year he forged the Giant, in his own image, so that he might rule and maintain peace over this great land. In the sixth year he uploaded Sentience and Symbiotics; he breathed life into his creations and set them free. He looked down upon his work and knew it was good.

In the seventh year, spent from his task, the Toymaker lay down and died.

It was seven more years before the Giant went mad; the animals knew this because their springs and gears always kept perfect time (apart from the wind-up monkeys, who never cared for time). First the Giant lost his reason, then his sanity, and then his sense of purpose. Some said a virus had scrambled his wiring. Some said he was losing his power. Some said he had lost it long ago. Some said the world would die without the Giant to lead them, but they did not die, and the world went on, perhaps only a little less harmonious than it should have been.

No one asked the Giant about his notable lack of sanity, mostly because he was so much bigger. He was too much stronger. He would tear them all to pieces, or stomp on them until they were nothing more than crumpled scrap, or grind their bones to make his crown. They were all afraid of him… all save one brave little unicorn.

As you know, unicorns are not wound-up like the monkeys, nor do they collect and hoard mighty power like the miserly dragons. No, each unicorn is born with a star burning bright and pure in his heart. You can tell how old a unicorn is by the glow of its horn: a young unicorn's fire flashes raw and untamed; the fire of an elder unicorn is tempered, focussed, and controlled.

But there were no young unicorns left in the world. And there had not been, not since the Age of the Toymaker.

Many a unicorn had attempted to fly into the heavens upon their tiny wings, hoping beyond all hope to thwart the inevitable, but they all failed. When the light of a unicorn's star extinguished, his body and soul died right along with it. It became an empty shell, a hollow reminder of his brethren's brief time in the world.

And so it would have always been, but for that one unicorn.

It was twilight when the brave little unicorn came upon the Giant weeping in the forest. It did not occur to him to be afraid. Now, you might think him silly—many would—but it was not ignorance that drew the little unicorn towards the deep, creaking sobs. What drew him was curiosity, and kindness. For this unicorn was the youngest unicorn, the last fashioned by the Toymaker before his untimely absence, so his heart burned the brightest and the purest, the most compassionate of all.

"Poor Giant, whatever is the matter?" he asked the Giant humbly.

The Giant, as tall and as loud and as hollow as his head was, did not hear him. The unicorn, only as large as the Giant's longest finger, stepped a bit closer. He lifted his head, but kept his wings folded back in reverence.

"Is there anything I can do to help?" the unicorn asked again, but again the Giant did not hear him.

Undaunted, the unicorn flew up into the tree beside the Giant's head and landed precariously in the branches closest to his ear. They shook as his hooves strove to find purchase on the smooth bark. The leaves tinkled and flashed with starlight.

"Pardon me," he said.

The Giant bellowed a roar that echoed from one end of the Box to the other. It made the grass sing and the leaves clank, and it blew the unicorn clear out of that tree.

"Ho," called the Giant. "Is someone there?"

The unicorn shook out his wings, dislodging stray leaves and hoping the grass hadn't punctured anything vital. "Hello," said the unicorn.

It took the Giant a moment to find the tiny voice that squeaked up at him. "Hello, little one," said the Giant. "You should be afraid of me. I could tear you and fold you and crush you, and I probably will."

"You are sad," said the brave little unicorn. "You were crying. If you cry, you will rust. And the Toymaker did not mean for us to rust."

"No," the Giant replied, "he meant for us to live."

"And so we shall," the unicorn finished the scripture. "Tell me, Giant, why are you crying?"

"I am crying, little one, because I am mad. I have lost my mind. I have lost myself. I'm afraid I am losing my soul." He laid his enormous gray head in his enormous gray hands with a clunk. "And my head hurts something fierce."

"I am very good at finding lost things," said the unicorn, "so if you will tell me what your self looks like I will keep a sharp eye out for it. Your mind as well, for that matter." The unicorn bravely pushed through the blades of grass and took a step closer. "And if you will tell me where your head hurts, I would be happy to fly up and take a look."

"But you are small and fragile," said the Giant. "I could crush you with a toe. I could rip your wings off with a sneeze. I could crumple you up between my fingers and toss you to the far ends of the Box."

"You could do all those things," said the unicorn, "but your head will still hurt, and you will still be sad."

"So true, little one. So true." The Giant moved a heavy arm and lowered his head and shoulders. "Go on, then. Have a look."

The unicorn backed up and then ran to the Giant at a gallop, spreading his wings and letting them heft him aloft until he had settled on the Giant's proffered arm. He walked respectfully along the Giant's shoulder, careful not to scuff his hooves, until he came around to the back of the Giant's neck. It was full dark now, but the brightness of his horn lit the way. He could feel the whir and tick of the Giant's heart beneath his skin.

He saw the problem immediately.

"Giant?"

"Yes, little one?"

"Why would you have grass lodged in your neck? How did it get way up here? Did the monkeys throw it at you? They do have a tendency to throw things."

There was a gentle wheeze and creak as the Giant's shoulders shook, and the unicorn spread his wings, straining to keep his footing. "No," laughed the Giant. "But I lower my ear to the ground now and again. Sometimes I can hear the animals approaching. Sometimes I hear my own ticking heartbeat. Sometimes," the Giant whispered reverently, "I think I can hear the soul of the Toymaker himself."

"I should like to hear the soul of the Toymaker someday," said the unicorn.

"It is a mournful sound," said the Giant, "a lonely sound. But it is a sound full of love for the Box and hope for the future."

"Then it is a good sound," said the unicorn. "Now, if you don't mind, I'm going to remove some of this grass."

"Okay," said the Giant.

"I'd appreciate it if you don't try to swat me or smash me while I'm working," said the unicorn.

"I'll try to remember," said the Giant.

The unicorn turned back to the blades of grass sticking out of the Giant's neck, and not for the first time he wished he had hands instead of hooves. There were three blades, long and sharp and wedged deeply into the Giant's skin. The first two he removed easily enough with his teeth, using his hooves and wings as leverage to wrestle them free. The third, however, was lodged between the Giant's baseplate and his circular power supply.

This was the nuisance responsible for the headaches, the unicorn decided, and judging by the scars it had been causing the Giant trouble some time. It looked as if the Giant had snapped branches off trees and tried to scratch the offending splinter away. Unfortunately, the damage that had caused, coupled with the damage already done by the grass to begin with, seemed to have unalterably weakened his once bright power circle.

The Giant was dying.

Like a unicorn's star, when the light from that circle faded, the body and soul of the Giant would fade with it and he would indeed be no more. The land would never again have a king; it would never be restored to order and its shining former glory. Instead, the Box would fall into darkness and they—every one of them from the dragons to the bears to the trees and the pesky blades of grass—would turn to rust.

The Toymaker would not have wanted it that way.

Without giving himself time for further introspection, the unicorn bit the offending blade of grass and pulled it free. Then the unicorn knelt on tight joints and touched his horn to the Giant's neck. In a rush of heat and light the unicorn poured his heart, his soul, his star into the dim circle there.

The Giant did not see the unicorn fade, nor fall. He did not hear the small whisper, or the tinny crumple as its body hit the grass below.

Darkness flooded the Giant's eyes and ears as the old life leaked out of him. His mouth turned down and his lids slid closed. The Giant slumped forward and the last pulse fled through his fingertips. Blue lines sparked between the blades of grass around him and lit the dark night.

In that moment the Box marked the passing of its ruler, and it began the countdown to Entropy.

In the next moment, the Giant's power circle blazed to light once more. There was a whir and a tick and a shimmy, and the Giant's heart beat again. His eyelids opened with a clatter and he looked down at the empty shell of the unicorn…and he knew.

The Giant gently lifted the unicorn in one hand, and ripped up a blade of grass with the other. He turned the unicorn over, its segmented wings clinking as they unfolded beneath him. Carefully, the Giant inserted the blade of grass into a join in the unicorn's side and pried up the plate over his belly.

Then the Giant stood, stretched his arm up into the heavens, and pulled down a star.

He pressed the bright star into the unicorn's belly and maneuvered it into position with the point of the grassblade. Fixed in concentration with his mind intact now, the Giant repaired the inherent flaw in the unicorn's feedback loop and upgraded him.

He closed the belly circuit board and let one finger hover above the still form of the unicorn. One bright, blue pulse emitted from his fingertip, enveloping the body of the unicorn, electrifying every wire, every plate, every segment and synapse inside and out.

There was a whir. A small shiver. And finally, an almost imperceptible tick. The unicorn got to his feet in the Giant's palm, lifting and testing every one of his hooves in turn. He stretched his wings out and retracted them again. He lowered his head until he could see the bright tip of his horn reflected in the Giant's silver skin. Then he stared up at his enormous savior.

"Giant?"

"Hello, little one," said the Giant.

The unicorn blinked once, twice, a third time. He looked at the trees with their silent leaves, and the shadowy blades of grass shimmering with reflected starlight. "Is this the Afterlife? I hope not. It looks an awful lot like the old world." He turned back to the Giant. "And if you're here, it means I didn't fix you."

"Don't worry," said the Giant. "You fixed me more than you know. Better than ever. And I fixed you right back."

"You fixed me? But wasn't I beyond fixing? I gave you my star."

"Yes, you did. So I gave you another one."

"I have a new star?" The unicorn's wings twitched again. "But I am not a new me."

"And I am glad of that," the Giant chuckled. "For a short time after a unicorn's passing, his soul is stored in his horn. Fortunately, I renewed your power supply quickly enough to save it. To save the you that was you. The you that will always be you."

"Always?"

"I fixed that too," said the Giant. "If you should ever happen to lose your star's power for any reason, your horn will store your soul indefinitely. In time, that bit of power will be able to even recharge you. You will never have to worry about power again. You will never fade."

"I will never turn to rust?" the unicorn asked incredulously.

"Never," said the Giant. "You will live. As the Toymaker would have wanted."

"You are truly a benevolent King." As he named him, a line of skin across the Giant's forehead glowed a bright gold, the gold of his power. In the center of the circlet was the unicorn's star, shining bright as a diamond. The unicorn bowed. "I thank you, Giant," he said humbly.

"I thank you too," said the Giant.

"One good turn deserves another," said the unicorn. "It was my duty."

"It was something only you were brave enough to do," said the Giant. "It is what a friend would have done."

"I am your friend?" asked the unicorn.

"You gave your life for mine," said the Giant. "I can think of no one more worthy."

"I am honored," the unicorn bowed again. "And you have repaid me most generously. I only wish my empty brethren might have been so lucky."

"I cannot bring back the old unicorns of the past," said the Giant, "but I can give their bodies new life if you would let me."

The unicorn pranced in merriment. "It would be my dearest dream. You do not need my permission for that."

"Oh, but I do," said the Giant, "for someone will have to teach these new unicorns about the world and the Box. Someone will have to teach them the ways of the Toymaker, and guide them into their new lives." He laid a finger in front of the unicorn. "Would you accept such a role?"

"I would," said the unicorn without hesitation. He touched his horn to the Giant's fingernail, and the shape of a five-pointed star etched itself upon it. The bright spot upon the Giant's brow twinkled.

"Then it is I who is honored," said the Giant. "And you will always be welcome at my Court, little friend. I hope you will visit and tell me tales of your brethren."

"I will," said the unicorn. "And perhaps one day you shall teach me to hear the soul of the Toymaker."

"As any friend would do," nodded the Giant. "It is full of love for the Box and hope for the future. It is a good sound. Though I believe if you listen to your own heart, you will hear it."

So that is how the King of the Box and the brave little unicorn became friends, a friendship that would last until the end of Time and the coming of Entropy.

It is also how unicorns became immortal.

How they came into our world… well, that's another story.

New York Times bestselling author **Alethea Kontis** is a princess, storm chaser, and Saturday Songwriter. Author of over 20 books and 40 short stories, Alethea is the recipient of the Jane Yolen Mid-List Author Grant, the Scribe Award, the Garden State Teen Book Award, and two-time winner of the Gelett Burgess Children's Book Award. She has been twice nominated for both the Andre Norton Nebula and the Dragon Award. She was an active contributor to *The Fireside Sessions*, a benefit EP created by Snow Patrol and her fellow Saturday Songwriters during lockdown 2020. When not writing or storm chasing, Alethea narrates stories for multiple award-winning online magazines, contributes regular YA book reviews to NPR, and hosts Princess Alethea's Traveling Sideshow every year at Dragon Con. Born in Vermont, Alethea currently resides on the Space Coast of Florida with her teddy bear, Charlie.

"The Giant and the Unicorn" was originally written for a steampunk Aesop's Fables anthology—it's based on the tale "Androcles and the Lion." As a fantasy lover raised on fairytales and folklore, she was never going to pass up the chance to invent a clockwork unicorn!

Ningyō

Laura VanArendonk Baugh

"Haul it down!" Musashibō shouted over the storm, throwing his weight against the ship's helm. "She's got too much windage. Down faster!"

The sail bellied, wet canvas straining as the ship heeled. Takeshi slacked the halyard, but the sail remained aloft and full. "It's stuck!" He changed to the downhaul, hemp biting his palms, but the wind wouldn't release its jealous grasp. "Saburō! Come and help!"

Saburō clung to the mast, his face pale even in the failing light. The storm had darkened the twilight to nearly full night, cut by flashes of lightning. Takeshi prayed lightning did not strike their airship. They had a thunder-rod with a long length of chain let out over the side, to disperse the fearful great sparks into the storm, but such measures were only moderately effective.

He wanted to touch his prayer beads, but his hands were full of soaked line and he could only move his lips against the rain.

The mast groaned as Takeshi fought grudging sail. "Saburō!"

Saburō peeled himself from the mast and came to help. Takeshi left the jammed downhaul, and together they freed the main sheet from the cleat. "Careful! Don't let it get away!" They eased the line through the block, and the tension slackened.

If they could get into the lee of the mountain...

A sickening crack and Musashibō shouted in alarm, flung aside as the wheel spun free and the ship's bow swung downwind. "We've lost steering!" He scrabbled to his feet. "Slack that sheet or—"

Saburō let go suddenly, and the line scorched through Takeshi's hands, taking flesh so fast he didn't have time to cry out. The ship veered downwind, and the mainsail bellied full despite the slack sheet. Musashibō let loose a bellow of very un-monkly language.

The ship broached, heeling hard as the sail groaned, and the men were thrown sliding to the deeply canted deck. Takeshi grasped for any handhold, keenly aware of how far he would fall if the ship rolled too far.

Musashibō shouted instructions but thunder drowned them. Lightning tore open the sky and illuminated the hillside a stone's-throw from them.

Takeshi ducked his head and whispered the name of the Buddha, and then the ship shattered around him.

***

Takeshi was alive. He could feel pain in his hands, his back, his head, his everything, so he must be alive.

He could hear Musashibō swearing, so the other monk was alive, too.

Takeshi rubbed cold water from his eyes. He was in a pine tree, which must have cushioned his impact. Above him, the tree trunk was splintered and bent jaggedly. He wriggled out of the tangled branches and worked his way to the ground about fifteen feet below.

The little airship hung in the dark sky, broken and fluttering. Torn sail flapped in the wind, and with the strain relieved the ship rolled slowly from side to side, balancing herself despite her shattered boom. She was still in the air, rebounded from the trees, though wounded—but they weren't aboard her. Her bow's figurehead turned out to the dark sky as the ship drifted in the storm.

To Takeshi's left, Musashibō was getting to his feet, minimizing the weight on one leg. He saw Takeshi and nodded a relieved greeting. Then he looked toward the drifting ship. "Think you can make that jump?"

Takeshi needed a moment to realize the senior monk wasn't serious. "Maybe Saburō's still aboard. Saburō! Saburō!"

He heard a moan, and he turned to see Saburō curled against a tree. His heart sank; no one left to throw down the rope ladder. He limped over to the servant. "Come on, Saburō. Nothing will be helped down there."

Saburō lifted his head. "Are we dead?"

"We are not dead." Takeshi answered with irritation despite his own wondering just a moment before. In the next flash he looked at his rope-burned hands, stinging in the rain.

Musashibō swore again. "Come back!"

But the little airship was pulling away from them, wobbling as it was carried by the storm, dragging its damaged hull across the treetops. The oil lamps along the sides disappeared behind branches and rain, flickering out of sight like last hopes.

"We're lost here!" wailed Saburō.

"Hush and look." Musashibō pointed through the storm. "Do you see that light?"

There was a flickering orange downhill, a fire.

"We can beg shelter," Takeshi said. "They will not turn away monks."

"And their servant," Saburō added quickly.

Musashibō lifted a hand to indicate the departed airship. "We won't be making many miles tonight. Let's find what rest we can and tackle the problem of travel in the morning."

They walked toward the flickering orange light, stumbling in the dark, bent under the wrath of the storm, shivering with cold and spent fear. Musashibō did not complain but Takeshi could see how he favored his right leg, and he put himself near the monk to be within reach if necessary.

The light seemed to die, falling and quieting until it went out. But by then they were near enough to see other lights, smaller pinpricks of candles or lanterns. "We're nearly there," called Musashibō encouragingly.

A house rose out of the darkness. It was not grand, but it was not small, a house as a merchant might have, if a merchant built a home beneath a dark mountainside—though Takeshi guessed they might be near to the sea. It was impossible to hear waves or smell salt through the storm, but they should still be near the coast, unless the storm had blown them too far. A storage building or workshop was attached behind, barely visible in the dark, but candles showed through the sliding doors at the front.

Musashibō kicked off his shoes at the base of the steps and mounted the porch as he called, "Please, let us in! We are monks begging shelter!"

There was a long moment, and then one of the candles moved, and a woman opened the door. "Hello? Good evening?"

"We are two monks and a servant, wrecked tonight on our journey. We beg shelter from the storm until the morning."

The woman bowed. "Of course, of course, come inside."

Takeshi had not realized how dangerously cold he was until he came near the sunken hearth near the center of the room. He was shivering uncontrollably as he stretched his hands to the irori's flames. The heat stung his burned palms and fingers, and he pulled them back, trying to flex them against their dried ooze and the cold.

Opposite him, Saburō extended his arms greedily to the heat, soaking up the warmth. His hands were unmarked, and Takeshi felt an uncharitable surge in his chest.

The woman knelt to the side between them, feeding more wood

to the flames. She adjusted the jizaikagi, lowering a hanging pot to the fire to warm. The carved fish lever seemed to stare out through the smoke.

"Thank you for your kindness," Musashibō said, settling on the fourth side of the irori.

"I will prepare a meal for you," she answered, her eyes on the fire, "and you can tell me how you came to my home."

"Is it only you here?" Saburō asked.

She did not look at him. "I have my work."

"Where have we landed?" asked Takeshi. "Are we near the sea?"

"Very near," she said. "I will serve you fresh fish."

"That will be wonderful." The words came broken through his chattering teeth before he remembered. *All living beings we eat today might have been our fathers and mothers in the past; therefore, we should refrain from eating them as much as possible.* How quickly his old habits returned under distraction, even after so much time and practice.

"Strip your wet clothes," Musashibō said, without comment on his unseemly eagerness for meat. "You'll warm faster."

"We can hang them to dry," said the woman. She rose and brought a kimono stand near to the irori.

The three men stripped to their fundoshi, unwilling to shed this last before their hostess. She hung their dripping clothes over the kimono stand, over several baskets, over a shellfish trap. Takeshi leaned so near the fire he thought he might burn, and his shivering slowed.

"Be careful," the woman cautioned. "Your skin is fine."

Takeshi looked at her and then immediately away, feeling his face warm without the fire's influence. He had not noticed before—he must have been too intent on the fire—but she had well-shaped features and sleek dark hair. He had thought her the age of his mother, but now in the firelight he thought she was younger than he had mistaken. "Ah," he said stupidly, and regretted it.

Musashibō grinned in gentle mockery. "My fellow monk is young and not yet so far removed from the world," he said. "I'm afraid it's still too easy to discomfit him."

She shook her head. "That was not my intent, and I apologize. I notice only as an artisan."

"What is your work?"

She bent over the fire, head down. "I craft men." She straightened and smiled. "Mechanical men."

"Ah! Is it possible we have come near Adachigahara?" asked Musashibō. "That is the first market in automata."

"You are not far, only a day's walk," she answered. "I sell my work there."

"What do you mean by mechanical men?" Saburō asked.

"You will not have seen them in the countryside," Musashibō explained, "but in the great cities one may find kikai shikake no ningyō, mechanized servants in the form of men. They are used for labor—or for impressing one's guests."

Takeshi had seen them. His uncle had kept one to draw water.

Musashibō continued, "But the few I have seen have been of metal, and you said you work in skin?"

She looked down again, embarrassed. "My creations are different."

A memory pricked at Takeshi's mind, something he had nearly forgotten, a dream which had been real.

"Do your ningyō bear flesh?"

"My ningyō, if I may say so, may pass for men," she said to the fire.

Musashibō smiled, a little patiently. "Your work must be like that of Ajatasatru's guards for the Buddha's relics."

"What guards?" asked Saburō.

"Long ago in India, King Ajatasatru wished to guard relics of the Buddha, and he ordered made fabulous automata which neither slept nor conversed to distraction nor grew weary of watching, and for centuries they kept their ceaseless watch."

Saburō twisted his mouth, unsure if he was being mocked or if his master was gullible. "For centuries? And you make mechanical men like that?"

The woman lifted the lid and stirred the pot of rice. "I have made no guards for the Buddha. But I have made automata for the tenno himself."

Takeshi had seen them. The memory came back to him: he had been twelve, sitting in stifling robes behind his father and uncle, and the automata had come out to dance. Even sitting so far back in court, he had been dazzled by the smooth movements, the flawless synchronization, the utter credibility of them. They were machines— the way they drooped into senseless stillness once the dance was complete demonstrated that—but they moved more smoothly and gracefully than any automata he had seen in the great houses he had visited. The courtiers had applauded and praised and there had been much talk of the maker, absent from the display.

They had been three mechanical men, with different shades of skin but dressed in identical dancers' costumes, utterly still until activated. Then their performance had been flawless, their movements fluid in a way no other automata could achieve. Whatever gears were hidden within were far more intricate than the usual machinist's miracle of movement without life.

Takeshi adjusted to distribute the fire's heat over more of his body. He wondered if he should ask about the dancing automata. He had renounced that life, and he wasn't sure if Musashibō remembered he'd once had it, and he was certain Saburō did not know. It should make no difference, and yet...

The woman dished up three bowls of rice, compressing it into neat mounds. "I'm sorry I can offer so little, but I did not expect guests this evening."

"Whatever you have will be fine," Musashibō answered readily. "We are grateful for your hospitality."

She retrieved a bucket from the rear of the room. Again near the fire, she dipped her hand into the bucket and brought out a live cuttlefish. With a deft stroke of a knife, she dispatched the creature and placed it on a mound of rice.

The knife stroke cut Takeshi as he watched. Meat was not absolutely forbidden, but when eaten, it should not have been killed specifically for the devoted practitioner. He should refuse now—but it was already killed, it was already on the plate, refusing could not give it life again, and he was so cold and so hungry...

She dipped her hand again and this time brought up a sand lance. She killed the fish and added it to another bowl.

Musashibō held up a hand as she dipped a third time. "Rice will be sufficient for me, thank you."

Takeshi avoided his eyes and hoped the senior monk could not know how his mouth watered.

The woman nodded gracefully and arranged the three bowls before her. Before she handed them the food, she uncapped a small jar and poured a brown liquid over the bowls. Takeshi gaped in horror as the cuttlefish began to writhe and flail in its bowl. As the sand lance flopped out of its bowl onto the tatami, Saburō scuttled backward.

"What magic is this?" demanded Musashibō, eyes wide but holding his place. "What spell do you have in that jar?"

The woman laughed softly. "It is no magic," she said. "This is the liquid left when making hishio or miso paste. It acts on flesh and muscle, making them move as in life."

She set a bowl before each of them with a bow. Takeshi regarded his suspiciously, as the cuttlefish finally settled on the rim of the bowl.

Saburō shook his head. "It's magic. It's bad magic."

"It is no magic, I said. It is salt against the muscles, the same mechanism which moves your own limbs. You can see there is no life in the thing; you watched me kill it." She lifted the bowl. "It gives some amusement to see it dance after death. I thought to entertain my guests."

Musashibō spoke to cover Saburō's rudeness, and to press past the question of meat killed for them and made to dance for them. "If you are a maker of automata, then that must be your workshop near here. Was it perhaps your forge which led us to you?"

Her face shuttered. "Perhaps."

"Were you working? I would be very interested to see your craft."

"No, I'm afraid not," she answered, and it wasn't clear if she answered the question or refused the implicit request.

Takeshi picked up his cuttlefish and rice, freshly guilty but hungry. The salty brown sauce was good, though it burned his stripped hand where it had been dripped over the rim by the flailing cuttlefish.

She fed the rest of the wood into the irori, so that the fire leapt between them. Takeshi was grateful for the flames and smoke which shielded him from Musashibō's eyes as he ate. The clothes spread nearest were beginning to steam. The woman said, "Please, eat. I will go and fetch more wood. But keep your eyes on the fire, lest it escape for being so large."

"You have one guardian already," said Musashibō, gesturing to the carved fish on the jizaikagi. Fish, who never closed their eyes, made admirable guardians for the fire. "But we will be your second."

She nodded. "Thank you. And please, I must ask you to stay here, by the fire. Do not go to my workshop."

Takeshi slurped down the last of the cuttlefish and licked his lips clean of sauce. "Of course," he said, though it hadn't occurred to him to visit the workshop. He had no wish to leave the fire.

The woman rose—was she older, further from the firelight? But surely the dark would be more flattering, so it must be a trick of the smoke—and went out of the room.

Musashibō ate his rice. "What kindness she has shown us," he said. "We should pray for her tonight and when we are safely in Saitoyama."

"You haven't told me yet what our task is in Saitoyama," Takeshi said. They had gotten on the airship so quickly, with barely time to pack a few meals.

"Ah, well, that hardly matters now," Musashibō said with a rueful smile. "It's going to be quite a while before we arrive there. At least it sounds like we can reach Adachigahara in a day's walk, and we should be able to find a merchant to take us from there." He sighed. "Jyuuji won't be pleased about the loss of the airship."

Saburō scowled at his rice. His fish was gone, presumably down his throat once the woman had left. "Do you believe that about the mechanical men? For the tenno?"

"They are real," Takeshi said irritably. "Or didn't you believe Musashibō when he explained to you?"

Saburō scowled. "He never saw them at the court."

Takeshi had renounced that life, renounced that position, abandoned those memories, and yet Saburō's insolence and cowardice gnawed at his abraded patience. "I have seen such work," he snapped. "Dancers at the court, mechanical but wholly unlike any stiff machine."

Saburō snorted. "Dancers at court. And you watching them." He shoved the last of the rice into his mouth and spoke through it. "Because you know more sutras than me, because you can expect rich women to offer you hospitality, you think you can tell me tales and mock my ignorance. I'm not so ignorant, and—"

"Saburō!" snapped Musashibō, an edge to his voice as Takeshi had rarely heard. "Guard your tongue, lest it drag you to a chasm."

Saburō fell silent and sullen.

"Go and help her with the wood," Musashibō said.

Saburō made a sliding sound of protest like a child told to come home from play.

"Go," Musashibō ordered, and under his tone Saburō rose and retreated across the tatami.

Takeshi was uncomfortable with the exchange, with his

resentment of the recalcitrant servant, with the uncomfortable reminders that he had not wholly relinquished his worldly attachments and expectations. He wanted to ask Musashibō about it, but should he broach the subject while the older monk was also angry with the servant?

Takeshi had just drawn breath to raise the question when Musashibō spoke. "Now that he's gone, listen."

Takeshi swallowed his words.

"We go to Saitoyama on a matter of urgency. Matakaiji has gathered warrior monks to their temple and are preparing to move against us. We received word only moments before I called you to the airship. We have asked Yamanoi-dono to help us, but we have learned there is a spy in his house who will block or change our message. We must appeal in person, or our temple will fall without aid."

Takeshi's breath was tight in his throat. "So we can't stay long."

"We have to stay the night; we cannot make time on a strange road in the dark and in this storm. But we must leave at first light."

Takeshi nodded. "Why was this a secret from Saburō?"

"There is a spy in Yamanoi's house. We don't know that there isn't one in ours."

Takeshi blinked. He thought Saburō too lazy to be a spy—but then, that was what a spy would want, wasn't it?

Musashibō smiled. "And if you wonder why I trust you, that's simple enough. Your father is allied with Yamanoi-dono, not any of the lords whom Matakaiji courts."

Takeshi nodded once. So his earthly life was not so far behind, after all. Not even in Musashibō's eyes.

What sort of monk was he? What sort could he hope to be?

The fire settled and the flames lowered. They sat in silence, waiting. Takeshi flexed his fingers in the warmth, grateful that his body had absorbed enough to feel comfortable once more. He reached to feel his robes and found them only damp. They would be ready soon. "Hasn't she been out a long time?" he wondered aloud. "And Saburō?"

Musashibō frowned. "Yes. Even if they are together, they should have returned by now."

A moment passed, and then a shriek pierced the night. It came again, this time nearer a word. "Master!" Saburō burst through the door, stumbling and catching himself with outstretched hands, running again toward the fire. "Master! Help! She is an oni—her workshop—"

He was bleeding, his face streaked with mingled blood and water under his dripping hair. Behind him came the woman, arms full of split wood. She walked tall and angry, her clear features set in disdain for the noise and mess made in her house. Saburō looked over his shoulder and cried out.

Musashibō rose to his feet. "Saburō, what is this? What's happened?"

Saburō threw himself at the monk. "Save me, master!"

Musashibō put his hands on the servant's head and shoulder, looking down at him, and then raised his head to address the woman walking evenly toward the irori. "Kind lady, I am sorry—"

She opened her arms and let the load of split wood tumble free, spilling in all directions, save for the two triangular pieces she held in each hand. These she brought together in a smooth arc directly into Musashibō's face.

Takeshi gasped and leapt to his feet. She reversed her stance and swung the clubs toward him.

***

Takeshi returned gradually to the world, drowsy with warmth and lingering dark behind his eyes. Something nagged at him, some feeling of urgency, but he was warm and lying on his back, and surely he could sleep a few minutes more.

Something was in his eye, disturbing him even though his eyes were closed. He moved to brush it out and found his arm was trapped. He shifted, and there was pressure across his wrist, keeping it in place. His head hurt.

Memory returned.

Takeshi jerked awake with an intake of breath. His wrists were bound over his head to the end of a workbench. His ankles were similarly bound at the far end. He was near the fire of the great forge, flames leaping as the woman worked the bellows.

Takeshi looked from side to side, unable to grasp at first what he saw. Everywhere in the workshop were metal figures, false bones and skulls reflecting yellow and orange in the firelight. Other figures did not shine in the light, and Takeshi realized with fresh horror that they were bones, real bones, perhaps models for the machined parts.

Past the gasp and hiss of the bellows and the crunch of charcoal, Takeshi could hear the sobbing whine of Saburō. He turned and found the servant similarly bound on another table, half-hidden on the other side of the forge.

Where was Musashibō?

"Let me go," wailed Saburō. "Please let me go."

The forge heat was uncomfortably warm against Takeshi's bare skin.

The woman straightened from the fire, and her skin seemed to glow golden as if she were a machine herself. Takeshi could not tell if she was young and beautiful or old and lined with age and smoke. She spoke to Saburō without looking as she selected from a collection of molds. "You were told not to look," she said simply. "You were told."

"I did not think they were real," Saburō moaned.

"You did not believe my words, not about my work and not my warning." She set a long mold on an empty surface and took a metal implement from the charcoal, holding it up to examine the glow. Dissatisfied, she replaced it in the fire. "You should have listened."

"I know the truth of it," Takeshi tried, pushing the words through his tight throat. "I have seen your automata dance."

She turned toward him, eyebrows raised in a question.

"I saw them dance at court. Three metal men, perfectly attuned to music played from their own bellies, with movement like the most graceful of women."

She relaxed and smiled. "Ah, you did see them. Yes, those were some of my first great successes."

Takeshi forced himself to continue. "They were amazing. You were much praised that day. Why do you bind us here?"

"The court demands wonders ever new. You would like to serve at court again, wouldn't you?"

"I am a monk," Takeshi protested stupidly, as if that renouncement could save him.

Save him from what?

But he already knew, even if his mind tried to deny it. The dead cuttlefish had danced upon the rice, bathed in salt. The fabulous automata had moved better than any gears because they were not constructed of gears.

"Let me go," pled Saburō. "Keep the monks. They will be good servants, metal men to fetch and carry. I am a bad servant."

"You will be remade," she assured him, turning to his bench. "And then you will have so much more merit to carry into your next life."

"I don't want to!" cried Saburō.

She drew out the implement again, glowing with heat. "Then you are full of demerit, and you will suffer its retribution."

Saburō screamed. He kept screaming as the woman worked. The air smelled of charcoal and hot metal and roasting meat.

Takeshi strained against his bonds. His torso was slick with sweat and burning with the relentless heat of the forge. It did not seem he could ever have been cold. He twisted his head, trying to block Saburō's shrieks, but it was impossible to escape them.

There! Musashibō was tied in a corner, head bowed and bloody. But he was alive, or he would not be bound. Takeshi had to reach him.

Takeshi had to move.

Saburō fell silent. Takeshi did not know if he had passed into unconsciousness or if he had died. The woman continued to work.

If he could slip free of his bonds... His hands were wet with sweat, and he rolled them desperately against the cord. His eye caught his bare skin gleaming in the firelight and for one hysterical instant he thought he was already burning.

With Saburō's silence, he could hear other sounds now, pulpy wet sounds. He wanted to look, but the forge blocked most of his view, and he was terrified of what he might see. He turned his head, looking automatically for Musashibō, and for a moment he could not find the monk. But there! He was along the wall, bloody and still. Had he not been in the corner?

But then, as Takeshi watched, Musashibō eased out of his drooping huddle and crept across the floor, intently watching the woman as she busied herself with Saburō. Takeshi's heart leapt.

He must have made a sound, for Musashibō jerked his eyes to him and shook his head firmly. That movement seemed to unbalance and sicken him, and he spent the next moment crouching still, bound hands pressed to his mouth, eyes flicking between the floor and the craftswoman's back. The blow to his head had been severe.. Takeshi wanted to scream with impatience.

After a time Musashibō began to crawl forward again, until he came to Takeshi's bench. He took an implement from the nearby table and sawed at the cord on Takeshi's wrists. Takeshi felt the blade bite skin, but it brought only joy even as he flinched. When the cord parted and his wrists came free, he jerked away and twisted to take the knife. Musashibō sagged to the tatami as Takeshi, watching for the craftswoman to turn from her work, cut his ankles free. Then he rolled off the bench and knelt beside the injured monk to cut him loose.

"We cannot save Saburō," Musashibō breathed.

Takeshi nodded. Musashibō was in no condition to fight.

"There is nothing to save," Musashibō continued. His face was twisted with pain and sorrow.

Guilt lanced through Takeshi. He had thought of practicality, not possibility. With a start, he realized he had been willing in his terror to simply accept his senior's words and leave the servant to die.

That was something to put away for his next time of contemplation. Now to escape to contemplate again.

He grasped Musashibō under the arms and helped the monk to his feet, sheltered by the hot forge. They started toward the rear wall and the door. As Takeshi put his back to the forge, the blessedly cooler air of the door's draft slapped him.

Cold rain sliced into their unprotected skin, and Takeshi's battered head throbbed with his movement. Even with Takeshi's arms around him, Musashibō fell down the step to the ground. Takeshi managed to catch him enough to blunt injury and fatal sound, but the monk clung to him and gasped, "I cannot flee. Run, Takeshi, run without me."

He could not leave another, not so hard upon leaving the first. But Musashibō was correct—they could not hope to escape at his pace, much less manage the mountain and the long flight to help.

He turned to the house and its raised veranda. "Hide here," he said, lowering the monk. "Stay out of sight, and I'll lead her away."

How he would return for the senior monk he had no idea, but it was better than leaving him in the madwoman's hands. Musashibō wriggled into the mud and slid back. Muddied and in the dark, he vanished.

Takeshi wanted to say a blessing, to say anything, but his mind went blank. With Musashibō out of his arms, raw panic returned, and he wanted only to run.

An inhuman shriek came from the workshop, but it was not Saburō. The sound was born of rage, not pain, though it promised pain.

Takeshi fought every fiber in his being to hold in place. *Not yet.*

Not yet. If he was gone when she came, she would search and find Musashibō.

A figure loomed dark in the workshop door, silhouetted with leaping orange firelight, and a second uncanny shriek reached into the rainy dark, questing for them.

Now!

Takeshi choked on terror and ran straight ahead, his bare feet numbing on the wet ground as the rain pelted him.

She followed from the workshop, and something came with her. It moved like a man, but Takeshi knew better. For an instant he imagined it was Saburō, already fully an automaton of flesh, but he shoved that aside and thought of perfectly synchronized dancers.

That was hardly reassuring.

He was on the mountainside, running along the slope. His head pounded, but he pressed on. He should have run toward Adachigahara, should have run toward a port on the sea—but he had no idea which direction they might be. He would lose himself on the mountain, and if he survived this night he would try to walk for help in the morning.

Lightning flashed above him. He was naked and lost on an unfamiliar mountain in a storm, with a monster and its unholy creation in pursuit. He would not survive this night.

Despite the storm, despite the clatter of his stumbling over rocks, he could hear her behind him. He could feel her rage, hot through the cold storm. She was coming for him. He turned and saw a light glowing behind him, like kitsune-bi but borne by something even more terrible.

Takeshi would die here. Wounded Musashibō would die under the veranda, of his injury and the cold or when he was discovered. Yamanoi-dono would not receive the message, their temple would be attacked, and many more would die. They had failed utterly.

He slid and stumbled as he clawed up the mountainside. Rain slashed his exposed skin and stung his eyes, but he could see little in the dark between lightning flashes anyway. He was climbing by feel, hoping for some miraculous escape as he fled up the mountain.

One should be in a virtuous state of mind before death to aid in a better rebirth. But he could think of nothing but his terror.

The trees parted, and he came out upon a wide clearing of puddled stone, a section of mountain cleared by lava and not yet fallen to regrowth. Lightning flashed and he saw a broken edge perhaps a dozen paces away, vanishing into the rainy dark. He was shivering with cold and horror, and his hands and feet were bleeding into the rain.

Takeshi turned and saw her ascending, marked by the glow of her brass lantern shining in defiance of the storm. Its light was unnaturally steady, not a candle but an abomination of chemicals like those which powered her automata.

She stepped out of the trees and faced him.

His choice was clear. He could kill her—a violation of his vows, his character, all but his very human desire to live, and a difficult challenge given his condition and her vicious relentlessness—or he could take himself from her. The cliff was just behind him, undoubtedly plunging to stones below. A mountain crag was not so bad a place to die.

Takeshi gulped and choked. Rain pelted his face, mixing with his tears.

Namu Amida Butsu. He tried to focus on the name that would bring him to the Pure Land. *Namu Amida Butsu.* Man could not achieve liberation though his own efforts but must call upon offered help. Faith was all that could save him, even if only through death.

Oh, but he did not want to die.

The strength of his desire to live frightened him nearly as much as the monster pursuing him. What sort of monk could he be, considering whether he could kill a woman with his bare hands?

Namu Amida Butsu. But surely the Buddha would not hear so pitiful a devotee.

Takeshi stooped for a broken piece of stone.

The woman—how could he have ever thought her beautiful?—stepped forward, streaming like a murderous water spirit come on land. She had a harpoon in her hand, with a jagged hook facing him. Behind her, slowed by the mountainside but doggedly persevering, came the automaton, straightening upright as it came to the more level ground. Its face was mercifully bland, a figure of metal and stoicism. It raised bladed arms as she pointed and spoke a command.

If Takeshi meant to fight, he should do it now. He could rush her, strike her with the stone just as she had struck him with the wood. He sucked in a breath. He wanted to close his eyes, but he could not tear them from the bronze and brass death before him.

Namu Amida Butsu.

Lightning flashed, muting the electric lantern, and something enormous loomed over them in the sky. Takeshi looked up, trying to pick out the shape with dazzled eyes.

Lightning came again, and Takeshi saw a woman floating above. She was all white and gold, dazzling in the burn of the sky, and her robes hovered like birds caught in the wind. Floating lights streamed back on either side, dots of gold in the night sky.

Kanzeon Bosatsu. The bodhisattva of compassion and mercy, descending from the heavens. Takeshi gaped, rain falling into his open mouth.

The mad craftswoman saw her too. She leaned her head back and raised an arm to shield her eyes. She opened her mouth to speak.

Lightning cracked and the world went white. Incandescent power threw Takeshi backward, and he cowered on the ground, hugging the rippled rock and sobbing.

It ended in a heartbeat, but he could not move for much longer, blind and deaf and terrified. At last he pressed himself up and turned back, but all was dark but for the floating lights still in the sky.

The lights shifted and rotated, staying in perfect alignment, and then lowered. Takeshi stared as a dark shape between the lights came slowly into view—the swell of a hull. An airship. The mast was splintered and smoking, and the hull was jagged, and no one clung to the railing or responded to the fire. A ghost ship.

Their ship.

He blinked and saw, in the next flash, the trailing chain which carried lightning from the ship's thunder-rod out into the air. He scrabbled back as the ship came about.

Lightning flashed, illuminating the twisted molten sculpture on the clearing of stone. The woman hung stooped and motionless, one arm extended with the hand dangling grotesquely loose. Her automaton had partially vaporized and melted in the lightning strike, and they were fused together in a circle of slagged stone.

Takeshi's legs gave out and he fell back on the stone, stinging his hands. He looked up again for the bodhisattva.

But it was not Kanzeon Bosatsu. The woman, lit again by a flash, was the figurehead of the ship, wind-tossed with one merciful arm extended. Only a figurehead, on a ship which had intervened to prevent the death of his body or the death of his soul.

Takeshi crawled to his feet and went toward the ship, keeping his eye on the steaming chain as if watching it could prevent another strike and explosion. Rigging dragged from the broken boom, and as the ship drifted near the clearing, it hung low enough to nearly make a ladder up to the deck. He gritted his teeth against the pain in hands and feet and climbed aboard the ship.

He had to reach the workshop and Musashibō at the base of the mountain. He cut free a wedge of torn canvas and rigged it to a long rod, affixing both to the stern. A lashing to stabilize the sweep of the makeshift rudder made it easier to handle. Takeshi heaved, ignoring the searing in his palms, and to his amazement the ship responded.

He was not a good aeronaut at the best of times, and especially not when he was naked and shivering, spent with cold and exhaustion, bleeding from hands and feet and managing a crippled airship. He barely held the small airship on a line for the forgefire glowing bright against the night, but the shuddering ship stayed on course.

When he had found Musashibō, they would go into the empty house and sit by the fire. Not the fire where Saburō lay among all the pieces and parts, man and machine—no, they would sit by the irori and bathe in its homey warmth. They would wrap themselves in thick, fluffy kakebutons and drink hot tea and think of nothing, nothing at all.

In the morning, when the storm had cleared and the sun shone too brightly to allow for nightmares or memories, they would bury Saburō and the other bones. And then, on the way to Saitoyama, Takeshi would reflect on his fresh opportunity to live out his path.

Laura VanArendonk Baugh writes both award-winning speculative fiction in a variety of flavors and bestselling non-fiction about animal behavior and training. Though she has summited extinct, dormant, and active volcanoes, none has accepted her sacrifice. She enjoys travel and making her imaginary friends fight each other for made-up reasons. She lives in Indianapolis with her husband, her dogs, and a prepper stash of emergency dark chocolate. Find her (and free stories) at LauraVAB.com

ꜰATHER ꜰWORM

Adam Breckenridge

When she was a child, the ruby necklace Amber's mother had given her after her first bird ceremony would reflect the sunlight so brightly that even a glance at one of its faces would sear its anger onto her eyes for an hour or more. The vertical slits of fire they left behind when she blinked reminded her of her cat Hunter, and for as long as the glow lasted she believed herself imbued with the same predator's lust. She would pounce around the house, tearing at imaginary birds until she regained her human vision and became a docile girl again, sitting in the shadows and watching Hunter lazing in the sunlight, no doubt absorbing the inspiration for his next kill.

Though Amber had long abandoned this particular fancy, the association of the sun with bloodlust had never left her. Even now, after so many years of the sun's light dwindling until even on a summer morning such as this, her necklace barely glimmered in his wan light, she still imagined the old sun as a thing with teeth, consuming anything that dared venture into his firmament.

Amber stopped her examination of the necklace, dropping it back in place as she looked out the window, past the yard and its rows upon rows of long empty birdcages, to a hill on the other side of town where her new destiny awaited her. The Steel Swallow, the creature that would carry her and as many people of her town as she could still motivate to leave, waited to carry her into that same firmament, to seek some place in the heavens where the sun's glow was still fierce enough to bite. At noon she would take her place at the captain's chair, she and her crew the first humans to ever leave the good earth behind them.

Hunter lay in the sunlight, tail twitching, perhaps still absorbing the sun's fury, though neither he nor the sun had much fury left. Hunter hadn't brought Amber a kill in years. It was perhaps only fancy that she associated his aging laziness with the sun's waning light, but all the same Amber had a place for Hunter on the Steel Swallow alongside her. Even if the trip didn't reinvigorate her old friend, she would not let her duties as captain keep her from the obligation all keepers of animals have to see their beloved companions through to their deaths. She above all knew how sacred a task it was.

She scooped Hunter up in her arms. He was too old to give much protest and settled quietly into her embrace. She looked around at her ancestral home, taking the familiar walls in for the last time. For generations beyond measure her family had lived here and kept watch over the valley and its people. When two villagers had a dispute they would come to the manor for judgment. When crisis hit, whether flood or fire, it fell upon her family to lead the fight against it. And, most sacred of all, it had been their job to prepare the birds for their hallowed ceremony, and now she was set to follow in their path.

**

Some of Amber's earliest memories were watching her father walk among the ark of birds they caged in the yard, singing to them in whistlesong, his melody sowing some frenzy into them that she could only assume was patriarchal love. Amber knew how much she loved her father and, tiny as she was, tinier still was every bird who flitted around in their cages, burning a profound energy that she believed was their inability to contain their love for him within their frail bodies. She would run among the cages, trying to match the wavelength of their energy, whistling to them her own songs of love. She always stopped before she exhausted herself too much, because she feared that if she burned herself out she would have no more love to give.

At the end of every month her father would take some of the cages through the village to the hill on the other side of the valley. There he would release them in a ceremony she was forbidden to attend. "He's giving the birds back to the sun," her mom would tell her, the only explanation she was ever given.

On every occasion of this ceremony Amber would devise a scheme to slip away from the care of Whitlock, the family's mechanical servant, who could anticipate her plans as deftly as a grandmaster playing chess against a novice. Every time she thought she had mastered her escape she would turn a corner to find him waiting for her. "I have more eyes than you know," he'd laugh as he scooped her up and carried her back to the house on his shoulders, steam blowing in her face from the valve in the back of his head as he chuckled at his own cleverness. It always felt like rain to her.

"Why am I not allowed to watch the birds go free?" she asked him once.

"Because there is a truth to the ceremony that you are not ready for," he'd say, "and when you learn it, you will long for your innocence."

For most of the rest of the month Amber could forget her curiosity in watching her father sing to the birds and dig through the yard for worms to feed them with. This task Amber was allowed to help with. The dirt beneath the grass had a kingdom of worms, so many that Amber swore the ground sometimes wobbled with their movements. Even in her small hands a clump of dirt would have a whole family of them, squirming between her fingers, exploring her skin, slipping away sometimes to plop back into the earth. The feeling of them disgusted her, and yet she would sometimes crouch down to wonder at the little holes they made and where they might lead.

"They're beautiful aren't they," her father had asked her once while she'd been studying their movements. He'd been standing between her and the sun, so that when she looked up at him she was blinded even in the presence of his shadow.

"You don't mean the worms, do you?" she'd asked.

"What else would I mean? They're the only creatures brave enough to hide themselves from the sun." He paused a moment. "And we give their lives to these idiot birds."

That was the first time she'd heard her father express his love for the worms. That love was as repulsive to her as the worms themselves, but fascinating too in its way. The birds also loved them, so much so that they'd eat them. It was strange though, to love something so much that you would eat it. Surely that was madness.

Her dad never ate the worms, but he'd study them for long hours when he should have been tending to the birds, sitting beneath an umbrella running his hands through the earth, sometimes refusing to come in until the sun had set. His obsession with the worms was growing and it got to the point that her mother no longer let Amber out in the yard with him. She would hide in the house and listen to her mother out in the yard yelling at her father beneath his umbrella.

"Your duty is to the birds."

"Damn the birds and damn every feather on them. We were wrong to ever look to the sky for life."

Whitlock's thousand eyes would find Amber's hiding places when she eavesdropped, and he'd scoop her away to the kitchen to feed her bits of fruit and soothe her worry.

"Never a couple that hasn't fought," he'd say, putting a slice of apple to her lips, her eyes fixating on the miniscule gears visible between the hinges of his fingers, "and often over sillier things than birds and worms. I've always been partial to fruit myself. They grow from the earth and reach up to the sky and are beloved by birds and worms alike. Learn from the apple, my child. It contains true wisdom."

"But how can you love apples if you can't eat?" she asked him.

"Well how can I love you if I can't eat you?" was his response.

Her conversations with Whitlock, and the apples he fed her, kept her centered. She could grasp the madness that was consuming the house, and understood what it meant when dad moved out into an old, disused groundskeeper hut in the yard while mother started tending to the birds in his stead. Her mother spun fairy tales for her to try to soothe her: that dad wanted to live life more simply and spend more time gardening. Amber lacked the words to tell her mom she understood what was really going on, but her mother must have seen something in her eyes because in the middle of one of her stories she stopped and studied Amber for a moment before saying, "I think you're ready to help me take care of the birds now."

She led Amber out into the yard, walking her amongst the cages for a while before asking, "have you ever really listened to the songs we sing to the birds?"

Amber thought about how beautiful they were, but she knew that wasn't what her mom meant.

"Can I hear them again?" she asked.

Her mother began her whistle and, this time, she focused on the music, its melismatic cadence that veered from near supra-audible piercings to notes so gentle they were really just exhalations. Amber listened, and the longing the song wove into her was unbearable. She strained her back trying to sprout wings so she could fly from it, or rather fly towards the radiant source of her desire: the ever-burning sun, whose gigantic heat held the promise of a love bigger than anything this silly earth could possibly hold, all-consuming and transformative and out of her grasp only because she was a slave to gravity...

Then her mother stopped whistling and the longing left her as quickly as a ghost. Amber blushed, feeling stupid for allowing herself to fall so easily into its dishonesty, but the birds were still enraptured.

Her mother spoke.

"The song we sing them is about the divine love of the sun and the bliss they will feel when flying into his embrace. The song's power fades quickly for you because you are too smart for its tale to hold sway for any length. But the birds: they are gullible. They believe the song as completely as you believe in yourself. For generations it has been the duty of our men to sing to the birds, but your father...well the task is ours now. I must teach you how to sing to them, and at the end of this month you can attend the ceremony of the birds."

Amber saw the shadow that passed over her mother's eyes at the mention of her father. She had seen little of him since he had retreated to the hut, only occasional glimpses of him digging the earth for worms, which he now only did at night. She wanted to talk to him, but was afraid to approach the hut. Only slowly had she come to understand that she was losing her father, and only at this moment did she also understand how much heavier that loss weighed on her mother than it did on her.

Her mother went back to tending to the birds, answering their questions about the sun and feeding them, Amber observed, apples.

"We're not supposed to feed them apples," her mother said, "but I'll cut this hand off before I dig into this earth for even a single worm."

Over the next two weeks Amber's mother taught her the birdsong. It was a simple language for simple creatures, posing little difficulty for conscious minds. Amber took to the music of it, loved singing to them of the beneficent sun because when she did she could feel the euphoria as keenly as the birds did. There was no other time in her life when she was that happy, not even when preparing for her first bird ceremony.

***

The townspeople all knew of the insanity that had gripped Amber's father and quietly mourned for him. There were others whose minds had been struck from them by the sun's heat, who lived only for shade and night. The families of these people hid them away out of shame and, as best they could, tried to go on as though they didn't exist. But for the king of the manor to fall prey to this delusion: that was too big to ignore. It shook them deeply.

Thus it was that the procession through the town had the air of a funeral, mother and Amber leading the way, no sound except the hissing and cranking of the cart loaded with the birds who would be set free that day. The townspeople waited quietly outside their homes and stores until the cart passed before joining the procession. Amber had heard the echoes of their celebration in past ceremonies and their silence now was despairing. Was this dour affair really to be her first bird ceremony?

She began to whistle the birdsong. Her mother followed suit and they were joined soon by the townspeople. They didn't know the notes, but they had melodies of their own that wove between the old harmonies of faith, the discordant songs building into something as crystalline as the firmament and that Amber was sure she could pluck out of the air if she'd wanted to. Even the hissing of the cart's steam engine fit into the melody they sung.

They arrived at the hilltop in better spirits, her mother standing at its crest, surrounded by the cages. She spoke to the townspeople.

"Today we give these birds to the sun, who has waited to take them into his embrace as anxiously as they have longed to be embraced by him."

She began to whistle a song Amber hadn't heard before, one about arriving at one's destiny and the glory of finding yourself at the pinnacle of your life. This one didn't move Amber the way the song of the sun's love did, but she saw the tears in the eyes of the townspeople and saw the proud stature of the birds. For whatever reason this song was not for her. Or, perhaps, not yet for her.

The song over, Amber's mother began unlatching the bird's cages, moving quickly, not wanting to keep them from their destiny any longer than necessary. They flew straight up, towards the noonday sun, and were quickly lost in his glare. Amber had to look away, lest the sun take her vision of whatever was to come next. She stared down at the earth, feeling for the undulations of the worms beneath her, when someone shouted, "Here they come!"

Amber looked up, at first seeing nothing, but then, as though emerging from the sun himself, came little bundles of fire, dozens of them, every flame a bird returning to earth. The sun had seared them, turning them back homeward bound in ash.

Amber felt tears form. This was deception. This was betrayal. But by god it was beautiful. It was as though the sun were sending his own children to rain down on them.

The carcasses of the birds thumped to the ground, the flames extinguishing on impact, leaving their blackened husks to litter the earth. Amber's mother picked one of them up and ripped it open. The townspeople around them were doing the same.

Smoke drifted out of the birds' breasts and Amber watched it vanish into the firmament. She held back her tears. At least some part of the bird would ascend to heaven.

Her mother removed the bird's heart. It was cooked through but the simmering heat gave it the illusion that it still beat. She thrust it towards Amber.

"Eat," she said.

Amber took the heart, uncertain, but she could see in her mother's eyes that this was something she had to do. She ate. She could taste the bird's love and terror in its flesh. It was the most delicious thing she had ever tasted.

When they returned home her mother disappeared into her room and returned a moment later holding something glimmering in her hands. It was a necklace with a ruby in it that, depending on how

Amber held it, resembled either a heart or an apple.

"I wept for hours after my first bird ceremony," she said, "your strength today was astonishing."

"But why do we do it?" Amber asked. "Why do we kill the birds?"

"Because the sun truly does love them," she said, "but he has only one way to show it."

***

Not long after, it became the norm to wake up every morning to fresh holes that had been dug in the yard during the night. There was only one person who could be doing it. Amber tried to stay awake many nights to catch him at it, keeping herself occupied with books on the mechanics of flight and the mysteries of the firmament, but Whitlock always arrived with a glass of milk that had been warmed by the heat of his coils to put her to sleep when she climbed out of bed to stare out the window, always tucking Hunter in alongside her too.

"Sometimes madness is only a stage someone has to pass through," he'd said to her once while tucking her in.

Whatever mystery lay behind the holes was chipping away at her mother. Amber could see her skin sagging, her frame bending. Amber feared she was getting ready to succumb to some madness of her own and tried to talk to her about it but would always get cut off.

Finally, Amber decided to take matters into her own hands. She waited until her mom had gone into town and approached the gardener's hut. She knocked on the door.

"It's open," she heard her dad's voice say.

Amber went in. It was dark inside, made all the darker by her sun-kissed vision from tending to the birds all afternoon. She could only see shadowy hazes, but there was one in particular that she was sure was her father.

"Shut the door," he said. His voice was gentle.

She closed the door behind her, casting the place deeper into darkness.

"The sun has taken your vision," he said, "you'll need some time to be able to see properly again."

His shadow moved towards her and she felt his hand on her arm. It was her father's touch. She let him guide her to a chair.

"Your mother has been causing you undue worry," he said.

"She's been worried herself," Amber said.

"This may seem like madness to others but the sun got to be too violent for me. I needed to get away from him for a while, maybe for good."

Amber still couldn't make out anything in the shed but she felt something crawling up her shoe and onto her leg. A worm. She reached down for it.

"He won't hurt you. He only wants to know you. Worms have to experience the world by touch. They don't have any other way to understand things."

Amber let the worm be and tried to sit still as it crawled around the rim of her sock. It was soon joined by another.

"I've been learning how to communicate with them," he said, "like we do with the birds, but their language is nothing like ours. They have no vocalizations. They speak through movement. I've had to retrain my mind to understand it but in a way it's more beautiful than birdsong."

Her eyes were slowly adjusting to the darkness. Her father's outline was clear but his features were still muddled in shadow. More worms were feeling at her legs.

"Do worms have anything to say?" she asked.

"More than the birds," he said. "We've been so dedicated to the sun that we forget he's only half the world. Less, really. He's only one layer of the firmament but, in his vanity, he works so hard to outshine the rest of the heavens that we have to wait until nightfall to see what the cosmos has to offer us. It was a mistake to think the sun represented wisdom. The sun, really, is the light of arrogance. But the worms, their holes take them to places beyond our world."

Amber thought of the birds falling from heaven in flames. She had attended several more bird ceremonies since her first and the pain of the betrayal was dulled considerably since that first experience, and the flesh of the birds' hearts had tasted sweeter each time. Could the night, and his worms, really have anything better to offer?

"You've been to the bird ceremonies now, I can tell," he said. "You've made peace with the lies you tell the birds already. It's easy to rationalize it. Believe me, I still haven't shed my taste for those innocent hearts, but the night demands no sacrifice. He lets everyone pass in peace."

The hut was finally coming into focus. There were rivers of worms moving along the floor, many of them gathering around her shoes to take their turns at feeling the new arrival. Many more were gathered at her father's feet and they showed the affection of dogs. They loved him. They were crawling up the legs of his pants. She could see their movements beneath his clothes, under his shirt. Then she saw his face and screamed.

The worms had eaten holes into his skin, highways in his flesh that they burrowed through with the familiarity of home. They were living in him. They were part of him.

"Don't be afraid," he said, trying to soothe her, "they don't hurt me. They're gentle, they are—"

But she was already running for the door and was outside before he could say anything else. She heard him calling after her but she ignored it.

The sun was blinding. She had to close her eyes, finding her way by touch until she crashed into the birdcages. She held onto one of them, listening to the worried song of the bird inside and slowly opening her eyes until the sun no longer hurt. She looked around.

Her dad had closed the door to the hut. He was back in the darkness, which was where she wanted him.

There was a worm still exploring her ankle. She felt the rhythm of its movements for a while before picking it up. She had no interest in anything it had to say. She opened the door to the cage she had been gripping and offered the worm to the bird, who took it gladly. She reached in and pulled out the bird. She was crying. She held the bird to her chest and sang to it, thinking about the taste of its heart.

***

Amber never told her mother about the state her father was in. Indeed they never discussed him at all except to the extent that occasional uncomfortable glances towards the hut and the unspoken tension itself counted as any sort of communication. If her mother knew how he had given himself over to the worms she gave no indication and Amber, though she was growing ever older and wiser, still lacked the perception to guess the extent of her mother's knowledge. When she pried Whitlock about it, he would only tell her that her mother carried heavy burdens.

They lived for years with this unease, Amber growing into womanhood, distracting herself with her studies of aviation and the firmament, and her mother growing into tattered fragility, with nothing but the bird ceremonies to keep her going, until they started going wrong.

The change was gradual, a slow deterioration of the heart meat that few noticed until, after awhile, it was plain to all that the blood dribbling between their teeth was from undercooked hearts. The sun seemed to be losing heart, drifting away from his duties. Was it only their imagination to think he was getting further away every year? It seemed absurd, but they couldn't deny that it had never been so easy to look at the sun without punishing your eyes.

It was on the walk back from one of these dismal ceremonies that Amber's mom said, "We have to talk to your father."

Amber followed her mom to the shed.

"Why do we need him now?" Amber asked as they approached the door.

"He was in communion with the sun far longer than you or I and the sun's secrets have always been handed down to the men of the family. We need that knowledge now."

She knocked and they sat and waited a long while with no sound beyond the door. She knocked again. After more silence she reached for the handle. Amber backed away.

"Mom, you…"

But her mother had already opened the door before she could say anything else. The shed was as dark as before but it was clear there was no motion here. Amber blinked at the darkness, trying to make it come into focus. Her mother was forging ahead but took only a few steps before she vanished with a yelp.

Amber ran in after her, stopping short at her mother's mistake. There was a hole in the middle of the hut, big enough for a man, and her mother had fallen into it. She had not fallen far, her head and shoulders were still above ground, but she was groaning in pain. Amber grabbed her under the arms and pulled her out.

"Are you hurt?"

"I think I twisted my ankle," she said. "What is this hole?"

Amber went to the boarded windows and started prying away at the slats, allowing little worms of light to make their way in as she broke them free. Soon the sun was back in the hut, and he showed them the details of the scene.

It was a worm hole, or at least what a worm hole would look like if worms were as big as men. Amber stared at it, understanding intrinsically what this meant, but her brain refused to confront the implications, to grasp how deep her father's transformation had gone. Her mother was staring at the hole too.

"He can't have… he would never… he was…" She looked up at Amber. "Did you know how far gone he was?"

"I haven't seen him in years," Amber said. She crept forward to the edge of the hole. It went straight down about four feet and then turned sharply. From there who knows where it went. The thought of following the path made her sick.

Her mom was crying.

"I could have stopped this. If only I had known. Why didn't I check on him in all these years?"

Amber helped her up and back into the house, the whole way listening to her mother cry, "I should have known, I should have done something…"

Later that night Amber was awoken by a light outside her window. A fire. She ran to the window to see the shed in flames and the shadow of Whitlock standing beside it. Amber ran downstairs and out the door, not even bothering to put on shoes. She ran until she stood beside Whitlock, who was far too calm.

"It needed to burn," he said to her. He stood silent a moment. Amber hadn't noticed until now that Whitlock too had been aging, rust forming at his extremities, his gears clanking in ways they never had before. "I failed your family. The madness was planted deeper than I realized, and I failed to root it out. It's best for me to move on now. This," he indicated the fire, "is my last duty to your family."

Amber looked up at him. Even the reflection of the flames dancing on his glass eyes couldn't mask the sorrow there.

"You can't go," she said, "we need you."

He looked at her, and the fire didn't reflect in his eyes when he turned to face her.

"No, my child, you have no more need of me. Keep your mother's grief from consuming her and pay careful attention to the sun. He is softening, and the people will look to you to take action as he fades." He turned back to the fire. "I built it carefully. It won't spread. By the morning it will only be ash and smoke, but stay and watch it if you wish. A good fire can burn away so much. Goodbye, my child."

He turned and walked into the shadows, seeming to vanish far too quickly. Amber wanted to chase after him but she stopped when she felt something rubbing against the soles of her feet. The earth was moving, tracing a pattern on her skin. It was her father, speaking to her in worm-motion, the language so intrinsically simple that she understood it almost immediately.

"Daughter, it is peaceful down here. Do not fear for me. Take care of your mother."

The message tickled. She lifted her foot, examining the dirt coating her skin. She could just make out faint, wormlike patterns in it, and the flickering flames seemed to give them life.

***

Amber tried to make good on the requests from her father and from Whitlock to care for her mother, but she was beyond any care Amber could provide. Her husband's transformation had broken her mind, sent her inward to spiral around her failings. She went through her daily motions so mechanically she hardly noticed the ashen remnants of the gardener's hut or the fact that her daughter now went everywhere barefoot, even to the bird ceremony. Even the birds seemed less receptive to the sun song, or maybe it was just the general atmosphere that hung about the manor that dampened their spirits.

Fewer people were attending the bird ceremony and none but her mother still ate the hearts of the now only lightly singed birds that fell back to the earth. Not even Hunter, on those occasions when he followed them to the ceremony, would touch the carcasses. Amber was obligated to go through the motions to appease her, palming the heart and pretending to chew, digging her feet into the earth hoping to hear word from her father. Occasionally she did feel him greet her through the ground beneath her, but his attentions came far too rarely to give her much comfort.

The bird ceremony was the one tenuous thread of sanity her mother still clung to, and it seemed to Amber that as long as she could delude herself they were going well she could keep it together, maybe even rebuild herself. But there was now no denying that the sun was getting colder and dimmer.

The end came shortly before Amber's eighteenth birthday. Her mother trudged through the village alongside the cart as usual, Amber helping, trying not to look the villagers in the eyes as she passed. They were growing more lethargic with the retreating of the sun.

Most of them just sat at home, not even bothering to run their businesses. They were looking sick and scrawny and showed Amber and her mother none of the accolades they used to enjoy whenever they came into town. Curiously Amber herself felt little of their demotivation, and her mother was too much in the grip of madness to notice it either. Amber looked up at the sun. It was now possible to stare directly at it without hurting her eyes.

Only eight villagers joined them on the hilltop, all of them younger men and women who still found it easier to cling to their energy. Her mother recited the usual words, then opened the cages. The birds flew off towards the sun. They waited a long time, the wind getting colder as they stared up at the sky. Amber wondered whether keeping communion with the earth was worth exposing her skin to this chill.

Her mother was the last one there to understand that the birds weren't coming back. They had fulfilled the promise of the sun song, finding paradise somewhere in the firmament.

"No," her mother said, "no no no, this isn't—that's not how this—"

Her hands were shaking and soon her whole body was trembling. She was trying to work her mouth, but she was somewhere beyond language now. She collapsed, curling into herself, emitting an anguished cry that could easily have been mistaken for the wind. Amber knelt down beside her, trying to comfort her, but her mother had retreated too deep within herself.

One of the villagers helped Amber load her mother onto the cart and helped her back to the manor. It was all Amber could do to coax her mother into walking through the door and up the stairs to her room. After she laid her mother down Amber went outside and started stomping the ground and pounding it with her fists, trying to get her father's attention. Now not even the worms bothered to answer her. She was alone now. It was on her to do something about this situation.

***

The next day she marched into town, stood in the middle of the street, and spoke to whoever would listen to her.

"We must follow the sun," she said, "follow the birds. If we stay here we'll die. Can't you feel the life draining out of you?"

They had of course felt it, but lethargy was a hard thing to cure. Inspiration, however, was a good panacea for it, and those listening felt some small stirring of their old vigor returning.

"I have been studying the heavens these past years, and I've been studying the machinery of the great minds of man. There is a way. We can build a bird of our own, one of metal that can carry us to the heavens, to a higher layer of the firmament, put us back in the warmth of the sun. But it needs all of us working together to get it done. There will be no more bird ceremonies. There will only be our steel bird."

Amber found she could work the same magic onto the people that she had worked into the birds with the sun song. She could reinvigorate them, get them moving again. She instructed them to collect everything metal in their possession. It was a brutal sacrifice, for everything beautiful and precious they owned had some bit of metal in it, but the people gave up their heirlooms and trinkets, their gadgets and machines for this project. Amber looted the manor for her own family's metal too, sacrificing everything except the ruby locket around her neck.

Telling her mother about this project was, she would quickly learn, a grievous error. Her mother had not left her bed since Amber had put her there. She would no doubt have starved if Amber hadn't been bringing her apples from the yard. She'd had some hope the apples would help her mother recover some of her sanity, but even apples proved to be just useless flesh. Instead Amber told her that she was building a machine that would let them follow the birds.

"Follow the birds?" her mother asked.

She sprung out of bed, so quickly that Amber couldn't react, a well of latent energy driving her down the stairs and out to the backyard. Amber chased after her. Out in the yard she heard cries of "Follow the birds!" and the sound of flapping wings.

Her mother was opening the cages, beckoning the birds to break free. Most of them stayed put, fearing perhaps the unwarranted freedom or the madness of one of the soothsayers that was so plain even they understood it for what it was. Some seized the moment to fly to the sun, ceremony or no, because why miss the chance to return to your beneficent provider?

"Fly, fly," her mother shouted, flapping her arms. She looked at the ground, then at Amber. "But how are we supposed to fly, my dear?"

"I'm building a ship of metal, mother."

"But metal can't fly, my daughter. The birds will have to carry us."

Her mother whistled a command to the birds to come to her. They flitted from their cages, landing on her outstretched arms, packing themselves in so tightly they could barely move, much less spread their wings when her mother gave the command to carry her into the air with them.

"Mother, stop this," Amber shouted, "this is insane." She started picking the birds off and setting them free to do as they please, most of them returning to their cages. Her mother fell to her knees.

"We're earthbound, wormbound," she said, "the sun is never ours. Unless…" She looked up at the sky. "…they carry us in pieces."

Amber slapped her mother, an action that shocked even her, but at least it stopped her insane reasoning.

"Let's take you back upstairs," Amber said.

Her mother went quietly and allowed Amber to guide her back to her bed.

The next morning Amber awoke to a far-too quiet house. There was no sound from her mother's room and no sound outside, not even the rustling of the birds. Amber went to the window, and what she saw in the yard was a horror beyond anything.

She ran downstairs and out to the yard. The dew and her mother's blood were frigid against her skin. In her right hand her mother held a blood-spattered meat cleaver and her left hand was gone, a few wayward bits of flesh showing that she hadn't done it in one clean chop. Her feet, too, were gone and slices and chunks were cut from her legs and face. There was no telling how long she had been at it before she had succumbed to her own injuries.

The birds had taken what they could on their flight to the sun, but left behind far more than Amber could bear.

She doubled over, puking up the bits of the apple she had eaten the night before. She wanted to forget all of this, wipe it from her memory, but even after she looked away her mother's body was still there. It would never not be there. It was a permanent scar on her mind.

She stayed on her hands and knees, eyes closed against the horror, wishing the sun had the decency to warm her. The air against her back stayed cold but the ground was getting warmer, trembling. Amber opened her eyes to see a flurry of worms pulling her mother's body into the earth.

"Daughter, look away," her dad's voice rumbled through the earth, "do not remember your mother like this. I will keep her close to my heart down here. You must do the same."

Amber looked away again until the trembling stopped. She was alone now: her mother, her father, Whitlock, even the birds, they were all gone. She lay there until the earth grew cold again. She heard footsteps approaching.

"Ma'am?" A voice said.

Who was calling her ma'am? She wasn't a ma'am, she was only nineteen, ma'am was her mother...

She looked up. It was one of the young men from the village, doing his best not to show his discomfort at the sight of her in a nightgown and haggard from crying.

"We're ready to begin work," he said.

There was no evidence of her sorrow anywhere now. The worms had even taken the blood off the grass. But she still had her work, the ship they had come to call the Steel Swallow.

"I'll be there in a moment," she said.

***

Work was the only thing that could stave off her grief. She sang to the workers the same songs she used to sing to the birds. They didn't understand the bird language, but the melody provided the light the sun failed to bring, kept them energized, kept the project going.

The elderly of the village died off quickly, their will to live whittled down to naught until they couldn't even be bothered to raise food to their lips. Within a few months no one over the age of sixty was still left alive in the village and even many of the middle-aged residents began to die off too. The creeping despair of the sun's retreat even worked its way into some of the younger workers. By the time the Steel Swallow neared its completion, the population of the village was less than half of what it had been in warmer times.

Amber lived apart from them, retreating to the manor when the day's work was done and quietly nursing her grief for her lost family, only the aging Hunter to keep her company, until the following morning when she emerged again to direct the labor. By the time the Steel Swallow was completed there was almost no one left for Amber to lead into the firmament, but the task was all she had left in her life.

And then the day came for her to look one last time around her ancestral home and, for the first time in years, slip her feet into a pair of boots for the journey to the Steel Swallow and beyond. If her father had anything to say to her today, she wasn't interested.

The village was far too quiet for such a day. What was left of the people should have been emerging to greet her. This should have been a new sort of bird ceremony, but she was met only with silence. Then in the road she saw a hole as big as the one her father had disappeared into all those years ago.

She ran into the nearest house, Hunter nearly jumping from her arms in alarm, bursting through the door to see the floorboards torn up and another human-sized worm hole there beneath it. She ran back outside, now with nothing more than to get to the Steel Swallow as her aim, dodging many more man-sized holes along the way. The earth was rumbling now, so harshly that even through her boot soles she could hear her father's voice.

"Daughter," he said, "daughter you are going the wrong way. Why chase the sun? The earth has always stayed loyal beneath your feet."

She continued to run, watching the earth stretch like fingers running against cloth.

"Do you not remember the fate of the birds who flew to the sun? Why should you be any different? Am I to lose my wife and my daughter to his love?"

"I would never get that close," she said, no idea if her father could hear her or not. She was nearly to the Steel Swallow. Its door was open to her, her ship alone to navigate. Right next to it a hole opened in the earth, big enough to drop the Steel Swallow into it if she'd had the strength to pick it up.

"The earth is warmer than the light, daughter. The heat you feel is what radiates from beneath you."

"I'm loyal to the sun," she said, but until now she had never realized how dishonest those words were.

She was through the door, which she sealed behind her. She checked the soles of her boots for worms before making her way to the pilot's seat. She plopped Hunter down in the seat next to her, then put her ruby locket in the ignition and started the Steel Swallow. The great machine rumbled to life, the churn of its engines imitating worm-speak. Only now did she realize the irony that she had given her mighty bird no way to sing. It spoke in ground language, but its words resembled the old song of destiny they would sing to the birds before releasing them to the sun, a song that Amber understood now in a way she never had before.

And through its rhythm still she could hear her father beckoning, his voice rattling the Steel Swallow's frame: "is the solitude of the sky really better than the embrace of the earth?"

She pulled back the lever to launch herself into the firmament. The Steel Swallow took off, setting course for the old promise of the sun. She was beyond her father's reach now, soaring into the heavens, or so she thought, until from somewhere above her a worm plopped down into the co-pilot's chair. She eyed the pink swirl on the chair. Where had it come from? The worm was moving. She picked it up. It spelled out on her hand: "Every bird who truly loved the sun returned to the earth in flames."

"That's not true," she said, thinking of the birds who carried all those little pieces of her mother into the firmament with them. She could feel the warmth of the sun returning, heating up the interior of the ship. Amber felt its energy, her life vibrating within her, heating her up from the core, the sun warming her from within, the heat searing her organs.

The sun did love her, but that love was more fury than she could hold. She would die if she kept to this path.

How could that not have been clear to her before?

Her dad had been right: the sun could only love with violent fury that would destroy anything that got too close to it. This plan was folly. There was only one path open to her.

She pointed the ship back down to the earth; to the worm hole her dad had dug for her. It was more than adequate to fit the Steel Swallow. The light vanished as she passed through, the darkness as hungry as the sun. The world behind her was gone, she was flying blind, no idea where she was, no sense of direction, but the air was warm and gentle, the ship vibrating to the tune of the earth, her father's voice echoing around her in a cry of love, welcoming her home.

Adam Breckenridge is a traveling faculty member of the University of Maryland Global Campus, moving around the world to teach members of the US military stationed overseas and writing whatever comes into his head while he's at it, and is currently based in Tokyo. "Father Worm" is an original creation, stemming from even the author is not sure where in his mind.

THE COACH GIRL
M.L.D. Curelas

Tara upended her canteen into her mouth and was rewarded with a single drop of warm water. The stories about The Crossing had not prepared her for the reality. It was dry. It was dusty. Her hands resembled snakeskin, fine diamond patterns etched on her skin. She couldn't ration her water, gulping it down as soon as her flask was filled. She had never been so thirsty in her entire life.

Maybe she should request a stop; after all, they'd been on the road since breakfast—the driver could probably do with a rest, too. Tara grabbed her walking stick, raised the knob towards the roof of the coach, and hesitated. Sienna, the driver, wasn't the most pleasant person. Maybe Tara could wait a while longer.

Her nose twitched. Tara peeled back the curtain. An oasis! Not an inhabited one, unfortunately, because she would have enjoyed warm food and pleasant company, but there would be fresh water. Her tongue seemed to swell at the thought. Tara rapped the coach roof.

After a moment, the hatch slid open. "What?"

"Sienna, I noticed that we're passing an oasis. Could we stop?"

Sienna huffed. "Did you drink all your water again?"

Tara's face warmed. She considered retracting her request out of sheer embarrassment, but changed her mind again. "Yes."

"Cripes." The hatch slammed shut.

Steam hissed and burbled through pipes as the coach veered towards the oasis. The land was rougher here, and Tara was jostled against the wall.

Soon the coach wheezed to a halt. After a few scrapes from above, the coach dipped and rose with Sienna's departure. Tara waited for the door to open, and when it became clear that it wasn't going to, she fumbled with the latch.

She gave up in seconds. "Sienna? I can't open the door, could you help me?"

The door swung open with a squeal. "This damn dust," Sienna said, peering at the hinges, voice muffled by the bandana that covered her lower face. "I'll have to oil those again, or you won't be able to get out at all." She tugged down her bandana, revealing a wide smile. For a moment she resembled a shark. Tara shivered.

Sienna pressed a button, and the coach whirred and clanked. Stairs unfolded from a slot beneath the door. Grasping the jamb, Tara descended the steps. It was tricky, because of the dress she wore. It took nearly a minute. She gazed at the smudge of water and calculated how many tiny steps it would take to reach it. Desperately, she held her flask out to Sienna.

The driver blinked, and a vein in her temple pulsed. "I've got to oil that door and restock the burner." Sienna jabbed a finger at each object in turn, shook her head, and climbed back on top of the coach, where the tool kit was kept.

Tara glanced down at her canteen, tears pricking her eyes. Her dress, while the height of fashion in Dunston, was impractical for a journey like the Crossing. It cinched in tightly at the knees, limiting her movement. With small, hesitant steps, she walked to the water. It was a marsh, she noticed with surprise. The last oasis had been a charming spring, where a couple ran a government way station and fruit tree orchard.

Cattails and lizard tails grew along the edge of and within the shallow water; a few shrubby willows provided some shade. Tara crouched awkwardly and plunged her canteen into the water. Bubbles rose to the surface with a satisfying gurgle. "Ha! Nothing to it." A pleased smile lightened her face, until it occurred to her that she would now have to stand up in her blasted dress.

She scowled and peeked over her shoulder at Sienna. Why hadn't Mama sent one of the servants along on this trip? Someone to help with her clothing? "And it would be nice to have a familiar face in my new home," she admitted aloud, quietly, to her canteen.

Tara drained the flask in a few unladylike gulps, then re-filled it, smiling again at the sound of burbling water, the sound of her success. She pulled out a handkerchief that was discreetly tucked into her bodice. It was plain white, of a cheap fabric, with one knotted corner. Her mama had given it to her as they had said their goodbyes, so Tara kept it close. Her mama was a formidable magic user and there was no telling what was stored in that knot. Tara dampened the handkerchief and patted at her face, throat, behind her ears, and the nape of her neck. She felt a little cooler.

She'd delayed standing for as long as possible. Spreading her feet apart as wide as she could, Tara rocked back on her heels and pushed upward, arms stretched in front of her. She felt silly, and knew she must have looked sillier, but she managed to get upright without falling. With mincing steps, she returned to the coach.

Tara eyed the stairs and sighed. Some of the steam coaches in Dunston had installed lifts to accommodate the hobble fashion raging through women's wear, but this coach spent little time in the city. Steam gurgled in the pipes, sounding almost apologetic. Grasping the handle, Tara prepared to hop on the steps, since it was nigh impossible to climb them normally.

"What're you doing?" Sienna asked. Her driving goggles, bandana, and flat-brimmed hat rested in a small heap on the ground.

"I'm getting back into the coach?" Tara cringed at the questioning lilt. "Don't we need to get started?"

"Oh, yeah, but a few minutes more won't make much difference. We'll make Sweetgrass tonight," Sienna said. She drew her hand cannon from its holster. "C'mon, step away from the coach or I'll shoot."

"I... don't understand."

"Look, sister, you got two choices: step out here next to me, or be forcibly dragged to this spot after I shoot you. Understand now?"

Tara's lips quivered. She bit down on the lower one to keep from crying as she complied with Sienna's order. Her eyes remained focused on the hand cannon.

Sienna nodded. "Wasn't so bad, was it? Now take off the dress."

"I won't!" Tara blushed.

The muzzle of the hand cannon dipped and the weapon coughed. The sand at Tara's feet spurted outwards and upwards. Tara screamed and her fingers flew to the column of tiny buttons on her back.

She struggled with the dress for several minutes before it slid off, leaving her in her silk corset and muslin bloomers. Although it was midday in the desert, Tara shivered and hugged herself. "Why are you doing this?"

Sienna grinned. She started to take off her own clothes with one hand; the hand cannon never wavered from its target. "You're selling yourself, aren't you, marrying some cattle baron that you've never met? What good are you going to do him, other than give him money? Help me into that dress, will you?"

Tara picked up her dress and took it to Sienna. With shaking fingers, she guided the dress over Sienna's head, pushed arms through sleeves, and started doing up buttons.

"The way I figure it, *you* have nothing of practical use to bring to the partnership, but I do. Besides, I'm tired of hauling you hoity-toity types back and forth across the Expanse." Sienna stepped away from Tara and admired the dress. "Very nice. A suitable outfit to meet my new husband."

Tara curled her hands into fists, ignoring the small pain caused by her nails digging into her palms. Her mama would have a fit if she knew about this. An image rose in her mind, one of her mama unloosing a knot and releasing a wind. Tara smiled. A charm would teach Sienna a lesson.

"You'll apologize for this insult," Tara said. She whipped out the handkerchief tucked into her bosom and tugged at the knot.

"What're you going to do? Flog me with that tissue?" Sienna laughed long and loud. Tears of mirth trickled from the corner of her eyes.

Tara hunched her shoulders. Her whole body trembled with fear. "B-blow, little wind, b-blow some sense into S-Sienna." She plucked at the knot, but the wet fabric refused to come undone. "Please?" she whispered.

"Well," Sienna said, wiping her eyes, "we really need to head out. So, put away your hankie, put on my old clothes, and I'll boost you onto the driver's bench." The hand cannon pointed the way.

Tara did as she was bid, her cheeks turning red and blotchy from her drippy nose and the tears streaming down her face. Not even the sounds of Sienna cursing at the useless dress which prevented her from walking properly could keep Tara's tears from falling. At last she placed a booted foot into Sienna's linked hands, and the woman pushed Tara up into the driver's spot.

"I've pre-programmed the coach," Sienna said. "All you got to do is push that green button and look smart—think you can do that?"

After suffering so many indignities, Tara couldn't muster any feeling about the slight against her intelligence. She nodded.

"Good. I'll get inside then." Sienna cocked her head. "Before I forget… Tara, if you tell anybody about what happened here, I'll kill you. Got it?" She patted the butt of her hand cannon, flat black eyes watching Tara with impersonal curiosity. Tara was reminded again of the sharks in the city aquarium.

Tara nodded again, a wave of revulsion rippling over her skin.

She sat with her hands folded in her lap, waiting for Sienna to signal that she was seated. When the rap sounded, Tara flinched, but leaned forward and pressed the green button. The coach gurgled and coughed. Tara patted the box. "If I can do this, you can do this," she said. As if it understood, the coach rumbled and stuttered forward a few feet before finding its rhythm. It trundled through the desert, steam percolating through pipes and tanks with contented hisses.

Tara clutched the edges of her bench, eyes squeezed shut. Sitting up so high, without the security of four walls and a ceiling, made her stomach roil. She hoped that nothing crossed the path of the coach, because she wouldn't see it and halt the coach in time to prevent a collision.

She moaned softly for many minutes until the sudden inhalation of a bug forced her to clamp her mouth shut. The acrid taste of the insect lingered on her tongue for a long time.

Eventually Tara cracked open her eyes, peering at the passing desert landscape. It wasn't as monochromatic as she had thought, with variations of yellow, brown, and even green giving the land a harsh beauty. The rhythmic sway of the coach lulled her into a light doze.

Sharp knocks on the coach roof woke Tara. The sun hung low over the horizon and the barest traces of pink and purple lined the sky.

Sienna yelled from the coach's interior, "We're almost there. Look smart!"

Tara straightened. Shading her face with her hand, she squinted. Sure enough, she could just make out a neat row of buildings. A town. Sweetgrass. She gulped. Her mama had surely sent pictures of Tara, hadn't she? Who would get married without at least seeing a picture of the prospective spouse? Other than herself. Tara wouldn't recognize her intended groom, Thomas Fairbanks, if her life depended on it. Remembering the hand cannon in Sienna's unwavering grip, Tara gulped again. It did.

Sienna hollered instructions on how to slow and stop the coach as it rolled into the town. Tara yanked on the black lever, slammed the red button, and lurched forward as the coach jerked to a stop. "Sorry!" Tara whispered. The pipes moaned, something clunked, and then the steam engine sputtered and died with a whine. Tara winced. The coach sounded like she felt: tired, worn out, and beaten down.

A group of people approached the coach, stopping a few feet from the coach door. After several seconds, Tara realized that they weren't there to help her down. She wasn't a lady here; she was the coach driver. Clutching the railing, she swung one leg, then the other, out of the box. Her toes scrabbled to find a perch, and then her arms began to shake. Her grip loosened, and she fell onto the ground.

Tara stared at the purpling sky, aware of a low buzzing that gradually separated into words. A pair of hands grabbed her shoulders. "Are you all right, miss?"

Tara coughed. "Y-yes."

The hands pulled her to her feet. Tara looked up into a lined face with hound dog eyes.

"I didn't know you needed help, Miss... ?" he asked.

Tara coughed again. She couldn't seem to get enough air into her lungs, and her limbs felt far away from her body. "It's been a long day."

"Sienna!" called the duplicitous driver from within the coach. "What happened?"

"Oh." Tara turned her head. "That's... I need to help her out."

She trudged to the coach and pushed the button that she had seen Sienna use. The steps whirred as they unfolded. Tara yanked on the door handle, and it opened smoothly. Sienna must have oiled it earlier.

Sienna slid-stepped down the stairs, muttering about the hobble dress, and shoved Tara out of the way. Her frizzy hair had been tamed into a smooth knot at the back of her head, and the travel grime had been cleaned from her face and hands. Tara gasped and raised her own hands to her face. Even if Thomas had been sent a photograph of her, he wouldn't recognize her. Sienna hadn't given Tara the goggles, bandana, or hat, and Tara had no doubt that her face was caked with dirt and bug guts.

"Tara!" The man with hound dog eyes walked to Sienna and clasped her hands. "I'm Jack Fairbanks. I'm pleased to meet you. Here's my son Thomas." Jack waved a hand, and another, younger, man stepped out from the small group.

Thomas bent over Sienna's hand and brushed it with his lips. He murmured some pleasantry that Tara couldn't hear. Then he tucked Sienna's arm around his own and led her away.

Tara was left alone in the dying sunlight.

Hot tears flowed from her eyes. So much for Thomas Fairbanks coming to her rescue. Tara sat on the folding steps of the coach, buried her face in her hands, and sobbed.

A polite cough alerted her to the presence of another person. She swallowed a sob and looked up, scrubbing at her face. A boy stood there, fidgeting.

"Uh, I'm supposed to bring Miss Tara's bags," he said. "What's wrong with you?"

Tara smiled at his bluntness. "I've never driven a coach before, and I don't know what to do with it now."

The boy's eyes widened, the whites gleaming in the dim light. "You made The Crossing on your first drive? Wow!"

Tara nodded. "And the coach made a funny noise when we pulled into town. I'm not sure it works."

"Huh." The boy scratched his head. "You can leave it for now, and we'll get someone from the livery to take a look tomorrow. I'll take you over to the inn. M'name's London, by the way."

"I'm..." Tara hesitated. She didn't want to take Sienna's name, but she couldn't use her own. "Lily." It was her middle name and should be familiar enough that she wouldn't forget it. "London? I don't have any money."

London nodded, as if that were completely normal. "Okay. Help me with Miss Tara's bags, and then I'll get you settled somewhere."

"There's just the one trunk." Tara peered at his gangly body. "I'm not sure—"

"I can carry it!"

Tara shrugged. She didn't want to alienate the only friend she had.

***

Tara stretched and winced. Her body ached all over. No surprise, really, after the uncomfortable coach ride, her fall, and helping London haul that damnably heavy trunk to the inn, which despite his boasting, proved too much for his small frame. She sat up, brushing hay from her clothes. Sleeping in the barn hadn't helped her body recuperate either, but it was free.

A horse thrust its head over the stall and whickered. "Thanks for the reminder," Tara said, reaching up to stroke the velvet nose. "Not free, but in exchange for work." The barn needed another stable hand.

Tara hadn't seen a living horse in years. She had fond memories of riding them when she was a little girl, but horseless carriages and coaches were all the rage, and the use of horses had dwindled in Dunston.

A couple of hours later she was hot, sweaty, and muttering curses as she shoveled out another stall. Although she wore gloves, her hands burned. Tara didn't believe she could work enough days to earn the money to send a telegram to her mama. Tears rose in her eyes again and she blinked rapidly to dispel them.

She thrust the shovel under a mound of hay and something gushed on her hand. Tara hissed and drew the hand back. A small dark spot dotted the glove. Blood.

She couldn't stop the tears this time. Why couldn't Mama, with all her magic, have foreseen the disasters of this trip? Tara sniffed, the tears drying up. Sienna hadn't wanted Tara's handkerchief; she hadn't understood its significance.

Tara reached into the pocket of her leather vest and withdrew the plain white handkerchief. The cloth was dry. She tugged at the knot. "Blow, little wind, blow," Tara whispered. But the knot did not loosen and the air of the barn remained still.

Tara stuffed the cloth back into her pocket. She needed money. Her hands were blistered and bleeding from unaccustomed labor, and her mama's charmed handkerchief wouldn't work. For a moment, Tara considered walking to the inn, where Sienna stayed, and denouncing her in front of everybody. The daydream played out, the shocked gasps of the guests, the gushing apologies from Thomas, the anger on Sienna's face… and then a gunshot and agony. Tara rubbed her stomach, massaging away the phantom pain. No, no exposure yet. Not that way.

A wisp of straw poked through her pants. "Ouch!" Tara plucked the offending stalk from her leg and twirled it. "Stupid straw." She glared at it, bending it easily, wrapping it around her fingers.

"Oh." Tara stared at the twisted straw, then bent and grabbed more from the floor. She looped two stalks around a finger, crossed the ends, and pulled. A knot.

Heart thumping with excitement, Tara grabbed two more stalks of straw. As she tied the knot, she whispered, "I need this barn shoveled, I need this barn shoveled." Her mama had more lyrical, rhyming chants, but all she really needed was intent. Tara tied another knot, repeating the desire for a shoveled barn. Not so much as a single stalk of straw stirred. Tara sighed. She'd never really had the knack of knot magic; her mama had despaired of teaching her. With a sigh, she picked up the shovel.

After a few more awkward and painful stabs at the straw, Tara tossed the shovel aside again. Her eyes lit on the steam coach. Nobody had checked it after it had been hauled to the barn last night. In a town of horses, there was no need for a steam mechanic.

Tara glanced at the work she'd done. More stalls needed mucking out, but she'd made noticeable progress. With her hurt hand, surely no one would begrudge her a break?

She stowed away the shovel and walked to the steam coach. It was filthy with dirt and sand. A horse would have been groomed after the long trip—why, even she had been allowed a basin of water to clean her face last night. Exploring the coach's storage compartments, Tara found cloths and polish. The polish couldn't go on until the grime had been cleared, so she set to cleaning the coach, pumping a bucket of water from the horses' trough in the paddock.

It was dirty work, and her muscles ached, and more blisters had burst, but the coach finally gleamed in the dimming light of day. It practically buzzed with pleasure as she rubbed a polishing cloth over the control box.

Tara paused. The coach *was* buzzing, no practically about it. And hadn't it seemed to hiss and gurgle in response to her remarks yesterday?

"Hello?" she asked.

The buzzing stopped.

Tara frowned. "I must be lonelier than I thought, talking to a machine. Of course, you weren't buzzing."

The coach's whistle gave an indignant toot.

I am talking to a steam coach, Tara thought. *I've had too much sun, or—or I fainted while shoveling!*

The coach hummed and the whistle moaned. The coach rocked.

Tara's eyes popped open. "Okay, settle down, coach. You're talking to me, I get it." She patted the control box. "Did… did you talk to Sienna?"

Disdainful whistle.

That lifted her spirits, although Tara laughed at herself. Imagine being more upset about the coach liking Sienna than her betrothed liking Sienna!

"So what's your name?" Tara asked. "I can't call you coach."

Air blew gently through the whistle, warm gusts that formed syllables. "Fa-la-da."

"Falada?" Tara repeated. At the coach's affirming toot, Tara smiled. "Nice to meet you, Falada. Now, you're clean, but something broke when we arrived in Sweetgrass. I apologize for hurting you. It was my first time driving, and I didn't know what I was doing. Can you tell me what's wrong?"

Falada's control box thrummed, and then something clanked below.

"Under the passenger box?" Tara guessed.

Falada tooted an affirmative, and Tara clambered gingerly to the ground. The descent was easier this time, now that she was more familiar with the coach. Lighting a lantern, Tara crawled underneath the coach and held aloft the light.

Some pipes had come loose, and a puddle of dirty water stained the ground. Tara reached out and touched one dangling pipe. Air rushed through the tubing, not forming words precisely, but communicating nonetheless. She could *see* how to fix the coach.

***

Tara was rubbing the soft cloth over Falada's chimney when London burst into the barn.

"Lily, what are you—" He blinked, mouth dropping open. "Wow. You musta worked all day on your coach. But," he tugged her arm, "there's a big to-do at the inn. That fancy lady married the boss's son. They're having a big dinner an' everyone's invited!"

Married already? Tara thought incredulously. She knew that was the purpose of the trip, that marriage had been the arrangement between her mama and Thomas's father, but she'd been expecting some time to become acquainted with her betrothed.

Falada gave a low whistle and Tara nodded. Of course, she wouldn't have needed to rush her wedding—Sienna had stolen Tara's life. A hasty ceremony before her deception was discovered was to her advantage.

Tara must have taken too long with her thoughts because London said, "There's lots of food. Even cake!" When she still didn't answer, he tugged at her arm again. "Come with me, it'll be fun."

Falada blatted, a cloud of soot puffing from its chimney.

London looked at the coach askance. "Is it… on?"

"No," Tara said. "Just dirt working its way out. The Crossing was pretty dusty." She placed the polishing cloth on the driver's bench. "All right," she said, patting the coach so that Falada knew it was included in her response, "I'll go to the dinner."

London didn't mention freshening up—and she didn't have any spare clothes anyhow—so she walked to the inn still wearing her grimy shirt and trousers. Tendrils of hair tickled her neck and ears, and she was fairly certain grease smudged her face, given the stains on her hands. Her mama would have had a fit if she knew, and Tara chuckled. For good and ill, her mama was very far away and had no influence on events here in Sweetgrass.

London eagerly pushed through the swinging double doors of the inn. Tara hesitated before following. Even in the dim light of evening, she could see the peeling paint, the dangerously sagging sidewalk boards. The inn, with its restaurant and saloon, was the social heart of the little town, and it was falling apart. Treading carefully on the cracked planking, Tara went through the door.

Everyone in the town must have been there, the room was so full. Tables laden with food lined the walls. Mostly plain, hearty fare: potato dishes, roast beef, several kinds of bread, roasted root vegetables. But there was also a cake, as London had promised, a snowy white, tiered confection which dominated a single table set on the opposite side of the room from the dinner fare. The little folding table sagged under the weight of the enormous dessert.

A beverage station was set up next to the cake table. There were a couple of large punch bowls of some presumably fruity drink and, she was surprised to see, a steam-powered coffee percolator. She smiled.

She was oddly fond of percolators and tea kettles—their burbling and chugging always seemed cheerful and never failed to lighten her mood.

Hmmm. Tara tipped her head to one side and considered the percolator. Had they *seemed* cheerful or were they *actually* cheerful? Had she been reading the moods of steam devices all these years and not realized it?

She walked to the table, squeezing between well-dressed women and men and stepping around children. She halted in front of the table and, feeling a little silly, waved to the machine. "Hello, percolator."

The coffee machine gurgled and its power button flashed. It was enormously pleased to see her and asked anxiously if she were thirsty, did she want some coffee, it would be *so honored* to warm up the brew currently in its canister, as it felt it had grown somewhat tepid in the last hour as most of the human-folk seemed to like that inferior fruit drink—

"I'd love a cup of coffee, thank you, percolator," Tara interrupted. As the percolator hummed in excitement and quivered as its heating element engaged, Tara stared at it in wonder. She could understand steam machines—had for a very long time, probably. She was her mama's daughter, but her gift lay with machinery instead of knots and wind.

She grinned foolishly to herself as the percolator re-heated the coffee and poured a cup out for her. It proudly directed her to a number of sweetening agents, such as pure granulated sugar, imported from a far-away island, and honey, harvested from local hives, and thick cream from the very cows that ate the sweetgrass for which the town was named, and even a fruit syrup, guava it thought, from some oasis that lay—

"Just a little honey, thank you, percolator," Tara said. She patted its beautiful copper lid and turned towards the collection of sweeteners, bumping into a person who was approaching the table.

"I do beg your—" Tara began, then gasped.

Sienna's eyes widened and the laughter which had been spilling from her mouth shriveled into a discordant jangle. "You," she hissed. "What are you doing here?"

She was wearing Tara's dress, beaded, hand-tatted lace, the highest of fashion in Dunston. Tara smirked at the poor fit. People being people, Sienna's ill-fitting dress would be the talk of the town tomorrow—at least among the women.

Thomas, the man who should have been Tara's husband, stood at Sienna's elbow and looked puzzled. "Aren't you the coach driver girl?" he asked.

Sienna fumbled with her heavy skirts. "I warned you!"

Tara took one moment to feel horrified that Sienna had mutilated the dress to manufacture a pocket for a hand cannon before dropping to the floor. The cup shattered, and her coffee streamed across the floor, splashing the hem of Sienna's dress.

"Tara, what in the world?!" Thomas shouted. He lunged for Sienna's arm, but she had already drawn the hand cannon.

"Percolator!" Tara shouted. "Spray coffee!"

Percolator was overjoyed to provide assistance for its friend, and coffee geysered from its spout, drenching Sienna's torso. She screamed, folding in on herself, but her outstretched hand still clutched the hand cannon.

Tara couldn't reach the hand cannon, but she grabbed the hem of the dress and yanked. Sienna teetered and wind-milled her arms, but in the restrictive hobble-style wedding dress, she couldn't maintain her balance. Sienna fell forward. Tara twisted out of Sienna's path and shoved her aside. Sienna collided heavily with the cake table. The tabletop collapsed and the cake slid onto Sienna's head. The hand cannon clattered to the floor.

Tara was vaguely aware of the din of the crowd, but she was focused too intensely on Sienna and the hand cannon to parse out individual words. Thomas knelt beside Sienna. He still appeared more puzzled than anything else, but he deftly pocketed the hand cannon while murmuring to his wife. He gently pushed the ruined cake onto the floor, and Tara couldn't help a giggle when a cluster of children led by London darted in for handfuls of the abandoned dessert.

"What is going on here?" demanded a new person. Tara peeked upwards and saw Jack Fairbanks, Thomas's father.

"I don't know, Pa," Thomas said, "but Tara needs a doctor."

"Her name isn't Tara," Tara blurted. "It's Sienna."

"And who are you?" asked Jack Fairbanks.

"That's the coach girl," Thomas said.

Tara stumbled to her feet. "Yes, well, no, I wasn't, but I guess I am now."

"Lying, jealous little cat!" Sienna shouted.

"No," Tara said quietly. "I'm not. I'm Tara Winthrop, and I can prove it."

Feeling a confidence she'd never felt before, Tara plucked out her mama's handkerchief. She didn't have her mama's wind powers, but her mama had given the handkerchief to her for a reason—it wasn't merely a talisman. "Blow, little wind, blow," Tara said firmly and blew on the knot.

The handkerchief jerked out of her hand and untied itself. A breeze swirled through the room, ruffling hair and clothing. Tiny dust motes coalesced into a human form—Mama.

The crowd murmured wonderingly, while Sienna went pale. Thomas patted her shoulder, but his face was creased with worry. Unsurprisingly so, as Tara's mama's wind magic was legendary.

"Greetings, Jack Fairbanks," intoned the ghostly figure. "I entrust my daughter, Tara, to you. Welcome to my family, and may the gods bless our—"

But the rest of her words were lost in the sudden cries of the onlookers. With the words "my daughter", a second cloud of dust motes had swirled into existence, one that bore no resemblance to the woman who had just married Thomas Fairbanks.

"I'm Tara Winthrop," Tara said again. "Sienna, the coach driver, threatened to kill me if I didn't swap places with her. And then threatened to kill me if I told anyone. As you saw, she was willing to shoot me tonight."

Thomas's hand dropped from his wife's shoulder to the pocket holding the hand cannon. He patted it.

The room was utterly quiet. Everybody stared at her. Tara shrugged. "I'll send a telegram to my mama."

Jack cleared his throat and awkwardly knelt on the floor. "Miss Tara, I know you were expecting a younger husband, but will you do me the honor of becoming my wife?"

Tara gaped at him. She would have accepted this proposal only yesterday—even this morning! But things had changed—*she* had changed.

"Thank you, Mr. Fairbanks. I appreciate your kind offer, but I must decline." He made to respond, and she hastily added, "My mama and I won't abandon your town. We'll still help, but that aid and support won't be tied to a marriage with me." She held out a hand. "What do you say… Jack?"

He stared at her hand a moment. Finally, he said, "I think that sounds promising, Tara."

He clasped her hand and she helped him to his feet.

***

It was a clear sunny morning when Tara loaded a small case of her belongings into Falada's storage compartment. She also had a full bin of coal, a hamper of food, and a full canteen plus an extra water jug. London had also helped her ensure that the coach tool kit was complete and in good repair.

She shut the storage compartment door and stretched. Falada gave a low whistle, and Tara turned to find Jack, London, and Thomas approaching. During the past week they had formed many agreements and arrangements with Tara's mama—and amongst themselves. Relations with Sienna were strained—Tara wasn't sure if her marriage to Thomas would last. But that wasn't her concern. What did concern her was Falada. Even though it could be understood that Sienna had abandoned the coach or given it to Tara, Tara had formally purchased the coach from Sienna.

After discussing it with Falada, they had decided to explore further into the Expanse, mapping the land and gathering information for her mama—for which she was receiving a salary. There were a few more known settlements out here, but she and Falada would hopefully update and add to the general knowledge of the area.

"You sure you don't need an assistant?" London asked.

"Yes, I'm sure," Tara laughed. "I need you here to keep the stables going. Falada will need a proper home when we return."

"And how long will that be?" Jack asked.

Tara shrugged. "That'll depend on what we find. Probably not for a long time. Don't forget about me!" Her light tone pinched a little and the last word squeaked, revealing her anxiety.

"We won't forget," Jack said.

Tara nodded, swallowing a lump in her throat. These would be the last familiar people she'd see in a while—they'd grown into friends and partners in the last week. She'd miss them.

"I better get going then, to take advantage of the daylight," she said.

She hugged London and then Jack and then Thomas.

"Tara," he said, "I'm sorry for—"

"It's okay, Thomas," she said, stepping quickly away from him. "I wasn't ready to get married anyway."

Tara climbed up onto the driver's bench and pressed the buttons on the control box that brought Falada's engines to life. She pulled on goggles and secured her bandana around her nose and mouth.

With a final wave to her friends, Tara steered Falada out of town. The coach whistled enthusiastically and Tara grinned. There was a lot of world out there, and she couldn't wait to see it.

M.L.D. Curelas lives in Calgary, Canada, with two humans and a varying number of guinea pigs. Thanks to a rather memorable* adaptation of "The Goose Girl" which she watched on PBS as a child (poor Falada!), that particular Grimms' fairytale has stuck with her through the years. She was excited to put her own spin on it for *Clockwork, Curses and Coal*, giving Falada an axe-free storyline.

*traumatizing

ABOUT THE ANTHOLOGIST

Like a magpie, **Rhonda Parrish** is constantly distracted by shiny things. She's the editor of many anthologies and author of plenty of books, stories and poems. She lives with her husband and three cats in Edmonton, Alberta, and she can often be found there playing Dungeons and Dragons, bingeing crime dramas or cheering on the Oilers.

Her website, updated regularly, is at http://www.rhondaparrish.com and her Patreon, updated even more regularly, is at https://www.patreon.com/RhondaParrish.

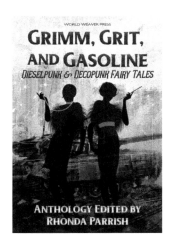

GRIMM, GRIT, AND GASOLINE
Dieselpunk and Decopunk Fairy Tales
Anthology edited by Rhonda Parrish

Dieselpunk and decopunk are alternative history re-imaginings of (roughly) the WWI and WWII eras: tales with the grit of roaring bombers and rumbling tanks, of 'We Can Do It' and old time gangsters, or with the glamour of flappers and Hollywood starlets, smoky jazz and speakeasies. The stories in this volume add fairy tales to the mix, transporting classic tales to this rich historical setting.

Two young women defy the devil with the power of friendship. The pilot of a talking plane discovers a woman who transforms into a swan every night and is pulled into a much more personal conflict than the war he's already fighting. A pair of twins with special powers find themselves in Eva Braun's custody and wrapped up in a nefarious plan. A team of female special agents must destroy a secret weapon—the spindle—before it can be deployed. Retellings of The Little Mermaid, Hansel and Gretel, Rapunzel, Cinderella, The Monkey King, Swan Lake, Pinocchio and more are all showcased alongside some original fairy tale-like stories.

Featuring stories by Zannier Alejandra, Alicia Anderson, Jack Bates, Patrick Bollivar, Sara Cleto, Amanda C. Davis, Jennifer R. Donohue, Juliet Harper, Blake Jessop, A.A. Medina, Lizz Donnelly, Nellie Neves, Wendy Nikel, Brian Trent, Alena VanArendonk, Laura VanArendonk Baugh, Sarah Van Goethem, and Robert E. Vardeman.

RHONDA PARRISH'S MAGICAL MENAGERIES

Featuring Amanda C. Davis, Angela Slatter, Andrew Bourelle, Beth Cato, C.S.E. Cooney, Dan Koboldt, Holly Schofield, Jane Yolen, Laura VanArendonk Baugh, Mike Allen, and many more.

Find these and more great short fiction anthologies at
WWW.WORLDWEAVERPRESS.COM
Also available at Amazon, Apple Books, BarnesandNoble.com, IndieBound, Kobo, and other online booksellers.

Thank you for reading!

We hope you'll leave an honest review at Amazon, Goodreads, or wherever you discuss books online.

Leaving a review helps readers like you discover great new books, and shows support for the authors who worked so hard to create these stories.

Please sign up for our newsletter for news about upcoming titles, submission opportunities, special discounts, & more.

WorldWeaverPress.com/newsletter-signup

World Weaver Press, LLC
Publishing fantasy, paranormal, and science fiction.
We believe in great storytelling.
WorldWeaverPress.com

Lightning Source UK Ltd.
Milton Keynes UK
UKHW020910050522
402542UK00009B/787